SPHERE SONG

THE ISLE OF DESTINY SERIES BOOK 4

TRICIA O'MALLEY

LOVEWRITE PUBLISHING

"The heart that gives, gathers."
– Tao Te Ching

CHAPTER 1

"*S*ister."

The goddess Danu opened her eyes to see her sister, Domnu, Goddess of the Underworld and leader of the dark fae who were currently wreaking havoc on the peaceful world that Danu oversaw. Danu wondered briefly if it would always be this way – the sibling rivalry – if the years in darkness had led Domnu to become a twisted version of the sister Danu had once known.

"Sister," Danu said, inclining her head briefly before standing, her shoulders thrown back, her gaze hard as she measured what her sister had become.

Domnu was dark to Danu's light – no less beautiful, but so very much colder. Where humans would weep in joy at the sight of Danu's purest form – should she ever allow herself to be fully seen by a human – they would be strangely intoxicated by Domnu's dark beauty. Her sinuous aura beckoned, promising a sweet ecstasy, but only in exchange for one bite of the apple. If anything, Domnu had become more beautiful with every evil she'd implemented from being a fierce and unrepentant ruler. It was as if Danu were looking at an icicle, with a cold, crystalline beauty and the sharpest of points that could pierce a warm heart without a thought.

They circled each other, each keenly aware of the other's powers, each unsure of the other's next move. Held here, in this in-between space relegated to the most powerful of beings, they paced. Seeking truths or seeking power, Danu wondered briefly, but held her tongue, waiting for her sister to explain why she'd sought her out. Not that Domnu had tried a usual route – like sending a messenger. Instead, she'd all but ambushed Danu as Danu had worked to sneak through the middle world to find safe haven in a lighter realm.

Safe haven for the treasures she carried, that is, not for herself.

Distinctly aware that the fate of the world as both her fae and humans knew it rested solely in the treasures she had tucked in a chainmail pouch beneath her cloak, Danu refused to blink, her eyes tracking Domnu's every move.

"I'm surprised you'd come here – to this in-between place," Domnu purred, the length of her dark hair seeming to coil and twist of its own accord around her shoulders.

"It's the only way," Danu shrugged, not finishing the thought. For Danu to move the treasures to a safer world, she must first pass through the middle realm. One in which many dangers lay, including her sister. Danu had expected it, was prepared for it, and now she waited to see what would happen.

"You're foolish," Domnu said, her dark eyes snapping in anger and perhaps even disappointment. Did she think

Danu had made it too easy for her? "To risk losing the treasures – to open the doors to my people? I'd almost think you'd planned this, or had a reason behind it. Except you never were that dark – were you? It's why, when the worlds split, you went to the light and I went to the dark. It was always in me, you see?"

"Yes, I know," Danu said, somewhat surprised to find that even after all these centuries, it still saddened her. "But there was also good in you. We all have duality, both humans and gods alike. It's what side you let win."

"Let win?" Domnu threw her head back and laughed, the sound like a glass shattering in a million pieces on the floor. "I didn't let it win. I embraced it. Don't you see, my pretty sister? Nothing is more important than what I want. I chose my destiny and now I will decide yours."

Danu blocked the first spell Domnu flung at her – not that she'd put much oomph into it anyway. She was testing her strength, trying to see if Danu would use dark magick to protect herself.

Understanding that it was futile, but still wanting to try, Danu sought to appeal to the light still buried deep within Domnu. "Sister, I see the light in you. It's still there. I know you've enjoyed your reign of terror, but this – this curse, these treasures, the future of our worlds? It will change the history of mankind and fae alike. Kingdoms will fall; magickal beings of all kinds will destroy, pillage, and battle. There will be no order, no natural way of being. Even you, my dear sister, will be subject to attack from those wishing to dethrone you. Don't you understand that to allow this to happen – to force it, even – will unleash utter chaos in all the realms as we know them?" Danu said, her eyes never leaving Domnu's.

When she saw the spark of madness deep within the dark depths of her sister's gaze, Danu knew all was lost.

"Chaos breeds change. It's a necessary evil, and change, my sweet sister, is the only thing we can rely upon," Domnu said, her smile growing wider, maniacal, against the sharp angles of her face.

"You can choose. To be different, to live differently, to rule differently. None of this is necessary," Danu said, circling.

"My people would never forgive me. If it isn't me who leads them to a new world, then it will be another ruler. I refuse to let anyone, even you, stop me," Domnu hissed, and Danu knew the time for conversation was over. She had a half-second to throw her arms up and block herself from the wave of spells that Domnu began drowning her in.

Lightning bolts flashed. They battled, matching spell for spell, light magick clashing against dark. The skies rumbled and time seemed to stop, held on a gasp of breath, as the world waited for what would come next.

And when Danu fell, the treasures torn from her side, she worked the last spell she'd brought with her – the only one that could save them all – and prayed it would do as it was meant. For Domnu planned to take the treasures to the underworld, along with the Seekers themselves.

Danu slitted her eyes open, her energy drained beyond belief, to see Domnu raging as she raced away, dark magick surrounding her as she tried spell after spell to break Danu's light. When she couldn't, she turned to scream at Danu.

"If I can't take them with me, then I'll lock them away until time runs out and the walls to the worlds crumble. You. Will. Not. Stop. Me!"

Domnu winked from sight and Danu closed her eyes, then worked a spell of light and love, whisking it down to her Seekers along with a prayer.

"I'm sorry, my Seekers. It's the only way the last treasure can be found…" Danu whispered, her hand clutched to her chest as she watched the women she'd come to admire so much being torn from their beds in the middle of the night and ripped away, the dark magick surrounding them before any had a chance to fight it. Only one protector, Lochlain, was able to put a dent in the spell, and it was enough to track his Seeker. For now, the Na Cosantoir would have to stand once more on their own.

CHAPTER 2

*C*lare's eyes popped open and her breath was all but torn from her as she was pulled – by nothing she could physically see – straight from a shouting Blake's arms. What had they been doing? Clare shook her head groggily, trying to determine if this was a dream brought on by an overindulgence in wine earlier that evening, or if it was reality. The last thing she remembered was curling into Blake after a particularly passionate night – be it the wine or their mood – and dropping immediately into sleep, spent and satiated.

"Blake," Clare gasped, a half-whisper, half-shout, as silver Domnua zipped around her at such speed that she could only see a cyclone of silver, her body stuck in the middle, as she was pulled... somewhere. Clare pivoted to lash out, to fight, to do anything, but it was as if the Domnua were holograms and her fists kept sliding through a silver wall into nothingness.

A piercing shriek of curses shattered the wall, the Domnua breaking into pieces like a wine glass shattering on the floor, and Clare was left kneeling on cold, damp stones. Lifting her gaze, she gasped at the woman who stood before her.

Impossibly beautiful but so very cold, her dark hair raged around a face made of edges and eyes made of ice. Clare knew instantly that this was Danu's long-lost sister, and the one who had sent her minions to try and kill Clare when she was seeking the stone. Refusing to bow before this cruel mistress, Clare jumped to her feet, grateful that she'd pulled a thin t-shirt over her head before sleep. Holding her hands up in front of her in a classic boxer's pose, she said nothing.

Domnu threw her head back and laughed, her hair twining about her shoulders and bouncing with laughter as well.

"You humans never cease to amaze me with your sheer stupidity." Domnu's voice, a whiskey-soaked razor blade, cut through Clare.

"I'd be saying it's more stupid to kneel before an adversary than it is to stand and ready myself for battle, no?" Clare asked, causing Domnu to laugh once more.

"Aye, the lot of you – stupid to the core. It's why I need to bring my people forward and shake this world arse over end," Domnu muttered.

"What do you want with me?" Clare asked, since it seemed Domnu was in a chatty mood, and she'd clearly not brought Clare here just to kill her. If she'd wanted Clare dead, she'd be dead by now.

"What I want is nothing of your concern, as for now you'll do as I say," Domnu hissed, pacing, which gave Clare a chance to look about the room. It seemed they were in a rounded tower of sorts, much like an old castle lookout tower. With only a few little slits for windows, the tower room was empty but for herself and Domnu.

"Isn't doing what you say the same as doing what you want?" Clare asked.

Domnu's eyes narrowed. She raised her hand, which shook visibly, and clenched her fist once before lowering it again.

"No, because if I had what I wanted, you'd be in the underworld with me, along with the treasures," Domnu said, her voice mocking as she began to pace the room.

Ah, Clare thought, now who was the stupid one? Domnu had just revealed to Clare that she had a bigger plan, but something was stopping the goddess from fulfilling her agenda. And the only thing that could thwart power of that level was a magick spell leveled by another goddess. Sending up a quick prayer of thanks to Danu, Clare leaned back against the wall and crossed her arms, pretending a pose of nonchalance.

"Danu stopping you, huh? Must be tough having a sister who's stronger than you," Clare said – but when Domnu zipped across the room and lifted her by her throat, she immediately regretted pushing the dark goddess too far. When would she learn not to speak every thought that entered her head?

"If my sister was more powerful than I, she would have the treasures. Instead, I have them. And you, and your precious stone, will be left here to die," Domnu hissed, enunciating every word carefully, her eyes sparking in rage as she held Clare suspended in the air. Shaking her once more, Domnu dropped her to the floor;

Clare barely caught herself from falling as she gasped for air.

Domnu laid a pouch on the floor in the middle of the room. "Here. It's yours, Seeker. Too bad it is of little use to you now. Your final days will be stuck in this room, with your magickal little stone, until the time has run out on the curse – until the walls crumble, and the Domnua once again rule the earth."

Clare gaped at her, but the room was empty. As quickly as she'd come, she'd disappeared, leaving Clare to run and grab the pouch from the floor. Holding it, she turned in a full circle, her eyes scanning every possible part of the room for any escape. Aside from the slits that allowed small shafts of light to penetrate the darkness, there was no exit.

She was officially stuck.

"Shite," Clare whispered, shivering as the cool damp began to seep through the thin cotton of her shirt. Pulling out the stone, she moved across the room to sit, tucking as much of the t-shirt below her bum as she could.

"I really need you right now. I need you to work for me," Clare said to the stone, holding it up to her face. "I believe in you and your magick, I pulled you from my heart. And for now, I just need you to keep me warm and send out your magickal vibe. Please. I know you needed to remain hidden until I found you, but I did find you. I fought for you and for the lives of everyone in this world. I fought for the light. Please, I beg of you, show me your warmth. Send word to Blake. Send up the Batsignal. Something," Clare begged, and held the stone to her heart once more. "I believe in you."

Tears blinked into her eyes when the stone began to hum, a comforting glow emanating from deep within its core, and warmth surrounded her.

"Thank you," Clare whispered, bringing it to her lips for a kiss. "Thank the goddess Danu. For I will survive to see the good win this battle. Blake, my love... come for me. I won't die on you."

Tightening her hands around the stone, Clare concentrated all her mental energy on Blake – her love and her life – and closed her eyes.

"I won't die this day. I'm here. Find me, Blake. Find me."

CHAPTER 3

*N*eala O'Riordan met her opponent's gaze across the worn wood table of the cozy corner pub tucked down a narrow street in Kilkenny.

"Aye, let's see it, Jack. You've been talking a big game for ages now. I'm growing a wee bit tired of all the talk but no action."

The youth, barely eighteen if he was a day, raised his chin at Neala.

"That's 'cause I was giving ye a chance to bow out, what with you being a lady and all," Jack said, and the regulars huddled around the table burst into laughter. It was well known that while Neala was indeed a lady, she was the type of lady who would cuss a man out with a nice turn of phrase while holding a knife to his throat should he ever get too fresh.

Or, in this case, that she could down a pint of Guinness faster than any man between Kilkenny and Dublin.

"Ahhh, don't be doing me any favors, son," Neala

chuckled, shaking her mass of auburn hair back over her shoulders. "We'll meet on this battleground fairly."

Jack, encouraged by the razzing of the lads in the pub, straightened his shoulders and nodding, raising his pint before him. Neala winked at his friends and then, matching his pose, raised her own.

"Sláinte," Neala said, and laughed when Jack sputtered, his pint but half-finished while Neala's now sat empty in front of her as she primly wiped her full lips.

"But... but..." Jack said, a thick line of foam from the Guinness hanging over his top lip.

"That'll teach you to underestimate your opponents — lady or no," Neala said, holding her hand out. "Now, pay up."

"But... but..." Jack just looked back from his pint to her empty glass, as his mates thumped him on the shoulder and guffawed around him. Neala quickly summed up that he didn't have the money to pay for his bet. However, knowing that Irish pride demanded a bet be honored, she leaned forward and dropped her voice low.

"Come by the shop in the morning. I'll have a few chores for you and we'll call it even," Neala said.

"Aye, miss, I appreciate that," Jack said, but his eyes weren't on hers. They were now centered decidedly on where her blouse gaped open and her generous cleavage was cupped in a midnight blue silk bra. Sighing, Neala straightened and cuffed Jack upside the back of his head, sending his cap flying and his mates into another peal of laughter.

"Keep your eyes proper now, young man," Neala strode away, nodding to where the bartender worked behind the long wooden bar tucked under a beamed ceiling. "Pints are on me tab, Stephen. I'll settle up this week."

Stephen waved a hand in acknowledgement, and Neala slipped out with barely a word of goodbye, knowing she'd be stuck for hours chatting with everyone in the pub if she didn't just leave at once. A perfect goodbye, done the Irish way, would be to slip out without anyone noticing, but that could be hard to accomplish when there was a tab to pay.

Neala nodded at a few regulars smoking outside and strode on her way, barely noticing the people who called for her to wait. They all knew she had to get up at four in the morning. It was rare she stayed out past eight in the evening, unless it was a Sunday, as her one day off a week was Monday.

Ah, Neala did love her Mondays. Not that she took much of a day off – oh no, but when a body loved what they did for work it was barely a hardship. Neala smiled as she stopped at the storefront of her bakery, Sugar & Spice, and looked up at the delicate gold letters, etched in a swirly antique script on the tall glass windows. Her bakery, housed in a beautiful stone building close to Kilkenny's main drag, ran a brisk business and soon she'd need to hire more employees – if, that is, she went ahead with opening the second location she'd been eying up on the other side of the city. Maybe, just maybe, if she budgeted well, she'd be able to swing it by the end of next year.

Unlocking a door with a thin column of etched glass in the middle, Neala slid inside and locked the three locks on the door behind her – a girl living in the city could never be too safe – and clambered up the stairs that led to the two-bedroom apartment on the second floor of her bakery.

She loved living above her shop. When the apartment had opened up for lease, she'd hounded her landlady until she'd promised not to show the place to anyone else before Neala had walked through it. It had taken but one look around the apartment – high ceilings with old tin inscriptions, large windows, and exposed stone walls – and she'd been sold. Neala had put down a deposit and moved in that very day. Since then, she'd formed a friendship with her landlady; there was even talk of Neala one day owning the building she now lived and worked in.

Neala sighed as she dropped her keys in a little flower dish on a shelf by the door. So many dreams, so little time. But it was how her mind worked. Why dream small when she could dream big? Wasn't that the entire point of dreams? She tossed her purse on the floor and moved into the small galley kitchen so she could get started on her favorite part of the day – the one hour a day where she didn't need to talk to anyone or answer to anyone's demands but her own. Pulling out her pan, she poured oil in it, tossed some popcorn kernels in, and covered it. Typically her favorite time also included stove-popped popcorn, a glass of red wine, and an hour of salacious television that required none of her brain cells to think about.

It wasn't a bad life, Neala mused, keeping an ear out for the kernels as she all but bounced to her room. She pulled off her jacket, shirt, and pants and tossed them on the ever-growing and endlessly full armchair that stood next to her bed. Snagging an old t-shirt, she pulled it over the midnight blue silk panties – just because she wore an apron all day didn't mean she couldn't be sexy underneath her clothes – and sauntered back into the kitchen just as the pot was filling with popcorn.

Thinking about sexy underwear made her think about sex... which reminded her that it had been entirely too long since she'd had any fun in that department. But who had time for complications when she had a fun and prosperous business to run? And as far as Neala was concerned, relationships always equaled complications. She liked her life just as it was – hectic, satisfying, and rich with friendships. Anything above that could be a bonus, but typically ended up being nothing more than a headache.

Humming, Neala took her popcorn – sprinkled liberally with salt and Kerry gold butter – and her glass of wine, and made her way to the bedroom, shutting the door on the outer room – and the unadorned windows therein.

Closing out those who watched from the outside.

Waiting for their orders.

CHAPTER 4

*N*eala had already been baking for at least an hour when her assistant baker and counter girl, Sierra, waltzed in. With electric blue hair and tattoos running up her arms, Sierra was a lightning bolt in motion. Neala always appreciated her energy in the mornings; it was like a jolt of espresso when she walked in bubbling over with whatever story she had from the night before.

"You look well." Sierra paused and looked Neala up and down where she stood at the counter, pouring flour into a professional mixer.

"I do?" Neala asked, glancing down at herself: fitted denim pants, a loose white shirt tucked into her pants, and her hair, contained in a braid and hairnet, over her shoulder.

Sierra moved closer and studied Neala's face.

"Did you shag someone?"

Neala laughed and shook her head no as she concentrated on measuring out sugar.

"Just a good night's sleep is all. Oh, and I tried a new face polisher – plus a new plum eye shadow."

"Ach, that's it. You don't usually wear makeup. Not that you need it with those green eyes and dark lashes," Sierra pouted.

Neala smiled. "I'd kill for your high cheekbones and sunny blue eyes, my friend," Neala said. They'd had this conversation many times before. Sierra was slender, with a smattering of freckles and brilliant blue eyes, whereas Neala was her polar opposite – curves for days, a bosom that would make any man look twice, and rich auburn hair, which made her emerald green eyes pop. It wasn't uncommon for both women to get their share of compliments and phone numbers across the shining glass display case at the bakery. Sierra took every number that was slid to her across the glass, reasoning that it was best to sample the goods widely before settling down, while Neala rarely took a number or an invitation, deciding it was best not to lose a customer over the complications of an intimate relationship.

Content to work while Sierra chattered about her failed date from the night before – a horrible kisser, from the sound of it – Neala pulled scones from the oven, prepped dough for rising, and spooned chocolate chips into a cookie batter. Sierra worked on presentation, filling the bakery shelves quickly and moving any aging breads to the discounted basket. When it got just a touch stale, Sierra would take it with her to donate to any shelters that were in need, or to offer it to the swans swimming the river that wound through Kilkenny's lovely downtown.

In no time, the sun had risen and Neala's first

customers of the day – her regulars – were already not so patiently waiting at the door. Neala checked the clock; it was a few minutes shy of opening but, never willing to turn customers away, she unlocked the door and ushered people in.

"Coffee's just perking and we'll be with you shortly," Neala called over her shoulder, swinging behind the counter. She'd set her shop up so that people could linger over a tea and a scone or read the paper if they weren't in too much of a rush in the mornings. Several small tables hosted cheerful pots of flowers and the large windows allowed the customers to people-watch. Neala had picked a warm gold paint for the walls, then covered them with a mishmash of mirrors, funky artwork, sculptures – pretty much whatever suited her and Sierra's fancy. It looked both vintage and modern at the same time, striking a balance between homey and fun, and Neala quite simply adored her space.

It was several hours before Neala looked at the clock again, when the morning rush had finally quieted and there was a lull before her next group of regulars arrived, a group of mums who met for morning coffee. Stretching her arms over her head, Neala turned to Sierra.

"I want to try out a sweet potato muffin recipe I was reading about. I think I can add some nuts and maybe raisins to it."

"Sounds yum. I've got the mums crowd. Go for it," Sierra said.

Neala was almost back to the kitchen when she heard the door slam open, rattling the window. A mirror fell to the ground and shattered. At Sierra's shout, she whirled and raced back to the counter.

A man – or 'warrior' was the word that came to mind – stood just inside the door. He towered over the glass display case, his black hair wild, and his piercing blue eyes scanned the shop until they settled on Neala.

"You. With me. Now," the man ordered.

Sierra slid a look to Neala. "I'm calling the Garda," she whispered, her hand already reaching for the phone.

"Do not move," the man shouted and both Neala and Sierra froze, waiting to see what he would demand.

"I'm not going anywhere with you, sir," Neala said, trying to use her best customer-service voice, though her body was beginning to tremble. The man was radiating anger so palpably it was as if they were being seared by his rage.

"You will come with me now. Or I will take you against your will. It's not about you – it's, I have to save…" Neala was shocked when the man's voice cracked, his eyes looking for a moment like he wanted to cry. "Clare. She needs us. Please, I beg of you."

Sierra looked at Neala once more, unsure of what to do.

Realizing that the man must be a nutter, Neala rounded the corner. She stood back from him but tried to appear soothing.

"I'm sorry that Clare needs help. I'm sure if we just call the authorities we'll be able to help her in any way you need. Why don't we do that?"

The man laughed, running his hands through his hair,

and shook his head. "The authorities can do nothing. It's not their world to handle."

Neala shot a worried look over her shoulder, where Sierra was making a 'he's crazy' face at her and motioning for Neala to step back behind the safety of the counter.

"Neala!" Sierra gasped as Neala was wrenched by the arm and hefted over the man's shoulder as though she weighed nothing. Screeching, Neala began to beat his back, terrified by what was happening.

"Stop it," the man ordered. "I'm not going to hurt you. This isn't about you. It's about something so much bigger."

"Put me down!" Neala shrieked, determined to make a horrible scene as he carried her through the door and past the shocked group of mums with their strollers who immediately began to shout as well.

But it wasn't the mums who caused the man to pull up short. Oh no.

Neala craned her head to look, but all she could see was a pair of dusty leather motorcycle boots, worn denim pants that fitted legs as large as tree trunks, and was that...? Well, if it was what she thought it was, the man certainly had done something to be on the right side of the angels when he was made. Neala figured the blood must be rushing to her head if she had time to think about any of this as Motorcycle Boots spoke.

"Blake. You overstep yourself."

"I don't give one damn. My woman is in mortal danger and yours needs to save her. We don't have time for pussy-footing around waiting for Neala to figure out what she is. Clare will die."

Wait… what?

Neala began to struggle again, refusing to be discussed as if she weren't there, refusing to be subjected to whatever indignity this was – right in front of her own shop, no less – when the wail of the Garda's sirens broke through the sounds of the crowd gathering.

Thank goodness, Neala thought, an instant before everything surrounding them went dead quiet. Neala peered around, trying to see what had happened, then real panic set in, and she began to hyperventilate.

For everything was gone. Where, moments ago, they'd been standing in front of her shop, now they stood silently in a field.

Held captive by a madman, with only Motorcycle Boots to save her.

Neala closed her eyes and tried to breathe.

This had to be a dream.

CHAPTER 5

*N*eala gasped as she was unceremoniously dropped onto the ground in a heap, and the man called Blake turned to face Motorcycle Boots. Pushing herself up, Neala scrambled backwards on hands and feet – a fast crab crawl – to try and distance herself from the two, but also to see what was going on. When her eyes took in the full glory of Motorcycle Boots, she froze.

"Dagda," Blake bit out, crossing his arms as he glared at the man wearing motorcycle boots.

Dagda, Neala whispered to herself, caught in the moment, completely mesmerized by the specimen of man... warrior... otherworldly *whatever* that stood before her.

She'd thought Blake was large, but this Dagda, this man, towered above him. With deep brown hair shot with hints of gold and warm red, a ruddy beard, and shoulders easily double the size of Blake's, Dagda was a force of nature. He reminded Neala of depictions of warriors from days past. His hands alone looked to be the size of her head, and she shivered to think of the harm he could cause her.

Although, from the looks of it... he seemed to be trying to protect her?

Neala gaped as Dagda leveled a glare at Blake, his hands clenched in tight fists and his shoulders shaking with barely restrained rage.

"You will not touch my Seeker."

Dagda's voice sent another shiver through her and awoke something deep within her... something she had been ignoring for a very long time. Surprised at herself, Neala reprimanded the baser side of her mind, and scrambled up to standing, her gaze darting between the two men.

"Well, she needs to get off her arse and get moving. Everything's changed – the rules have changed. Don't you know? Domnu has the treasures. She's kidnapped the Seekers, taken the treasures, and all will be lost. Clare... Clare's gone," Blake said.

Neala heard it again, the sheer terror in his voice, and felt her empathy swell despite herself and this odd predicament she found herself in.

"Um, I'm not certain what this is about. Would anyone want to clue me in?" she said, stepping forward, just a small step, but enough to draw their attention back to her. She shivered as Dagda looked at her, his eyes leaning more toward stormy skies than blue, and she felt herself warm once again. Even though he looked like he could break her in two with his bare hands, she wanted to lean in and wrap her arms around him – just to see if it would feel like hugging a big bear.

"You see? She doesn't even know. And we don't have

time for this," Blake said, all but stomping his foot in the grass.

"Having a fit is not going to speed up Neala's learning process. It was not for you to interfere. It was meant for her to discover and learn in her own time," Dagda said, his words measured, his arms now crossed over his chest. Neala's mouth went dry as her eyes traced the thick muscles that bulged through the tartan shirt he wore.

"Seriously, lads, I'm going to need you to fill me in here," Neala said, exasperated that they continued to speak as if she wasn't there. When they both ignored her and continued their little stand-off, Neala flung her hands in the air, turned on her heel, and stomped across the field. She had no idea where she was, or what direction she was going, but it wasn't like the men behind her were brimming with information for her. At the very least, they'd be forced to go after her if she was so damn important to whatever it was they needed to to find this Clare person.

What she wasn't expecting was a flash of silver, ten glowing angry men, and her life zipping before her eyes as she crested the hill.

With barely time to gasp out a warning, the men before her were torn in half by an enraged Dagda and Blake – both of whom worked in a blind fury – and the men, or whatever they were, melted into silvery puddles in the earth.

Stumbling back, Neala gaped at the silver drops, then up at the two men who towered over her, and back down to the puddles.

"I... what... the... I..."

"Lovely. The lass can barely speak," Blake said.

Dagda shook his head, quietly furious as he chastised Blake. "You would be confused, too, if you'd had the rude introduction you provided her. It's best we go someplace safe. And soon."

"I know just the place. But let's not tarry long. We're needed."

Neala gasped as Dagda wrapped his tree-trunk arms around her – she'd been right; it was like being smothered, or trapped, by a bear – and in seconds the scenery around them changed.

"Where... what..." Damn it, Neala thought. She'd once been convinced she was capable of handling herself in stressful situations. Running a business and working in customer service all day didn't afford someone the option of being tongue-tied.

"Magick," Dagda said simply, his mouth quirking at the corner for a second as she slipped from his arms. They stood in front of what looked to be a castle, and a teeny tiny woman came out of the door, beaming and wiping her hands on her apron.

"Come in, come in." The woman gestured, and Blake rushed to hug her.

"I am so lost," Neala muttered.

"Pay attention. We'll get you up to speed soon enough," Dagda said, leaving her side and striding to greet the woman, who barely came to his waist.

"It seems I have no choice then," Neala said. Remembering the scary silver men who had just tried to attack her, she scampered forward. These two may have kidnapped her, but they hadn't killed her yet.

Better the devil you know...

CHAPTER 6

The half-pint of a woman beamed up at Neala, and despite her misgivings, Neala smiled right back. It was impossible not to smile at the impish face, twinkling in delight at having visitors. Her white hair was bound in two braids down her back, and her small form radiated welcome.

"I'm Esther. Welcome, sister," the woman said, holding out her hand and bowing when Neala took it.

"My name is Neala. And the term 'sister' is an odd choice, no? Unless my father had dalliances I was unaware of... and –" Neala tried to figure out how to word it discreetly – "at a young age?"

Esther threw her head back and laughed, her braids bouncing, and then reached up to wipe away a tear.

"Sister in our fight. You're a Seeker – same as I once was. Very few of us are chosen, you know. It's quite an honor," Esther said, ushering Neala into a room that resembled a great hall of yore. One end was dominated by a massive stone fireplace with a long table, which could easily seat twenty, sitting before it. Neala's stomach grumbled in response to the scent of heavy spice that wafted through the hall. It seemed Esther was a chef – and a good one, at that, if the heavenly smell was any indication.

"I'm sorry. I really have no idea what you're talking about," Neala said gently, understanding dawning that the poor woman must be addled. Though who was she to judge? If anyone asked her, she would swear she had just seen a group of men dissolve into silver puddles on the ground.

Esther shot Blake a disapproving look, but he just scowled from where he stood in front of the fireplace, stoking the embers.

"Your grandson," Dagda said, "took it upon himself to ambush Neala in her place of business, leaving me no choice but to intervene using magick. Now our brethren are left to clean up the mess magickally and try to alter what people think they saw. Neala will still be missing, though, and I'm sure that without an explanation from her, there will be some questions. It'll be best if you contact your employee to shut the shop down."

Neala automatically reached for her purse and cell phone, then grimaced. She'd been abducted in what she'd been wearing at the time – which meant her purse was back in the shop, her hair was probably still in a hairnet, and her bright blue apron with the lace trim was still tied over her jeans and white shirt. Casually, she reached up to feel if the hairnet was still on her head.

Of course it was.

Neala grimaced and snatched it off, running a hand over her head to smooth any flyaway hair.

"I can't exactly contact anyone when I don't have a phone, nor do I know exactly where I am. Would it be so difficult for all of you to stop talking in riddles and fill a body in on just what in the hell is going on?"

Esther sighed and clucked her tongue, ushering Neala further into the house.

"I'm going to take her to wash up. You boys figure this out. When we're back you'll best be explaining all this to the poor lass."

Neala followed Esther as she chattered her way through the great hall, pointing out various paintings and artifacts as she went. Shooting a glance over her shoulder, she met stormy grey eyes with an equally stormy scowl. Neala could swear she felt her blood heat when she looked at Dagda. The man should be on the back of a battle horse leading his clan into war – or in this era, perhaps astride a massive motorcycle, leading his gang into trouble. His eyes seemed to take her measure and find her lacking, but Neala couldn't be sure what he thought. If ever there was a man who fit the saying 'Still waters run deep...' Dagda was like an enigmatic bear, deceptively quiet and deadly fierce.

"I'll just be in the kitchen. You're welcome to join me once you've freshened up," Esther said, and pointed to where a pretty arched hallway wound away from the door to the washroom they stood in front of now.

"Thank you," Neala said, and watched the tiny woman walk away. They clearly weren't worried about keeping her captive or they wouldn't have let her out of their sight with this diminutive woman, so Neala decided she would reserve judgment until someone was kind enough to fill her in.

Plus she was dying to get a taste of whatever was cooking in that kitchen and making her mouth water. She hurriedly tended to the necessities, then, with a quick sigh at the state of her hair, she unwound it from its braid, letting it hang loose around her shoulders so it could finish drying, having still been wet from her shower early this morning. That was the thing about thick hair – if she bound it up wet, it stayed damp all day long.

"Oh my," Esther breathed when Neala joined her in the kitchen. The woman was standing on a small stepstool and cheerfully stirring a bright red pot of stew. "That's a gorgeous head of hair you have on you. Dagda's going to be enchanted when he sees it – if he isn't already."

"Dagda… why?" Neala asked. She leaned against the counter, comfortable in the kitchen – any kitchen.

"Well, he's your protector, dear. Sometimes the chemistry just works. And if you do come together – if it's true you're fated for each other – it's for life and beyond," Esther said.

Neala felt nerves trickle through her stomach.

"Then I'm sure that's not the plan for us. I've other things to attend to – like running my business. And, since we're on the topic, figuring out why I've been abducted in the middle of my morning shift. And… even more importantly, just what is in this stew? It smells divine." Neala couldn't help herself. She had a lot of questions, but inevitably, food always won out.

Esther laughed and scooped up a spoonful, which she handed carefully to Neala.

"It's pho. I've been working my way through a new cookbook Blake brought me – it has recipes from around the world. I'm responsible for a large Sunday dinner for all the people who work my lands and we've all decided we want to become more cultured and worldly. Isn't that a hoot? We're starting with new cuisines. I cook a new meal and then one of the other women will read off facts on the country we're dining from that night, and another will introduce a game or perhaps a famous story or song from that country. It's really been a fun way to expand our knowledge."

Completely charmed with Esther, Neala beamed at her.

"You've done a fabulous job with it. I'm certain this will be a hit."

"Oh, good! I was just doing a test run today to make sure. Let's bring it out to the boys and see if they've murdered each other yet."

Instantly alarmed, Neala looked toward the great hall, where all was silent.

"Do you think they would?"

"Boys will be boys," Esther chuckled and pulled a tray out. "Now, let's fill these bowls."

And so Neala found herself once again in a kitchen, in her comfort zone of feeding people, with no idea where she was.

Or even what she was anymore.

CHAPTER 7

*D*ag watched Blake pace and said nothing, though a part of him wanted to drop the man on his head for the way he'd gone after Neala. It took quite a bit to make Dag boil over into rage, but he'd been decidedly close when Blake had slung Neala over his shoulder and stormed from the bakery.

Dagda had been conscious of his imposing size since his teen years, when a single punch during a typical teenage-boy argument had knocked the other lad out. His mother, disapproving as she was, had pulled him aside and roughly explained to him that he must change his expectations of others because he carried more power than most. And not just physically – the fae blood ran strong in him. It had come as no surprise to anyone when he'd been chosen as Na Cosantoir. Since that time, he'd worked tirelessly to hone his abilities, from strength to magicks, knowing that one day every ounce of his knowledge and skill would be called upon to protect his Seeker in his sworn duty to the Goddess Danu.

To have another protector step in and try to abduct his Seeker was unheard of. Dagda's fists clenched again as his blood began to boil.

"Just what were you thinking ye'd be accomplishing by having off with Neala, then?" Dag asked, schooling himself to keep his voice calm. There was something about seeing another man's hands on his Seeker that made him want to lock her away forever. As protectors and Seekers were typically not supposed to become romantically involved – though judging from Blake and Clare, that wasn't always the case – he didn't want to examine his thoughts of jealousy overmuch. It was best he stayed in his role, honored the goddess, and finished his mission. Then he would be free to start his life for real, outside the boundaries of any expectations set upon him by his duties.

"Domnu has Clare. She was stolen in the middle of the night. From... my arms," Blake's voice cracked, and Dagda averted his eyes, pretending not to notice the shimmer of tears that the flames of the fire picked up. He gave Blake a moment to collect himself before clearing his throat.

"You're certain it was Domnua?"

"I'm certain. I saw them. It was the first time I was unable to stop them. The magick was so dark – beyond any I've encountered – that I wasn't able to do anything. I've never felt so helpless in my life. It happened instantaneously, too. She was there, then ripped from my arms and whisked out of sight."

"How do you know the treasures have been stolen?" Dagda asked, turning once more to stand in front of the fire, studying the way the flames flipped and moved, a seductive dance all their own.

Blake dug in his pocket and held out a small scroll of paper, which Dagda took and unrolled, holding it up to the light.

It was only a matter of time
Before the treasures were mine
Perhaps you'll find it a relief
To know the key is Clare's belief.

"Not the most eloquent of poems," Dagda remarked.

Blake snorted. "Domnu isn't known for her brains," he commented.

Dagda raised his eyes to the windows, where lightning shattered the sky in fury. "Wards are up?" he asked.

"Aye, the lands are protected. Strong magick here. Otherwise, I'd never be able to leave Esther on her own."

"Speaking of…" Dag turned as he heard Neala's peal of laughter, the sound rich and earthy, and now his fists clenched for a different reason. Her hair tumbled loose over her shoulders, the warm mahogany accented with deep red undertones picked up by the firelight. It was the type of hair that made a man want to bury his hands in it while he watched her writhe in ecstasy beneath him. Closing his eyes and taking a deep breath, he cleared his mind of such images before moving forward to help the women with the dishes they carried.

"Go on, go." Esther shooed him away. "I may be small, but I'm strong. Why don't you pour us all a whiskey from the sideboard and we'll have ourselves a nice chat."

Dagda did as he was instructed, grateful for a moment to gather his thoughts and to remind himself, once again, that his was the most important mission of all. This was the end of a centuries-old curse – the very last leg of it – and it was entrusted to him to see that his Seeker found the treasure.

Or the fault would lie with him.

CHAPTER 8

"Soooo…" Neala drew out the word once they were all seated in front of steaming bowls of pho. "While this is delightfully cozy and Esther is a supreme hostess, I'd be appreciating it if you could tell me what the he –" with a quick glance at Esther she amended the word – "heck is going on?"

"You really shouldn't have gone after her like that, Blake," Esther chided, and even Neala winced a little at the disappointment in her voice. "You know it's best that these things happen in their own time."

"There is no time. Clare's been taken. All the treasures we found are lost to us again. We're back to the beginning – even worse, as we've only got one Seeker, and a lazy one at that." Blake gestured angrily at Neala.

"Excuse me? I'm not lazy. I run my arse off all day long at a business that I own, manage, and work endless hours in. You can call me a bitch if you want, but lazy I'll not accept."

"Well, is it too hard for you to see the signs that have

been sent? Open your eyes, woman. The Danula have been trying to reach you," Blake countered, his eyes dangerous over his bowl.

"Since I don't know what a Danula is, I guess I can't be accepting signs from one, now, can I?"

"If ye'd open your eyes once in a while, you'd have that answer," Blake countered, and Neala was about to jump to her feet when Esther slammed her hand on the table, silencing them both. The only one who remained unperturbed was Dagda, who calmly spooned up pho and held his tongue.

"Blake. That's enough. You'll not be insulting a guest at my table. Now, from what I can gather, Clare's missing, Neala needs to be brought up to speed, and Dagda is a man of few words," Esther said.

Neala caught Dagda's mouth quirking in a hint of a smile before he nodded once at Esther.

"Look, I'm sorry your girlfriend's missing," Neala said, deciding to smooth things over in order to get answers, "but I truly have no idea what you are talking about or who you are. If I've missed any signs, I'm sorry. My life is incredibly busy and I barely have downtime to check an email, let alone look for signs from something or someone that I don't even know. I'm just buried… in fact, I need to hire more help. But what you did today was scary and awful, and I'm certain my customers were terrified."

"We've taken care of that," Dagda said, and saw Neala's fair skin go even whiter.

"You've killed them?" Neala said, dropping her spoon into the pho, where it made a little plopping sound when it landed.

"What? No. We've used magick to amend their memories is all," Blake said, shaking his head in disgust. "Don't you know we're the good guys?"

"No. I don't know that. Because good guys don't come running into a place of business, shatter my favorite mirror, and forcibly abduct me in front of my regular customers," Neala said, each word dripping with venom.

"If I may interject," Esther said, drawing the attention back to herself, "Blake's not normally so careless and I've taught him to be respectful toward women. So, first he'll be apologizing, and then we'll tell you about the curse."

Neala shivered at the word 'curse,' her eyes meeting Dagda's across the table. The man was like a silent force of nature, his gaze steady, power emanating from him. Now she shivered for a very different reason.

"I apologize if I am distraught that the woman I love more than life itself was ripped from my arms in the middle of the night," Blake said. "Perhaps I've been a bit overzealous in my need to find answers."

Neala met his eyes. "You'll be calling that an apology then? Sounds like it's more about yourself than it is about me," Neala said easily, spooning up more of the pho. It really was delicious. She'd have to get the name of the cookbook from Esther.

"I'm sorry I scared you and broke your mirror. Now, can we move on?" Blake bit out.

Neala sighed, waving her hand for him to continue. She was tired of discussing this anyway, because it still wasn't giving her answers as to why she was sitting here on a rainy Tuesday afternoon, eating pho and drinking whiskey with strangers in an unknown location.

Neala cringed when the two men jumped to their feet and swiveled to look across the great hall, their hands automatically going to the knives they both wore at their belts. Nothing looked amiss to her.

"The wards sounded," Esther explained.

"Wards?"

"Like a magickal security system," Esther twinkled at her.

For a moment, Neala almost believed her. Surely, though, the darling old lady was just dotty. Or perhaps this was one of her more vivid dreams. Life had been catching up with her lately, and the stress was beginning to take its toll. Maybe she'd better schedule some time off when she woke up.

"It's Bianca and Seamus," Blake called from where he peered through the door, and Neala almost rolled her eyes.

"Oh good, a party," she growled.

Esther laughed and stood. "I'll just be getting a few more bowls."

"Do you need help?"

"No, stay. Meet your new friends. As they will soon be your best of friends and very much needed on this journey," Esther said, and then paused, laying a hand on Neala's shoulder. "I ask that you listen with an open mind. I know this sounds like we're all nutters, and you might think you're dreaming. But I can assure you: All of this is very real, deadly serious, and your help – help that only you can give – is desperately needed. We're on your side, Neala."

With that Esther trotted off, humming to herself, while Neala turned to greet the new arrivals, nerves pinging their way through her body. It felt like she was standing at a party where everyone was laughing at a joke she hadn't heard the punch line to.

When a sunny blonde walked in and immediately clenched Blake in a hug, Neala crossed her arms and waited. Behind the blonde came a lanky red-headed man, all elbows and knees with a cool hipster street style, and he hugged Blake as well. They murmured together, huddled in front of the fire, shaking hands with Dagda.

Neala felt like a little kid who'd been left off the team and she wanted to shout at them to pay attention to her. Fed up with the lot of them, she sat back down and spooned up more pho. Why let good food go to waste?

"I'm sorry, that was incredibly rude of us." The blonde, whom Neala assumed to be Bianca, materialized at her side, her expression contrite. "I'm Bianca, and that tall drink of water is my boyfriend, Seamus. I'm sorry we're a bit late to the party. We're here to help you on your quest – sent by the goddess Danu. We had some trouble locating you though, which I now realize is because our stubborn friend over here decided to take matters into his own hands. Can I just say that I am so sorry about that? I doubt he's apologized. But I can imagine just how scary and traumatic this all was for you. I can't promise that there won't be more scary or traumatic days ahead, but I can promise you that Seamus and I will be with you the whole way to help."

As introductions went, it was a hell of one, Neala thought, leaning back to gape at the blonde. Bianca was unwinding a scarf from around her throat and peeling off her jacket the entire time she burbled along, chattering about how concerned they were that she'd disappeared.

"It's nice to be meeting you as well," Neala finally said when she could get a word in edgewise. "My name is Neala, I own Sugar & Spice in Kilkenny, and I have no idea what I'll be needing your services for – unless you're interested in taking up baking?"

Bianca laughed with delight, and then clapped her hands when Esther tottered back into the great hall.

"Esther! I've missed you!"

And just like that, Bianca buzzed her way over to Esther, leaving Neala hanging once more, and wondering just how scary the road ahead of her really would be.

But at least she wouldn't be starving, she thought, glancing down at her bowl.

Small blessings. She'd take them where she could get them.

CHAPTER 9

*N*eala was quickly introduced to Seamus, who shot her a charming grin which completely eradicated the label 'awkward' that she'd originally assigned to him. He may have been all elbows and legs, but the man had his own quiet charisma. She could see where he was a good foil to Bianca's bubbly personality.

She raised her hand, effectively silencing the table, and everyone looked at her.

"Listen, I know this is all the usual for you guys and you all seem clued into whatever is going on. But since I'm not entirely convinced I'm not in a dream right now, I'd really appreciate it if people brought me up to speed now. As in immediately. Or I will be leaving out of that door in five minutes, passing through your little magickal security system or whatever, and hitchhiking my way the heck home, and you all can continue on your mission or whatever it may be without my help. Understood?"

"I'm so happy that I like you. I was nervous the last Seeker would be difficult like some of the others were...

not naming names." Bianca held up her hands and Seamus mouthed the name "Sasha" at her across the table.

"You have one minute," Neala said, pushing back from the table.

"Sit," Dagda ordered.

Neala put her hands on her hips, refusing to be intimidated by the man, even though he looked as though he could break tree trunks in half with his bare hands.

"I will not. Explain yourselves. Now," Neala said, and it seemed like her tone finally got through to everyone.

"When I called you 'sister' earlier, I meant it," Esther said, drawing Neala's attention to where she smiled gently from the head of the table. "We are sisters in a unique group of women who have been tasked with trying to break a centuries-old fae curse. The good fae – under the goddess Danu's authority – are working to break this curse. The bad fae, the Domnua, are working against us, in order to have the curse work in their favor. In other words, the walls of the underworld would fall and they would roam freely on our earth, creating bedlam and the end of the world as we know it." Esther paused to sample some pho and beamed in delight at her spoon. "Yes, yes, I think I hit the mark there. Anyway, you, my dear, are part of a group of women who have been given the honor of seeking the treasures that have long been hidden by this curse. They are the great treasures often read about in the Four Treasures Celtic creation myths. You'll see them used in a wide variety of ways across many myths, though Bianca would be the one to tell you more about that."

"One of the things that I went to uni for," Bianca chimed in.

"These two," Esther continued, gesturing to Blake and Dagda, "are protectors. Each Seeker has her own protector assigned to her to help her on her quest, to kill any Domnua that attack and to, well, protect her along the way. Some have been protecting their Seeker silently for years; some meet their Seeker the day the quest begins. In my case – ah yes, he had been protecting me for a good bit of time." Esther's eyes lit with love. "One of the best men I'd ever met, and I had the privilege to love him for many years."

"He was a great man," Blake agreed.

Neala glanced between them both, seeing the love there.

As stories went, it was a doozy, and Neala knew she'd have a lot of questions and probably a gazillion holes she could pick in the story. But what radiated from all of them was that they believed this story to be true. One hundred percent, no bull shite, honest truth. Irrespective of whether it was or not, this was their truth and Neala needed to tread carefully here.

"Aye, well, that's quite the tale you're weaving. But I'm sure I'm not the woman you're looking for. I've never had magick or been involved in any of that" – she waved her hand a little helplessly in the air – "and so I'm certain you've made a mistake, then. I'll just be seeing myself out and wishing you all the best of luck on your journey. Or curse-breaking. Or whatever it is you believe yourselves to be needing to do."

Pity, Neala thought as she rose from her chair and backed away from the table. She could see herself liking these people, especially that big bear of a man Dagda. But she had no time for crazy, as she had a business to run. They would need to recruit a different person to their little cult.

"You'll be marked," Bianca called after her, stopping her in her tracks.

"Marked?"

"A tattoo of sorts. It will be a quaternary knot. A four-sided Celtic knot. The other women had them under their hair," Bianca said. "Can you feel it on your scalp?"

"I... no, I don't think so," Neala said, confused by her question, but her mind automatically jumped to a bump that she'd been touching for the past month or so when she'd combed her hair. She'd been meaning to take a peek at it in the mirror, but had forgotten each time.

"I think you know," Dagda said softly.

Neala reached to run her hand over the bump at the base of her neck below her heavy tresses.

"I can't really be determining that, can I? I've got no eyes in the back of my head." Neala held up both hands to the table of people who looked up at her, decidedly ignoring Dagda's patient gaze. "Listen, I don't believe in any of this. I'm just a simple woman with dreams of expanding my business and making people happy with my cakes and pastries. That's all. Magick and curses and all that don't really factor into my life. Best of luck with this all, really – and Esther, thank you for the pho. It was delicious."

Turning to leave, she screeched as a mirror materialized in front of her face, hovering inches in front of her nose, attached to nothing. Neala gaped at her own shocked image in the mirror and then slowly craned her head to see how it was held up. She went a little lightheaded when she saw it was floating of its own accord. When a second mirror showed up over her shoulder, she froze.

"Look beneath your hairline," Dagda said, his voice low, almost a growl.

Neala gulped air, but did as he said, lifting a shaking hand to her hair and pulling it up. She piled it all over one shoulder and began to feel for the bump. Quickly locating it, she moved an auburn lock away until she could see what it was. And gasped.

"It's a quaternary knot. On my body. Like a tattoo I've no recollection of getting. Did I get one?" Neala babbled. "Did I get a tattoo one night after too many pints and just forget about it? Have I gone totally crazy? How could I have a knot on my head and be completely unaware of it? This is mental."

"I'll happily give you a knot on your head if you don't sit back down and help us out," Blake said.

Neala saw Dagda quirk that sexy half-smile again as both Esther and Bianca began to berate Blake.

"Fine, fine, sorry," Blake said, leaning over to pinch his nose and sigh. "I'm really worried about Clare and I'm not sure what this clue means."

"A clue!" Bianca exclaimed, clapping her hands in delight. "This is early on for a clue. Let's have it then."

Blake handed it over and Bianca peered at it. Nobody looked at Neala. The mirrors had disappeared of their own accord and she had a decision to make. She took another step toward the door.

And stopped.

Turning, she met Esther's look – a sympathetic one,

but also one that brooked no nonsense. There was a part of her that felt oddly compelled not to let Esther down. And when her eyes travelled down the table to meet Dagda's, she felt something even more.

A challenge.

And she'd never been one to resist a challenge.

"Okay, you nutters, I'm in. Bring me up to speed."

CHAPTER 10

"*H*onestly, I'm not entirely sure if you're all mental or if I've gone mental meself," Neala sighed. She leaned back, having moved onto a second glass of whiskey while Bianca had eagerly filled her in on the previous Seekers' stories. The bit about the mermaids and sirens had made her get up, cross the room, and grab the whiskey bottle from the sideboard, but she was doing her best to follow along without judgment.

"Listen," Bianca said, and leaned forward, her pretty blue eyes dancing in a face flushed with excitement. "I get it. I'm not magick – not like these guys are, anyway. But I've always believed in it, and have been endlessly fascinated by the rich mythological history of magick and fae our country has. To find out that it's true? Well, it's like a scientist proving aliens are real. Hey…" Bianca turned to Seamus. "Are aliens real? Do you guys like talk and stuff?"

"None that I've met, aside from that weird looking fellow in the pub a few years back," Seamus mused.

Bianca squeezed his arm. "You'd tell me, right?"

"Anything for you, my sweet," Seamus beamed down at her and Bianca laughed again, all but bouncing in her seat with love for him.

"That's my man," Bianca smiled and turned back to Neala. "But I get it. It's a lot to take in and the learning curve is steep. But here's the truth of it – people are dying, the Domnua are deadly serious about winning, and we need your help. Whether you can fully believe it or not, I just ask that you suspend your disbelief and trust us. I know it may be a lot to ask, but we wouldn't be here if we didn't believe in this," Bianca said.

Everyone at the table nodded in agreement with Bianca, and Dagda raised his glass in a silent cheers to her.

"That's fair. Something you should know about me is that if I take a challenge on, I see it through. For better or worse. I'm not saying I'm always successful." Neala shrugged, pushing the collar of her shirt back up from where it had slipped past her shoulder. "But if I say I'll do something, I do it. For that, you can rely on me. I may screw this up, I may be more hindrance than help, but if what you say is true and our people are dying, I will help in any way I can."

"That's all we can ask," Bianca said.

Esther leaned over and patted Neala's hand in approval.

"You'll do just fine, honey. I've got a good eye for people and I see your spirit. You remind me of a fierce pirate warrior I once knew…"

"I certainly don't back down from much," Neala admitted with a smile.

"Can we discuss this clue? I think this needs to start with Clare," Blake said, his patience worn thin.

"Aye, let's sit by the fire," Esther said, and waved a hand at the dishes. "We'll clean up after."

They all settled in on the various armchairs and settees pulled in front of the massive fireplace – which could easily roast a cow, Neala mused. Once they had settled in by the flames, as the rain poured outside, Bianca pulled the clue out and read it once more.

It was only a matter of time
Before the treasures were mine
Perhaps you'll find it a relief
To know the key is Clare's belief.

"It seems childish," Bianca remarked.

"I agree," Neala said. "As though it's schoolyard taunting."

"I don't think Domnu is known for being very wise, which is why she doesn't rule up here," Seamus said, and they all glanced at the window when thunder cracked outside.

"See? She's bitchy," Bianca mused.

"We must remember to use her temper against her then," Neala said, and they all looked at her in surprise. "What? Isn't it smart to know her weaknesses?"

"Aye, that it is," Dagda said, his voice warm with approval. "She's vain, shallow, and easy to anger. All useful things to know."

"There's something drawn on here as well," Bianca said, lifting the paper to the light.

Neala leaned over the arm of the creased leather armchair she was nestled in and peered at the paper. "It looks like a compass," she decided, and Bianca nodded her agreement.

"It does at that. The quaternary knot set in a compass. But why?"

"Four treasures. Four cardinal directions. I'm assuming she's placed each treasure at a cardinal point then?"

Blake gaped at Neala, admiration lacing his handsome features.

"I'll be damned. I'm not sure I would have gotten that so quickly," Blake admitted. "But it makes perfect sense. And with Clare being the first – I'd say she'd be north?"

"East," Neala said automatically and then shrugged when they looked at her. "I don't know, it just came to me. I think the last treasure would be north, right? True north? The North Star, guiding us all?"

"That does make sense, in theory. The Cauldron of Plenty, none go away hungry, true north – leading us all," Bianca mused. "It fits."

"I still find it interesting that the cauldron is my treasure, being that I'm a baker and like to feed everyone," Neala said. She'd been shocked to learn that her treasure was the infamous Cauldron of Plenty. Even she had read a myth or two about it – a treasure that served others, left no one hungry, and could feed famished villages or battle-weary troops.

"Each of the Seekers is finely attuned to her own treasure," Esther piped up. "I had the same treasure as you."

"You did?" Neala asked, warmth infusing her at the bond she now held with this little powerhouse of a grandmother.

"I did. Though it wasn't in my fate to find it, we were

able to locate where it was being held at the time and provide more protection for the treasure. It wasn't until we found the location that we learned it wasn't meant for us to have. Instead, our job was to protect it with new magick – stronger magick, you understand?"

"So you know where it is?" Neala asked, delighted at this turn of events.

"No, I'm sorry, I don't. I knew the location of it fifty years ago. But it's magick – and fae magick at that – so it'll have been moved long since."

"Fae magick is mercurial and tricky," Bianca explained. "Nothing is as it seems, and they do love a good riddle or joke. For a treasure to stay in one spot for over fifty years would be unheard of. They move, get moved, or follow whatever spell is woven around them. Sorry, girl, but you're still at square one there."

"Ah, well, it was worth a shot," Neala said with a shrug.

"Cannon Rock," Blake said, looking up from where he scrolled on a tablet. "It's a small island off the coast that's famous for shipwrecks. There's a disused lighthouse on the island."

"What do you think, Neala?" Bianca asked. "Does it feel right?"

"I... I don't know. How would I know that? I'm worried that I'll lead you astray while looking for your love." Neala nibbled on her lower lip in worry as she watched Blake.

"Does it feel right? Yes or no, Neala," Dagda asked, his voice rough and commanding.

"Yes," Neala said, surprised that it did feel right – to the best of her knowledge, she supposed.

Blake jumped to his feet. "Let's be off then. No time to waste."

"You'll not go until I've packed supplies," Esther ordered, and though Blake looked like he wanted to argue, he stopped, helpless to disobey his grandmother.

"Yes, ma'am."

"I'll help. Also, any chance you have an extra jacket or a cloak of sorts? I've only this t-shirt, as I was taken from a hot kitchen and now it's pouring rain out," Neala asked, with a pointed look at Blake.

"Of course. I've got everything you need," Esther said.

"Then I'll help you with the food and supplies. It's what we do, no?" Neala said.

Esther beamed her sunny smile at her. "They do say a way to a man's heart is through his stomach."

Swallowing, Neala studiously ignored Dagda as she rose and helped to gather bowls. The man had been nothing if not courteous, aloof, and demanding when the moment called for it. But he exuded not a wisp of interest, romantic or otherwise. Neala would have been hard-pressed to even identify him as her protector aside from when he'd stopped Blake in the street in front of her bakery. Otherwise, she could have been a third cousin twice removed for all the interest Dagda had shown her.

Certainly, Esther must be wrong about Seekers and protectors ending up together. For while a quick tumble with that one would surely be delightful, it seemed like it would carry more strings than she was used to tying.

Deciding to change the subject, she smiled down at Esther on the way to the kitchen.

"Now, Esther, I need the name of this cookbook. The pho was delicious…"

CHAPTER 11

Though Esther had insisted they stay for the night, Blake had refused. Which was understandable, Neala supposed; she wouldn't want her man to sleep for a night before coming to rescue her either. If he loved Clare as much as he claimed to, she doubted he would get much sleep anyway. Best to just crack on and get the first leg of this challenge done, Neala thought as she stretched in the front seat of the Land Rover Blake was driving with a ruthless efficiency. They'd given her the front seat, though Neala had protested and pointed to Dagda's height.

"Aye, lass, I'll be fine with the bags," Dagda had said, and hopped into the back, stretching out easily among the satchels of food and other gear that Esther had deemed necessary for their journey. Neala had shrugged, not overly worried about his comfort if he wasn't, and snuggled into the flannel-lined canvas coat Esther had dug out from somewhere for her. The deep olive green of the canvas made her eyes pop, she'd decided when she'd stopped in the bathroom to re-braid her hair.

What did she care what she looked like anyway? They were on a deadly mission. Her looks would have nothing to do with this, Neala reminded herself, studiously ignoring the little voice in her head that was begging her to pay more attention to Dagda. For someone so decidedly quiet, he had a very large presence.

"This Cannon Rock – it's not attached to land? Is there any bridge or anything?" Bianca asked.

"No. I'll swim it if I have to," Blake bit out.

Neala marveled at that kind of love. For years, she'd always assumed she'd fall in love, marry, maybe have a baby or two if she was so inclined. Then, when she'd never really clicked with any of her boyfriends – or not for longer than three or four months – she'd slowly given up on the idea of love. Neala realized she'd grown a little cynical in that department. Being a baker, she was constantly designing and decorating everything from wedding cakes to pastries for bridal showers, and she was always happy for the excited couple. But a small part of her wondered if they really – as in *truly* – loved each other in a way that no other could understand, or if they were simply caught up in the rush of it all, wanting that feeling of inclusion that society forced upon you. Especially for women, Neala mused; if you weren't married by the age of thirty-five it was as though something was wrong with you. *That woman must be crazy – she hasn't been picked yet. The good ones get snatched up young.* It was a senti-ment that irritated her on her best days and infuriated her on her worst. What about the women who didn't hang their self-worth on whether they were in a relationship or not? What about the ones who viewed relationships as complementary to their lives, but not necessary? The dreamers? The entrepreneurs? The change-makers? They should be viewed as a catch. Any man lucky enough to spend time with such a woman, let alone date her, should consider it an honor.

Until she met a man who looked at her like that – with complete respect for her business and the dreams she held – Neala was going to remain cynical about love. There was no time for anything fake in her life, and she certainly had no interest in living life by society's rules.

But… still. Seeing Blake's absolute determination to save Clare, the love of his life, did make her heart twinge a bit. To be loved by someone so completely, so fiercely, to the point of risking harm, must feel incredibly comforting. Like a big warm safety blanket, always knowing that the foundation was there. Yeah, Neala could see the appeal.

"I know a guy. He'll get us a boat," Dagda said from the back.

Of course he did, Neala thought.

"My man," Seamus said, and did some sort of complicated fist bump with Dagda over the seat.

"Neala, I have about a million questions for you, but I think we'd better start with some basics," Bianca said. "Anybody who glows silver is bad. They will try to kill you without any hesitation. They are not programmed with a conscience, nor do they feel remorse. Understand me? He who hesitates, dies. I think, had I understood that more clearly when I first started out, I'd have been a better fighter."

Neala clenched her hands in her lap. She hated fighting – she always had. It wasn't that she couldn't hold her own in a fight – she'd been in enough of them, Lord knew – but violence left a sick taste in her mouth and reminded her of days past that she'd rather not think about. It was one of the reasons she'd been driven to create such a sunshiny, happy business to work in. It was really hard for people to be mean or rude to her when they were picking up chocolate chip cookies or a birthday cake. Although some customers still managed it, for the most part people were happy when you fed them sweets.

"I don't like fighting," Neala said softly.

"I'm sorry, but you'll have to if a Domnua jumps you. Do you have any weapons? Anything to arm yourself?" Bianca asked, her tone brisk.

"Nay," Neala said, shrugging an apology over her shoulder to Bianca. Though if the blonde could fight, so could she, Neala thought.

"I'll protect her. She needs no weapon," Dagda said brusquely from the back – and damn if the words didn't just warm Neala to the core.

"Aw, that's sweet," Bianca said, and handed a dagger off to Neala. "But here's a knife anyway."

"I said I'd protect her," Dagda all but growled.

"Goddess save us from men and their egos," Bianca said cheerfully. "When you're fending off a hundred Domnua and one sneaks past and gets to Neala, wouldn't it be nice if she had something other than her fists to defend herself?"

Silence filled the car.

"That's what I thought," Bianca said. "Now, I suggest

going for the eyes, throat, or heart. Do not hesitate. They are lightning fast, the dumb shites," Bianca said.

Neala found herself liking the blonde more and more. She certainly had spirit and a cheerfulness that was almost impossible to begrudge.

"Got it. Will try my best," Neala said, and meant every word. She hated fighting, but she was a survivor – a fighter – and would do what was necessary when the time came for it.

"Why do you hate fighting?" Blake asked.

"Doesn't everyone hate fighting? I don't know anyone who's thinking 'oh, let's have a wee bit of fun with the ladies and get in a row tonight,'" Neala said, shaking her braid over her shoulder and staring out at the passing countryside. The light was dim, nearing sundown, and the rain lashed heavily against the car windows.

"I suppose that's true. I always feel all icky after a fight," Bianca admitted. "But it sounded like there were other reasons. It's fine if you don't want to talk about it though."

Neala turned toward the window again and silence filled the car. Obviously they were waiting for her to fill them in. And what did it really matter? She didn't even know where she was, or what was magick or real anymore, so she might as well open up to these strangers.

"I was bullied growing up. No mum, alcoholic da, easy to pick on. Was overweight for quite a while there before I had a wee bit of a growth spurt. I was an easy target," Neala said, then looked over her shoulder at Bianca. "Until I wasn't anymore."

"I like a woman who sticks up for herself," Bianca nodded in admiration. "What... did your... your da – ?"

"Hit me? No, verbal abuse was enough for him. He thought all women should know their place. At home, in the kitchen, not having any opinions unless they echoed his own. Especially politically. You couldn't budge the man on his politics and he grew to be quite childish about it. He would needle everyone around him, all but begging to get into arguments and shouting matches about it. And what did it do? Nothing. It never changed anyone's mind or convinced people of a different way. Instead, it lost him friends and a family, and eventually me. I was his biggest disappointment. Owning my own business and being unmarried? Aye, he'd not a lick of pride about me, that's the truth of it."

"I'm sorry," Bianca said, patting Neala's shoulder.

"You said 'was'..." Seamus said.

"Aye, he died a few years back from too much drink. It was inevitable – really more of a question of when than how, you understand?"

"I do. Sadly, this is much the case for many. Many of us enjoy a drink, but some – well, they don't have the personalities for it. It takes to the brain and becomes their sweet escape. Eventually it becomes their curse, as they can't be finding any peace without it. Tough way of it, it is," Seamus said.

"Your mum? She's gone as well?" Bianca asked gently.

"Aye, I never knew her. Da's stories would swing often on who she was or how she died, but the truth of it is, it didn't really matter. If she was alive, she didn't take me with her or stick around to see that I was cared for. So either way, she's dead to me," Neala said.

"Rough," Blake commented, his eyes never leaving the road.

"Life's rough. You can complain about it or make the best of it. I won't lie that I get my fits of melancholy here and there, but to my mind there's no use moping about for things I can't change. The only thing I can control is what I do and who I chose to be. I'm actually quite happy in my life," Neala admitted – and in doing so, she almost felt a weight lift off her chest that she hadn't realized she'd been carrying. It was the truth of it though – she was happy – and maybe time had given her the gift of reframing her tough upbringing to be able to keep her eyes forward-focused.

"You're more than a survivor," Dagda commented from the back, and Neala turned to meet his gaze, his stormy eyes just barely lit in the dim light of the day's end. "You're a warrior, and anyone would be proud of what you've accomplished on your own."

"Thank you," Neala said softly, a smile breaking out across her face.

The moment pulled out for a beat or two before Bianca made a humming noise and Neala flushed, turning back around in her seat. The warmth stayed with her, though, heating her insides and making her want to climb in the back for a hug from the big bear of a man. A man of few words, but seemingly just the right ones at the right times.

"We need to address this clue," Bianca said, moving everyone neatly past the vulnerable moment, and Neala let out a small breath of relief. She caught Blake shooting her a small smile from the driver's seat.

"I don't understand what it means about Clare's belief," Blake said. "I don't think she has any strongly-held beliefs, other than about rocks and stones and the like." He chuckled when Neala looked at him in surprise. "She's a scientist. Geologist, to be exact. Which is why her treasure to find was a stone. I'm surprised she was even able to hand it back to the goddess when the time came, without studying it extensively in her lab."

"Maybe it's about believing in herself? She did find the stone in her heart, after all," Bianca said.

"So… what then? We encourage her to believe in herself to break out of wherever she is?" Neala asked, wrinkling her brow in confusion. "I'm just not seeing it."

"You don't have to have all the answers right now," Dagda said from the back, his voice like a benediction in the dark car. "Just trust that you'll know the answer when you need it."

CHAPTER 12

*N*eala worried over what Dagda had said while they followed his directions to a little shanty down an overgrown road by the water. She had a lot of voices going on in her head at once; it was what made her an excellent entrepreneur and businesswoman – the ability to multi-task and follow several streams of thought at once. But how was she to know which answer was the right answer, especially if someone's life relied upon it? It seemed like a lot of pressure for someone who was just joining along on this little journey.

But she'd made a promise that she would rise to the challenge. It seemed she was about to get a crash course in trusting her inner guide.

"You're certain this guy has a boat for us? One that can navigate these waters safely?" Bianca said, leaning forward to peer over Neala's shoulder at the crumbling cottage that was illuminated in the light of the headlights. The shutters were pulled tightly shut against the rain, though Neala didn't think that would compensate for the gaping hole in one side of the roof. She could just barely see the outline of another building set further back from the cottage.

"Trust me," Dagda said, and swung out of the back of the car.

Neala watched him stride confidently through the night, the rain not bothering him in the slightest. She liked the way he moved, with a smooth efficiency that belied his size. The door opened before he reached the cottage and Neala could just make out the shadow of a man outlined in the light. After a short conversation, Dagda turned and gestured for the Land Rover to drive back toward the building tucked behind the cottage. As the car rolled along the path, Neala was surprised to see a sizeable barn tucked among the trees and all but hidden from the main road. Not like they'd get many passersby on this old abandoned road, but still, it was a safe spot.

"Are they…" Neala said, tilting her head in surprise at Dagda and the man who walked toward the barn. "Are my eyes deceiving me or are they faintly purple? Is that an aura? Magick?"

"Och, my bad." Bianca brought her palm to her face. "The good guys with magick are slightly purple. The color of royalty. You've a tinge of it yourself, too, but you can't see it. It'll come out more once you figure out what your magick is."

"My magick?" Neala asked, but everyone was already exiting the car – with weapons in hand, Neala noticed, and drew her dagger as well. This was a good a place as any for an ambush, so she'd need to stay aware. But she made a mental note to pull Bianca aside as soon as she could and figure out what she meant by Neala's magick.

A little frisson of excitement zipped through her at the thought. Wouldn't that be just the neatest? If she, Neala O'Riordan, boot-strapping entrepreneur, independent woman, and the daughter of a drunk, had her own magick? It was the stuff little girls read about in fairytales. Not that she'd ever had fairytales read to her at home, but in school they'd read some and Neala had always been fascinated by the possibilities of it all.

And wasn't that essentially what a dreamer was? Someone who embraced possibility? She'd always been a dreamer. Neala decided to keep an open mind and went forward to greet Dagda's friend, dagger at the ready but a smile on her face.

"This is my friend, Sean. Owns a fishing operation out of Dublin with his wife, Margaret. Friends of yours, I believe? Some connection down with Grace's Cove. The lot of you stayed at Margaret's daughter and son-in-law's house – Keelin and Flynn?"

"Aye, we did. It was a lovely house and brilliant stay all around. Big magick there." Bianca beamed at Sean and offered her hand.

"Pleased you had yourself a nice stay," Sean said, his wide smile lighting a handsome face. "Word was there was some rumblings this way and anything we can do to be of service, we're here to help. I store some of my favorite boats up here, and 'twasn't much of a drive up."

Neala instantly liked him.

"Pleased to be meeting you, then, and we thank you for your help," Bianca said as Sean unlocked a large padlock and chain. He slid the barn door open wide, flipping a switch to illuminate the interior.

"Well, I'll be damned," Seamus breathed in surprise, and Neala nodded along with him.

Six boats ranged the length of the barn, from a small two-seater fishing boat to a larger luxury yacht. Each boat was impeccably painted, meticulously shined, and gleamed under the spotlights that hung from the rafters above.

"You'd never know these were here," Blake said.

"Aye, that's the point of it. Little risk of vandals when people think it's just a poor man's shack. I still keep a strong security system on it, but I pay a few locals to come by and check things out once a week. They need the money and it keeps people from digging around," Sean said, walking over to a medium-sized boat in the middle of the barn. "I'm thinking she'll be the best for what you have in mind. Cannon Rock is tricky to navigate, and you have to pull right up among the rocks on a small beach to even get to land. See how her bow flattens out here? We'll be able to get in without too much damage from the shoreline."

"We?" Dagda asked.

"You didn't think I'd be letting you go on your own, did you? How many years of experience do any of you have captaining boats?"

The group looked around at each other.

"I've done my fair share," Dagda said.

"Aye, Dag, I'd trust you. But I think you'll have more important things on your mind than driving the boat. From what I understand, we've got some danger ahead of us. You let me drive. I know these waters and I know this boat. You do your job and I'll do mine, understood?" Sean said, his tone brooking no disagreement.

"That's a lad, then," Dagda said, and that seemed to settle it.

Sean worked quickly, assigning everyone tasks, from removing the boat cover to hitching it to the truck. They worked well together, silent for the most part, but already as a united team. Neala would have happily hired any of them to work in her bakery.

"Your rain gear," Dagda said, approaching her with a bright yellow jacket and pants in his hands.

"Thanks," Neala said, looking up at him.

"Stay close to me," Dagda said.

"I will. Is there… do you have any words of advice for me?" Neala asked, feeling unaccountably shy in his presence. The man was just so big! He towered over her, and his quiet strength and absolute confidence in his abilities would be intimidating if they weren't being used for her safety.

"Head up. Heart open," Dagda said, his eyes holding hers until a warm flush swept through Neala and she unconsciously licked her lips. Dagda's gaze tracked to her mouth and then back up to her eyes. "And don't do that. It's distracting."

"Do what?" Neala asked, honestly confused.

"Lick your lips. It makes me want to kiss you breathless and I need to stay focused on protecting you." Dagda strode away before she could respond.

Neala brought her hand to her lips in surprise, and then felt a little trickle of pleasure join the warmth that now pooled in her belly.

A man of few words, but he certainly used them where they counted, Neala thought, a small smile playing on her lips. She pulled on the yellow rain overalls and jacket, knowing she would need the protection, for now the rain came down like buckets outside.

"You've got a look about you," Bianca said, a round sunshiny balloon of yellow rain slicker.

"No, I don't," Neala grumbled, tucking her braid back and pulling the hood over her hair.

"You do. I know that look. I get it when Seamus says something sweet to me. Ohhhh, what did Dagda say? I've been hoping there'd be some romance there," Bianca breathed, clutching Neala's arm in excitement.

"Would you hush? There's no romance to be spoken of," Neala said, shooting a glance at where the men gathered by the barn door, checking to make sure the boat was properly hitched.

"Oh, come now, I see how he looks at you," Bianca pouted.

"How he looks... does he look at me then?" Neala asked.

Bianca bounced on her heels. "See? You are interested."

"That wasn't fair." Now it was Neala's turn to pout.

"I know. But the truth has its way of working itself free, no?"

"He said he'd kiss me breathless if I licked my lips again." Neala rushed the words out, deciding to trust Bianca before she could talk herself out of it.

"Ohhhh." Bianca fanned her face. "I'm betting he's a

hell of a kisser too. Quiet man. But still waters run deep, you know?"

"I'd say." Neala blew out a breath.

"They're calling us. We'll talk about this after. For now, remember – kill anything that glows silver. You can be having a talk with your god or goddess about the morality of it when this is all over. If you're the religious type," Bianca said.

"I'm not," Neala said.

"Good. You'll be a better fighter for it."

CHAPTER 13

"You're certain this is safe?" Neala asked, her eyes taking in the waves that crashed against the shoreline. The rain continued to come down in impenetrable sheets, and it was all Neala could do to try and see a meter in front of her face.

"No," Dagda said, and hopped out of the car to direct Blake as he backed the boat into the water.

"Lovely," Neala breathed.

"Nothing's safe, honey. Be it going to the market or getting on a boat in a storm. It's an all-out war, don't you see? Be on guard at all times," Seamus advised.

"He's right. But you'll be fine. We are going to kick some Domnua arse, rescue Clare, and get out of here. Damn, I'm trying not to be worried," Bianca admitted.

Neala leaned over to squeeze her. "I'm sorry. I know she's your friend."

"My best friend. We've been friends for years and seen each other through a lot of tough times. But this may take the cake," Bianca admitted and then took a deep breath, wiping the expression of worry off of her face. "Not the right attitude. I'm refocusing my energy right now."

"That's the way of it, love," Seamus said and then opened the door to the rain, ushering them out of the truck. Automatically, Neala ducked her head against the onslaught of water, but it did no good. Every part of her not covered by the rain gear was instantly soaked.

So much for the new makeup she'd put on this morning.

"Everyone up," Sean shouted from where they held the front of the boat, pitching wildly in the waves and wind, and Neala gasped when she was lifted as though she weighed nothing and deposited on the deck. Her waist burned where Dagda had lifted her, his energy seeming to pierce the cold and the rain to heat her core.

Soon everyone but Dagda was aboard, and Neala gasped when the engines started.

"Dagda's not on the boat," she said, trying to rush to the bow.

"Stay with me, lass," Blake ordered, grabbing her arm and pulling Neala close to his body. "He's walking the boat out. He'll be on board shortly."

Dagda nudged the boat forward, the waves crashing around him, but his height helped and he guided them out until he was waist deep in the water, then clambered on board as easily as if he were a young lad climbing a tree. Neala decided she didn't want to examine the feeling she'd had when the boat was pulling away from Dagda too closely, so she bent her head against the onslaught of rain instead.

Dagda moved to stand behind her, just pressing close

enough that she could feel him there, a cocoon of safety at her back. Seamus stood in a similar position behind Bianca, while Blake took the front of the boat, his eyes scanning the dark water.

"How can he see anything at all?" Neala shouted against the wind.

"Running lights, plus magick, plus Sean knows the waters and he's monitoring his gear," Dagda said, his mouth at her ear, and Neala nearly jumped at having his lips so close to her skin.

Sean stood tall against the onslaught of the rain, his shoulders braced, his hands steady on the wheel. A small shade cover sheltered him partly, but the rain was flying all but sideways, and no one was exempt from getting soaked. The rest of them huddled together at the back, forming a semicircle, their eyes staring out into the darkness as waves slapped the boat, rocking it on its keel.

It was there, in the darkness of the waves, that Neala caught a glimpse of it.

A flash of silver.

She strained her eyes to see if there was more, but saw nothing.

"I think I saw…" Neala said and then shook her head, not wanting to appear foolish.

"Saw what?" Dagda demanded.

"Just… a flash of silver, but now I see nothing. I'm sure I'm deluding myself," Neala shouted.

"On guard," Dagda shouted, and everyone on the boat went into action, pulling knives, daggers, and various weapons out of pouches and satchels. Even Sean pulled what looked like a machete from beneath the steering wheel.

For an eerily long moment, the waves and rain seemed to quiet, and all was silent.

When the Domnua hit, they did so with the force of a vengeful hurricane.

CHAPTER 14

*B*ianca had been right about the Domnua being fast, but Neala had no way of truly understanding what she meant until they poured over the side of the boat, an endless stream of silver warriors, as dense as the rain that once again fell from the sky.

The battle exploded instantly, with Bianca and Seamus diving into the flurry of Domnua, holding onto each other or the side of the boat for purchase as they fought both the rocking waves and the attacking Domnua. Blake, his back pressed to Sean's, fought off an ever-increasing onslaught of fae while Sean held the wheel steady, persevering though a battle raged around him.

That's a sea captain, right there, Neala thought dumbly, crouched against the rail as she held the dagger in front of her, her eyes trying to track every movement, though it was virtually impossible to do so.

But oh… Dagda. Dagda was a sight to behold, in his element like every warrior doing what they were born to do – fight to protect what was theirs. He was, quite simply, magnificent. Domnua that attempted to jump on his back were tossed easily over the side of the boat, while others, approaching from the front, were felled four at a time with one stroke of his sword. Dagda lifted his head and howled to the sky, his hair slick with rain, his eyes alight with battle, and all Neala could do was stare in awe.

And be thankful that he was on their side.

She didn't know if she should jump into the battle or stay where Dagda had deposited her with the strict order to stay put. Not knowing which was worse –ignoring his orders or not fighting – Neala finally decided she needed to do something, anything at all, to help. Sucking in her breath, Neala stepped forward.

She was instantly grabbed from behind. "Dagda!" she screamed, and struggled against the grip that banded her arms to her waist like steel.

So, that would have been the wrong voice to listen to, Neala thought as she gasped for air and kicked against the knees of the Domnua holding her, trying to angle her foot backwards to kick him where it would hurt a man most.

Silver liquid exploded around them, covering her, and Neala dropped to the floor. She narrowly missed slipping when Dagda grabbed her arm, the sword raised in one arm.

"I told you to stay put," Dagda said, his face furious.

"I can't just sit there and not help," Neala shouted.

"You are helping. By staying put. Don't you under-stand? They're after you! The more we have to track you around the boat, the more likely one of us will die. Sit. Down." Dagda pushed her back into her hiding spot and stood in front of her, at the ready.

Neala instantly felt foolish. He was unequivocally

right, though she hadn't really understood that the Domnua would solely be seeking her out. She'd thought they would come after all of them – that was why they were trying to rescue Clare, wasn't it? But now she felt awful for having put the others at danger with her own misguided voice.

Great, and they wanted her to trust her instincts? So far, she was not doing a good job.

"Cannon Rock," Blake shouted and almost instantly, all the Domnua disappeared, blinking away as if someone had turned the light out. The rain slowed, but still hung on, and Neala could just barely make out the rocky shoreline of a small island.

"There's no way we can land a boat there," Neala gasped, wiping silver blood from her face, watching as it dissolved in the rain at her feet. It was almost like ecto cooler blood, all neon and glowy, but silver instead of green.

"We'll land it. Trust me," Sean called back.

Seeing as how he'd kept the boat from capsizing amidst a raging storm and a fierce battle, Neala figured she could count on him. Pushing the worry aside, she eased up from where she crouched on the floor of the boat.

"I'm sorry," Neala said, addressing the group.

"That's okay. It's hard to resist the urge to help. But in that case, Dag was right. It's best you stay protected. If something happens to you – all is lost," Seamus said.

"Great, so no pressure, right?" Neala grumbled.

"Just don't be stupid," Dagda said.

Neala turned to glare at him. "Nobody told me I was the one they were after," she pointed out.

"Then maybe you should just listen when orders are

given," Dagda said, his tone even, his eyes on the looming rocks. "Get up to speed. You're the one who can make or break this quest. Putting the people who are here to help you in unnecessary danger is unacceptable."

Dagda moved to the front of the boat to confer with Blake, and Neala blinked back the threat of tears.

"Don't let him get to you. I sense he's more bark than bite. Probably just scared for you," Bianca said, squeezing her arm. "You know how men get."

"I am sorry. Truly. I just wanted to help."

"Trust me, you'll help in a lot of ways along this quest. But you can't help in the ways you want to all the time. We're a team, okay?"

Neala drew in a shaky breath and watched Dagda jump fearlessly into the water, pulling the boat to a miniscule patch of flat shoreline with ease.

"You're right. I'm used to calling the shots. I'll be better at it next time," Neala said, offering Bianca a contrite smile.

"No worries. Let's go get Clare."

"How will we know where she is?" Neala asked as they hefted knapsacks onto their shoulders and walked to the front of the boat.

"It's a tiny island," Sean said, turning the engines off, "only a lighthouse on it. I suspect she'll be in there, unless there's some underground cave I don't know about. We'll be onto her quick enough."

"You know the way?" Blake asked as they stood at the front of the boat. Seamus hopped easily onto the beach and reached for Bianca. Neala once again was faced with

Dagda, who wrapped his arm around her waist and swung her smoothly onto shore.

"Aye, I know the way. But turn your head lanterns on. The lighthouse isn't functioning, and the path up the cliff is rocky."

Lights on, they turned into the night, and worked their way to find Clare – the first Seeker to find her treasure.

CHAPTER 15

*D*agda did his best to ignore Neala's presence, though she was right there in front of him, trudging along in the rain. Even covered in a yellow rain slicker – all but a shapeless sack, really – she enticed him. He swore he could smell her scent on the rain, a mouthwatering blend of vanilla and cinnamon, which he assumed came from being in a bakery all day long. It made him want to nip at her neck, cuddle her close, and dive into exploring all the dips and curves of her generous body.

"I'm sorry," Neala said over her shoulder, sounding for all the world like a puppy he'd just kicked.

Dagda sighed and continued to scan the rocky landscape around them, looking for any sign of Domnua.

"Live and learn."

"I know. I'm a fast learner, but this is all so new to me. I don't think I really understood the scope of it all, or just what we were walking into. I'm not used to being the focal point, nor having someone else look out for me. I've done everything on my own, you see? It's hard to turn off that switch and follow orders, especially if I feel like I can be helping."

It made sense to him, even though he'd wanted to throttle her after he'd destroyed the Domnua who had been trying to pull her into the water. Seeing her in harm's way had only reinforced his belief that he needed to keep as much professional distance between them as possible. The thoughts that had gone through his head at the possibility of her being hurt or killed had chilled him to the core. Dagda was a one-man band, used to flying solo, and he preferred to keep it that way. He'd spent his life roaming the world on motorcycles and wandering free until the goddess Danu had called him home to serve his people. It was a post he'd taken freely, and happily, but not with the expectation of developing any sort of attachments in his life.

In fact, it had seemed like the perfect job to not form attachments. He needed to be ready at a moment's notice, slip in and out of magickal worlds, and destroy Domnua when necessary. He needed to be smoke in the wind.

Not thinking about bedding Neala.

At first, he'd tried to pass it off as an entertaining possibility. The woman was a knock-out – one of the most beautiful he'd seen in all his travels, and he'd certainly spent time with many a woman. But something about her had beckoned to him, a sweet innocence lying beneath her no-nonsense exterior, that had made him yearn for some-thing more than a quick tumble with her.

Which was why he was determined to keep his distance, and to not examine his feelings on that front too deeply.

"I understand. I'm much the same. Having done everything on my own, as well. But believe me when I say that if I tell you to stay put, I damn well mean it. I need to know you are where I told you to be. What if I'd swung around blindly and hit you with my sword? There are deeper ramifications to your actions now. Just be glad that nobody was hurt, and learn from it."

"I will, I promise," Neala said.

They continued on in silence for a while, moving as fast as they could in the beam of their lights, the rocks slippery beneath their feet in the still misting night.

"Where were you that you did everything on your own? You're fae, no?" Neala asked, and Dagda almost sighed. Women, always wanting to talk.

"Exploring the world. I'm a rambler; I don't set down roots. I pick up a motorcycle in whatever country I'm in and hit the open road. Meeting new people along the way, learning new cultures."

"How did you end up here then?"

"The goddess asked."

Dagda saw Neala shake her head.

"I'm still getting used to this whole goddess thing, if I'm to be honest. Not out of disrespect or anything, it's just... wow. The goddess asked you to do something. What was she like?"

"Beautiful beyond this world. Light and awesomeness in a manner most difficult to describe. You don't just see her light and beauty, it's something you feel deep within. She's what I imagine a butterfly's laughter looks like."

"That's... completely charming," Neala laughed and shot him a smile over her shoulder. The look in her eyes would have dropped a lesser man to his knees to beg for her attention.

"Aye, well, when the goddess calls – you answer. But this is a high honor and I'm happy to be of service to my people, as I've wandered for years now and haven't always been around to help."

"Family?"

"Not much in the way of that," Dagda said, shutting that door.

"Ah, I understand you there. Though I've never been much of a wanderer. I think I needed a home, which is how I ended up opening a bakery. I wanted a place that was all my own."

"It's a lovely shop," Dagda said, and almost kicked himself. It's a lovely shop? He was going to make himself sound like a weakling.

"Thank you. I'm quite proud of it."

"Enough talking. Best to keep your eyes ahead. I suspect we're walking into a trap," Dagda said, shutting the conversation down. It was more talking than he'd done in weeks, and it wasn't helping his plan to keep himself distanced from Neala.

If anything, he suspected his heart was already ensnared in its own trap.

CHAPTER 16

A butterfly's laugh, Neala thought, replaying the phrase in her head. It was exceptionally charming, but also invoked a feeling of playfulness and joy that she hadn't expected from a gruff man such as Dagda. She wondered if he was sentimental, or what other layers could be found beneath his tough guy exterior.

Oh, but she could just see him, muscles bulging, riding a motorcycle on the open road with wind blowing in his hair. She wondered if he had any tattoos, and added that to her mental image of him. Neala was surprised to find that she was picturing herself riding behind him on the bike, and for the first time really yearned for the freedom of the open road. Traveling had never been at the top of her priority list, and until a few years ago it had been virtually impossible, as she'd scraped and scrimped every penny together to keep her bakery alive.

But now? Oh, she wanted to see the world! A bit at a time, of course, but maybe once she opened a second store and hired a manager. Maybe she'd treat herself to the pasta-making class in Italy she'd always wanted to try.

"Lighthouse ahead," Blake called.

Neala looked up from where she'd been carefully watching her feet to see the outline of a murky stone lighthouse through the mist. If she strained her eyes enough, it looked like there was a faint glow at the top of the tower.

"The waves sound much further below us now," Neala commented.

Bianca turned back to her. "We're at the top of the cliff. This is the high side of the island. Be extremely careful with where you step. I really don't fancy diving into that cold water after you," Bianca said.

Neala felt put upon. "Hey, I said I was sorry about earlier, I'll follow orders," she said, just as her foot slipped and both Bianca and Dagda grabbed her.

Would there be any end to her embarrassment tonight?

"I swear you fae are just having your fun with me now," Neala grumbled but then smiled when she heard Dagda's low chuckle. At the very least, she'd made him laugh, which wasn't something it seemed like he did often.

"It's okay, I'm often clumsy too. But it really is slippery up here. Oh shite, there goes Blake," Bianca said. Soon they were all moving at a fast clip, trying to watch their footing while also keeping up with Blake. By the time they'd reached the lighthouse, he'd already begun trying to find a foothold up to climb the wall.

"Isn't there a door?" Dagda asked as the wind began to pick up, the rain blanketing them in thick sheets.

"It's been magickally sealed. No door. No windows that I can see either. Just little slits in the wall to let the

light in or out. I'm going to have to climb it. If I can."
Blake swore long and loudly as he slipped down the side
of the wall once more.

Neala tilted her head and looked up – a long ways up –
and back at Blake. There was no way the man would be
able to climb this and hang on in this wind and rain. What
was he thinking? She watched as he tried again, falling
once more to the earth, his curses getting louder. Dagda
circled the group, his back to them, his gaze tracking for
movement in the night.

"Is there any rope in the satchel?" Seamus called.

Neala dropped to her knees and flipped the pack open,
digging through it until she found a healthy cord of rope.
"Aye, rope here, but 'tis not long enough to scale the likes
of that, I fear."

"I'll think of something," Blake said, grabbing the rope
from her. His face was set in sheer determination laced
with panic. A cry from above stopped him in his tracks.
Over the howling of the wind, Neala could just make
it out.

"Blake!" Clare screamed from the tower.

"Clare! We're here! We'll get you out."

"Be careful," Clare shouted down again, but it was like
shouting at a man possessed. Blake began to scale the wall,
looking for a handhold with each step, the rope draped
over his shoulder. The higher he got, the more worried
Neala grew.

"How is he going to get her out once he's up there? It
doesn't look like there's a door. I don't like this," Bianca
said.

"I don't either. How can this not be a trap? Didn't the

clue say something about Clare's belief? Doesn't she need to be the one to unlock herself?" Neala demanded, growing angry with this woman who would allow her man to put himself in such danger to rescue her.

"But the clues aren't for her," Bianca said automatically, then her eyes widened as she turned to look at Neala, the rain slanting all but sideways in the light of her headlamp. "They're for you."

"Blake! Watch out! They're coming!" Clare screamed from the top of the tower just as the sky opened up and rained Domnua upon them. The group sprang into action – but not in time, and Blake fell from the tower, seemingly suspended in mid-air for a moment on Clare's scream, before going over the edge of the cliff.

"Do something!" Bianca shrieked and raced to the edge of the cliff, leveling Domnua on the way.

"Me? What do I do?" Neala screamed in panic, and looked to where Dagda fended off a slew of Domnua. He turned to her and pointed at his chest before whirling and taking out six more Domnua that came for him.

"My chest? I don't get it." Neala almost choked on her words, her panic was so thick, the voices inside her head all clashing together until one rose above the rest. Dagda had told her before they started out.

Head up. Heart open.

That was what the clue had been telling her. Clare had needed to look into her heart to find the treasure, but it was also that she needed to believe in love. Maybe Neala had been a bit cynical about love in the past, but nobody who had watched Blake scale a slimy, slippery wall, his hands scraped and bloody, while an army of Domnua rose to

attack – all to get to Clare – could ever deny the existence
of love. True, earth-shattering, world-ending love.

Neala raised her chin and held her hands above her
head, feeling as if she were a body outside of herself, and
called to the wind.

"I believe in love. In the beauty and pain of it, in the
exquisite life and light it both gives and takes. I call down
the wind."

No one was more surprised than she when the wind
whipped to a frenzy above her head, rolling into miniature
cyclone of sorts. Neala watched it wide-eyed, completely
unprepared for such power.

"Get Blake!" Bianca shrieked, and Neala realized she
could direct the wind –something she would have to
examine in much greater detail later. Rushing to the cliff's
edge, while Dagda fought off the Domnua that tried to
reach her, Neala saw Blake hanging by a single hand,
dangling from the cliff just outside of Seamus's reach. The
rope that could have helped him dangled from his
shoulder.

"Bring him up," Neala commanded the cyclone, and
closed her eyes for a brief second, praying that she hadn't
gone completely mad. She opened them in time to see the
cyclone of wind lift Blake and fling him none too gently
onto the rocks, where he lay panting for a moment while
Bianca bowed over him.

"Ah, darling, care to direct that little ball of wind
toward something useful?" Dagda drawled from where he
continued to fight the Domnua.

Neala started, realizing she was still in control. With a
whisk of her hand she ordered the wind to sweep the

Domnua away, and in a matter of moments their screams disappeared into the depths of the dark waters below.

"And it's time to blow away the rain. Bring us the moonlight, sweet wind of mine," Neala crooned, unsure if she was doing the right thing, but following that instinct in her head. The breeze brushed over her cheeks, a gentle kiss, and then flung itself into the sky, pulling with it the storm clouds and the rain, as if someone were opening a curtain so they could see the moon and the stars hanging brightly in the sky.

"Hell of a magick trick you've got there, darling," Dagda said.

"I had no idea I could do that," Neala gasped, panting as she knelt on the cliff's edge. Dagda grasped her arm and pulled her away from the edge, moving her closer to the lighthouse.

"Blake!" Clare yelled, racing around the side of the lighthouse in nothing but a t-shirt, her eyes only on her love, a small pouch hanging from one hand. Neala watched in silence as she streaked across the rocky land, oblivious to the pain to her feet, and collapsed upon Blake, where they kissed like lovers long lost. Neala supposed that even though they weren't long-lost lovers, they'd had a hell of a traumatic event, and she politely averted her eyes.

"The wind! That's so damn cool," Bianca crowed, dancing in front of Neala. "How did you think of that?"

"I have no idea. It just popped in my head. I'm learning to listen to the right voice, I guess." Neala shrugged.

"And for that, I am very grateful," Blake said, having

walked up with Clare on his arm. He pulled Neala into a hug and then introduced her to Clare who, even though she didn't look like a hugger, gave her one as well.

"There's a blanket in the pack," Neala stammered, pointing to Clare's bare legs, and Blake rushed to cover her with something warm.

"It's nice to meet another Seeker. I've a gift for you," Clare said.

CHAPTER 17

"*A* gift? For me?" Neala asked, surprised that Clare would have anything in the tower with her at all.

"Aye, from the goddess herself," Clare said and handed the pouch she carried to Neala. Neala almost dropped it, as she could feel the power it held pulse through her.

"Whoa."

"I know. Big magick," Clare said and they all gasped as Neala pulled out the truthstone. It was entirely round and glowed from within, almost seeming to sing with its own power.

"I can't take this," Neala said, offering it back to Clare, who held her hands up.

"It's not for me. As much as I'm dying to study it in my lab," Clare admitted.

Blake chuckled from where he'd wrapped his arms around her, cocooning her in the blanket, relief and exhaustion evident on his handsome face.

"But I can't... what am I supposed to do with this?" Neala said, terrified she would drop it or lose it.

"Take it with you. You may need it on your journey. There's more in there," Clare said, nodding her head at the bag.

"Um, okay." Neala held out the stone for someone to take it, but only Bianca would hold it for her, though Sean did lean over to study it, surprise and awe lighting his features.

"The Stone of Truth. Never did think that actually existed," Sean admitted.

"Is this a necklace?" Neala asked, holding up a chain with a large pendant on it. The pendant was in the same shape as the quaternary knot she'd found marked on her head, and seemed to have four metal petals. All but one of the petals were empty. The easternmost petal of the knot held a smoky pink stone.

"Aye, it is, and that's rose quartz. Used for belief in love and, combined with other stones, to attract love."

"It's beautiful, and yet odd. Only one part of the pendant has a stone."

"I bet you get a stone in each part of the necklace as you go along! Oh, this is going to be the treasure hunt to beat all treasure hunts," Bianca squealed. "We'll even have all this extra help on the way."

Clare seemed to sober at those words.

"We can't go with you," Clare said and the group went silent.

"I... I have to do this alone?" Neala's voice rose in a squeak.

"No, no, that isn't what I meant," Clare laughed.

"You'll have help. But Blake and I can't go with you. We've finished this leg of the journey and are forbidden to go further. I'm sorry. I want you to know that I owe you a debt of gratitude and for the rest of my life I will thank you for saving Blake for me. I would do anything to help you, but the goddess won't allow it. I think it may go against the rules or something."

"Don't you think the rules are thrown out the window at this point? What with Domnua coming back and stealing all the Seekers and the treasures?" Seamus asked, bitterly annoyed at the turn of events.

"I'm sorry. Please know I truly am. It's going to kill me not to come with and help you. Plus, I worry so much about Bianca and Seamus – my two best friends in the world. But I can't. I promise you I would if I could."

"Of course you would," Bianca said automatically.

"I think we should get off this island as soon as possible," Dagda piped up. "I don't imagine Domnu is going to be right pleased that we beat her already. The longer we linger, the more danger we are in."

Neala didn't have to be told twice to get her butt moving. She stayed silent on the climb down and let Bianca's and Clare's chatter fall on her shoulders, while the power of the stone and the necklace hummed around her.

She could call down the wind, Neala thought, and almost squealed out loud.

Wasn't that a miracle?

CHAPTER 18

*S*asha hadn't been asleep when she'd been captured, and she hadn't gone down without a fight either. Which was why she was now staring down a supremely angry dark goddess who was threatening to eradicate her existence completely.

"Lug was one of my best men," Domnu seethed, pacing in front of Sasha, who balanced lightly on the balls of her feet, waiting for Domnu's next move.

"He must not have been so great if I was able to take him out," Sasha said, and wiped blood from her lip with the back of her hand.

"He obviously wasn't expecting you to be armed," Domnu retorted, an angry flush on her icepick cheekbones, her hair whirling around her head in anger.

"A good warrior anticipates that everyone is armed," Sasha countered, refusing to back down, even in the face of such powerful anger.

"It doesn't matter, not really," Domnu said, ignoring Sasha's remark. "I have others. Stronger fighters. He was getting too lazy, and others shall learn from the price he paid. Just like you'll learn that your fighting was useless."

"I'll always fight the darkness," Sasha said, her chin up.

"Then you are going to have a very difficult time in the new world, aren't you?" Domnu hissed, stalking forward until her face was but inches from Sasha's, her dark power forcing Sasha's back to the cold stone wall.

"There won't be a new world," Sasha said, never lowering her gaze, though she could barely breathe.

"That's where you're wrong, my darling Seeker. You see, I've captured the lot of you, and taken your delightful treasures. I've but one more to gather and the world as you and I know it will be forever changed. Danu, my oh-so-perfect sister, will be condemned to the dark and I, oh yes, I will rule all." Domnu threw back her head and laughed, dancing around the room in her madness, her hair coiling and whipping around her head with every dip and turn she made.

"Doubtful," Sasha commented, causing the goddess to scream in rage.

"Oh, you'll be the first to go. Once I rule freely, trust me on this – you'll wish for death when I am done with you."

Domnu winked out of sight before Sasha could goad her further, and Sasha let out the deep breath she'd been holding and slipped to the floor. Perhaps it had been stupid to infuriate the goddess, but it wasn't in her nature to back down from a bully. All her training in martial arts and in the ancient history of swordsmanship had taught her to never show fear.

But she was desperately afraid – for Declan, for her friends, and even for the goddess Danu. Something horrible had to have happened for her to end up here. Wherever here was, Sasha thought, lifting her head to examine the room she was in. Much as she had suspected, there was no way in and no way out. A square stone room, with small square windows that perhaps a bird could fit through, and nothing more. Magick was at work here, and there wasn't much she could do about it.

When the Sword of Light appeared in a flash in the middle of the room, Sasha cried out and grabbed it, wrapping her hand around its hilt and feeling the power infuse her entire being. With it came hope.

"Declan, I'm here. I'm armed. I will not go down without a fight. I will fight for us, for our love, and for our people. I love you," Sasha whispered over and over, sending all the energy and power that she could to Declan.

She sat down, her back against the wall, the sword across her legs, a soldier ready for battle.

CHAPTER 19

"We'll need to sleep," Bianca insisted as they drove through the night, heading south on Neala's instructions.

"She's right," Seamus chimed in. "We do. Or we'll get sloppy and make errors that could cost us our lives."

They'd said their goodbyes – tearful ones at that – to Clare and Blake, who were driving back to Dublin with Sean. With promises to keep them updated and an extra-long hug from Bianca to Clare, they were on their way. This time, while they had a sense of direction, they didn't have a particular destination set.

"Why don't we stop at my place in Kilkenny? I can check on the bakery, let Sierra know I'm safe, and we can sleep in my flat," Neala suggested.

Bianca clapped her hands in delight. "Plus, fresh-baked yumminess!" she said.

"No," Dagda said from behind the wheel of the Land Rover.

"And why not?" Neala demanded, craving a shower and a fresh change of clothes.

"The Domnua will have your place staked out. We might as well wave a white flag of surrender if we go back there," Dagda said.

"Will Sierra be safe? My customers?" Neala asked, his words filling her with fear.

"Aye. They're after you. It's not quite time to let the world see them," Dagda reassured Neala.

Neala nodded and turned to stare out of the window, though there was nothing to see except darkness and the light of the occasional house or two on the horizon. She slipped her hand into the velvet pouch she carried, running her hands over the smooth stone, enjoying the pulse of power that warmed her, though the stone was cool to the touch. When her hand slipped over a piece of paper, she paused.

"I think there's something else in this bag," Neala said and dug out a mini-scroll of paper, something she had missed in all the excitement.

"A clue!" Bianca gushed, leaning over Neala's shoulder in excitement.

Neala read from the light of the clock in the car's dashboard, not wanting to blind Dagda as he drove in the dark.

The Sword of Light
Nay gave me a fright
But holding onto a slight
Makes me crow with delight.

"Domnu's really got to work on her poetry. She sounds like a four-year-old making up a schoolyard rhyme,"

Bianca laughed, but when a lightning bolt bisected the sky, she went still. "Ooops."

"She's also quite vain," Dagda said, gesturing with his hand to the sky, "judging from her response anytime we belittle her. We'll need to remember that. Childish and vain."

Another lightning bolt crackled across the dark sky.

"The southernmost point in Ireland is Cape Clear Island," Seamus said, looking up from his tablet.

"Can we get there today?"

"It's a five-hour drive. And, Bianca's right, we haven't slept in almost twenty-four hours. I vote we find a place to sleep for a few hours and carry on."

"Who will take us at this early hour?"

"I'm sure a hostel or a hotel will be open. Or we camp," Dagda shrugged, unconcerned.

"Or, Dag, you and I can switch off driving – we drive straight through, the girls sleep, and then we can check into an inn as soon as we arrive and rest for a few hours."

"Also an option," Dagda said.

"Let's do shifts then. I'll stay up with Dagda so he doesn't fall asleep, and then you two switch out in a few hours," Neala said.

"Sounds good. I'm about to drop as it is," Bianca admitted, snuggling into the crook of Seamus's arm in the back seat. In but a few moments, their breathing turned rhythmic and Seamus began to snore lightly.

"That didn't take long," Neala commented.

"Adrenaline crash. I'm fine to drive, you can sleep," Dagda said, the night cocooning them intimately in the front seat as he drove.

"No, I'll keep you company. Wouldn't be fair," Neala said, and stretched in her seat before turning to look at him. "You said you had no family to speak of. What does that mean?"

"Nothing to be said about them," Dagda said, his face a mask in the glow of the dash.

Neala just waited, saying nothing, until Dagda sighed.

"Women. Always talk, talk, talk. My family and I parted ways years ago. We didn't see eye-to-eye on things like the fae way of life, career choices, and whom I should marry. They are exceptionally conservative and feel that the fae world should not intersect with the human world. They are of the old sect, who will continue to live in magickal realms only, never meeting or interacting with humans. I didn't feel the same."

"I... well, that's fascinating. I never really thought about that. Granted, before a day ago I never much believed in fae to begin with, but to think about an entire society existing outside of ours, with no wish to interact with us... Is this belief held by most of the fae?" Neala almost pinched herself. She couldn't believe she was having this conversation – but hey, she'd just called down the wind, so anything was possible, really.

"The majority of the fae either encourage, delight in, or are ambivalent about intermixing with humans. There is a small sect that refuses to do so, thinking they are like peas-ants, and that we are destroying our bloodline by sleeping with or marrying humans."

The image of sleeping with Dagda slammed into her so forcefully that Neala had to consciously make herself breathe normally. Her entire body had flushed in desire.

She sincerely hoped he didn't have some magickal power that could read her lusty thoughts. Thanking the darkness, for she was certain her face would be flushed, Neala swallowed before answering.

"I suppose the mixing of races has been an age-old issue across many cultures. Why would it be any different with magickal realms?"

"Exactly. I didn't agree and so I left. We don't speak, and I think all of us have made our peace with that." Dagda shrugged.

"You're on your own, then."

"Aye. Just me, lass."

"I get that," Neala said, tucking a foot under her leg and wishing briefly for a cup of hot chocolate and a warm chocolate chip cookie from her bakery. "I'm the same. I think you end up having to create your own family then. Or just let it go."

"When did your da die?" Dagda asked.

"Going on seven years now," Neala said. "But our relationship had deteriorated by that point anyway. For the most part I just called him on holidays. He chose that time to rant at me about my politics and life choices, endlessly trying to needle me because I didn't agree with him."

"Why didn't you pretend to agree with him to mollify him?" Dagda asked.

"Not my style," Neala said, smiling over at Dagda.

"Aye, lass, mine either."

"And here we are, two loners on a mission to save the world – even those who don't share the same views as us," Neala said.

"You can't always pick and choose. We fight for the

greater good, to save those who are too blind to see. It may not feel good, but imagine if nobody picked up the fight? Then all would be lost."

"That's the truth of it, then."

"Are you angry with your father?" Dagda asked.

"Aye, I am. He was so fixated on himself, his world, and his wants and needs, that he couldn't see past that to try and form a real relationship – one of mutual respect. I was willing to allow him to hold his own views; why couldn't he let me have mine? It was childish and controlling, and, yeah, I'm angry."

"Anger isn't good for the soul," Dagda commented.

"Neither is regret."

CHAPTER 20

*T*hey found a little seaside bed and breakfast with two rooms available early in the morning. Dagda liked it for its location by the cliffside and the open land around it – not as easy for the Domnua to creep up and ambush them. Neala liked it for the cheerful blue front door and the yellow shutters that beamed like a beacon of friendliness on another gloomy day along the water.

"Girls in one, guys in the other?" Neala had asked brightly, expecting Bianca to easily acquiesce. She was surprised when the blonde shook her head adamantly.

"Sorry, love, but I want to cuddle up with my honey," Bianca said, and she and Seamus had disappeared up the stairs without another thought as to what position that would leave Dagda and Neala in.

Neala gulped as she climbed the creaky wooden steps and followed the innkeeper to their room. Dagda smiled at her small sigh of relief when she saw two double beds tucked under the eaves in a small but charming room.

"She's small, but will keep you cozy against the winds

today. Let me know if you need anything else. I'm thinking you'll be wanting some rest so I won't be bothering you." The innkeeper bustled out with a smile on her face.

"I'll be back in about twenty minutes or so," Dagda said, gesturing to the door to the small bathroom tucked in the corner. "Feel free to use the shower."

"Wait, where are you going?" Neala asked.

"Perimeter check. And to see about getting some supplies."

And with that, he was gone, leaving Neala to be grateful for a moment of alone time. While tired to the bone, her mind was whirling with all the new things she'd learned and experienced in the last day. She doubted she would be able to sleep anytime soon. Instead, the shower beckoned. Delighted with the hot water, which poured out in a steady stream, Neala took a long, luxurious rinse in the shower, combing through her hair with her fingers and allowing the warmth of the water to sweep any lingering tension in her muscles away. When she had finally dried off and wrapped her hair in a towel, exhaustion had done its work on her. Eyeing the only shirt she had, Neala pulled it over her head and peeked out into the room. Seeing that Dagda was still gone, she picked a bed, dove under the covers, and dropped off to sleep the minute her head touched the pillow.

By the time Dagda returned, Neala had tossed and turned enough that her hair had come unwrapped from the towel and the blankets were wound around her legs. He hadn't been prepared for the punch of her – the vulnerability of her face in sleep, at total peace, nor the way her hair tumbled across the bedsheets, its rich auburn against the stark white of the pillow. Though he knew it was rude, he couldn't help but follow the curve of her hip, down one luscious thigh that was exposed from the sheet, to a delicately shaped calf. It pained Dagda not to be able to cross the room and slide beneath the sheets with her, to entwine themselves until they were one, so that he could protect her and she him.

Silently cursing, he ran his hand through his hair and dropped a package lightly on the floor by her bed before crossing the room to squeeze himself into the impossibly small shower. Whenever he decided to settle down and buy a house, he was going to build himself a massive shower with enough room for six people and a bench to sit upon.

Or make love on.

Dagda groaned and forced himself to drown out the images of Neala that flashed through his head, and instead concentrated on the task at hand. Get a few hours' sleep, keep the group moving, leave few tracks behind. He had to remember they were at war, not on holiday.

Their lives depended on it.

CHAPTER 21

*H*e'd bought her clothes.

Neala almost laughed at the sheer absurdity of picturing Dagda in a clothing store, speaking with a saleswoman about sizes and the like.

"I can't believe you found a clothing store," Neala said in delight, pawing through the bag she'd found next to her bed. She was still under the hand-quilted coverlet, and still only in a shirt, but none of that mattered now that she had a change of clothes.

"I have my ways," Dagda said and sat up in bed, crossing his arms on his bare chest, which suddenly had Neala's undivided attention. The man was built. And she'd been right about there being some tattoos – none of which she could decipher, as they seemed to be in an intricate script she couldn't read. "Go on, see if you like them."

"Oh, right," Neala said, tearing her gaze away from Dagda's muscles. She pulled out a long-sleeved shirt in deep green, a beautiful softly woven wool sweater coat in a misty grey pattern flecked with greens, and a pair of brilliant green emerald silk panties. Neala held up the panties and raised an eyebrow.

"You didn't strike me as the plain white cotton type," Dagda shrugged, completely comfortable with buying sexy underwear for a woman – which immediately miffed Neala. Just how many other women had he bought underwear for?

"I'm not, thanks," Neala said, flushing a bit at the thought of him knowing what kind of underwear she wore.

"I didn't pick a bra, because, well, I haven't had that particular pleasure so I can't be the best judge of size and all," Dagda said, and Neala held up a hand to stop him.

"These are great, thank you. You like green?"

"I like you in green," Dagda said, his voice holding a sexy timbre that sent shivers through Neala's body.

"That's nice of you. My assistant is always telling me to wear more green, but I have a tendency to just buy white. I get a lot of stains at work, even if I wear an apron, so I like stuff that's easy to bleach," Neala said, then slammed her mouth closed, realizing she was babbling. "I'm just going to go put these on."

She realized she was holding the decidedly sexy underwear in the air, and flushed once again. Holding her head high, she got out of bed, tugging her shirt down to make sure it covered everything, and hightailed it for the bathroom, clutching her clothes in her hand. A quick freshen-up later, Neala came back out in her jeans, long-sleeved green t-shirt, and green silk panties that fit like Dagda knew every inch and curve of her body. His eyes skimmed over her, lingering at her waist, before meeting her gaze.

"Looking good," Dagda said.

"Thanks again. Everything fits. And, uh, yeah, it's nice to have a clean shirt," Neala said, refusing to bring up the underwear situation again. They were both adults; this was no big deal.

A knock sounded at the door, followed by Bianca's voice.

"Are you guys up? Am I interrupting anything? We've got visitors."

Neala gaped as Dagda jumped from the bed and threw the door open. Luckily, he was wearing pants – which she thought was odd, until she realized that a warrior was never unprepared. Which explained why he now held a dagger in his hand and was looking over Bianca's head down the hallway.

Bianca gaped at the muscled chest that met her eyeline, and then peered around Dagda to where Neala stood.

"Okay, just checking to make sure you had clothes on," Bianca said. "It's not Domnua. Meet us in the breakfast room. We're ready to move."

"Be down in five," Dagda said, and closed the door in Bianca's face. "Pack up."

"I've got like two things to be packing. I'm ready," Neala pointed out.

Dagda actually laughed. "You're right. I'm used to women carrying a lot of bags."

Neala waited for Dagda to use the bathroom, throw his things in a bag, and button up a red tartan shirt that made her want to snuggle into him. Damn the man for being impossibly sexy. She desperately wanted to ask about the women he'd traveled with who carried a lot of bags, but held her tongue, even though she was faintly annoyed.

"Say it," Dagda said with a small sigh, standing at the door of the room.

"What? It's nothing." Neala shrugged.

Dagda crossed his arms and blocked the door.

"It's never just nothing with women. Speak," Dagda ordered.

"I was just thinking it's remarkable that you were able to guess the right size of my clothing" – Neala refused to say 'panties' – "and that you seem to know so much about traveling with women, is all. Seems to me you've had a lot of women in your life."

Dagda's face split in a full grin and Neala wanted to kick him in the shin.

"Aw, darling, are you getting jealous on me? I didn't know you were thinking of me that way," he said, and Neala groaned.

She muscled her way past him, digging her elbow into his side as she went. "I'm not," she insisted.

"Sounds like you are," Dagda said, his tone decidedly cheerful as he followed her down the steps.

"If I even was, now I definitely would not be," Neala said, even more annoyed by him.

"The lady doth protest too much," Dagda said from behind her.

Neala threw up her hands in disgust as they entered the breakfast room, Dagda's low chuckle following her. Bianca was right. Goddess save them from men and their egos.

CHAPTER 22

A tall man with brown hair tied at the base of his neck and intense green eyes paced the breakfast room, with a decidedly purple tinge hovering around him. Judging from his tightly wound movements and mutinous face, Neala wondered if this was another protector.

"It's Sasha, then, that's been taken," Seamus said without preamble. Neala glanced to where Bianca was sitting next to an older woman with striking white hair, wearing an oversized button-down shirt and trim khakis. Whiskey-brown eyes smiled at her from across the room and there was something about her energy that made Neala feel immediately at home.

"Brother," Dagda said, striding across the room to perform some sort of complicated handshake with the impatient man.

"Aye, 'tis Sasha that's been taken. I'm Declan, by the way," Declan said, nodding across the room at Neala, "her love and her protector. And I failed her."

"You most certainly did not, young man." The older

woman spoke so sharply that everyone in the room immediately straightened their shoulders. "You can't be on
guard at all times. It's not your fault. It's that coward of a
goddess Domnu." Lightning cracked outside at her words
and the woman looked up at the ceiling. "Knock it off."

Neala raised both eyebrows at the woman. Whoever
she was, two things were certain – Neala didn't want to get
on her bad side, and she really liked her.

"I'm Fiona," the woman said, introducing herself to
Dagda and Neala, who were apparently the only ones who
didn't know her. "Let's just say I've had some involvement
in this quest you've all been on."

"You're Danula then?" Neala asked, sliding into a
chair across from Fiona and gratefully accepting the cup of
tea Bianca pushed across the cheerful blue wooden table
to her.

"No, I'm not fae. But that's not to say that my bloodline doesn't have a touch of its own magick." Fiona smiled
at her. "I'm a healer, among other things, and Danu has
entrusted me to help here and there along the way on this
quest. We're all fighting for the same thing, after all."

"A healer… as in, with magick? One of those 'you lay
your hands on someone and heal them' type deals?" Neala
leaned forward, genuinely interested. She'd read a book
about someone like this once and had a ton of questions
to ask.

"Aye, that's the way of it. A wee bit more complicated
than that, but close," Fiona smiled.

"So…"

"I hate to interrupt, but can we please go rescue Sasha?
I'm barely holding myself back from breaking every table

in this room," Declan declared, and the innkeeper popped her head into the breakfast room.

"It's best ye be moving along then. I won't be holding with no violence in my place of business," the innkeeper said sternly.

They all stood, muttering their apologies on the way out the door, while Dagda tipped her handsomely for the room.

"I don't know why you tipped her so much. It's not like we even stayed the night," Neala pointed out.

"She'll be less inclined to speak of us after I tipped her so well and said we'd be back on our way out of town so long as she kept our visit quiet," Dagda said smoothly as they made their way to the Land Rover.

"Neala, would you like to ride with us?" Fiona asked.

Dagda shook his head no. "She stays with me."

"I'll go with you," Bianca immediately volunteered, and leaned over to give Seamus a smacking kiss on the lips. "See you soon, handsome."

Seamus's eyes lit with love and his cheeks flushed, which told Neala all she needed to know about how Seamus and Bianca had chosen to spend their time in the B&B.

"You're certain about this island?" Declan asked.

"It's the southernmost point – well, southernmost inhabited point, aside from another tiny island with a lighthouse. We found Clare in a lighthouse already; I honestly can't imagine Domnu being so stupid as to put Sasha in one as well. But we'll have a boat and if we don't find her here, we'll head there next."

"And you, Seeker – this feels right to you?" Declan demanded, his tone still murderous, and Neala stiffened.

"Yes, it's right," Neala said, raising her chin to meet Declan's eyes.

"Then I'll be thanking ye when this is over." Declan nodded once and climbed into a sturdy looking SUV, and Neala was surprised to see Fiona take the wheel.

Together, the two cars left the B&B and trundled down the dirt road through a small village. Neala craned her neck to see if there were any women's shops around, and wondered just where Dagda had managed to find green silk panties from. She caught him smiling at her as though he knew what she was thinking, which immediately set her into a pout.

"If Declan and Fiona found us so easily, how come the Domnua haven't? Doesn't it seem eerily calm?" Neala asked.

"I texted Declan," Seamus piped up from the backseat, quickly ending the line of thought that Neala had regarding some sort of fae internet or otherworldly telecommunication system. "He'd already contacted me when we were rescuing Clare."

"You said Sasha is the difficult one?" Neala asked, and Seamus blew out a breath.

"Sasha is awesome. But initially, yes, she was difficult. She's a super tough badass woman who owns a specialty shop."

"Oh, neat. What kind of shop?" Neala asked, already drawn to this woman.

"Swords and daggers. Antiquities to present-day. She's

also an expert swordsman, and a martial artist. We do not mess with Sasha."

Neala let out a low whistle, and imagined what this woman would think of her own pastry-puff of a business.

"Her treasure, naturally, was the Sword of Light," Dagda said.

"Aye, and it was a beauty of a treasure at that," Seamus said. "I like her and Declan together as well. He's patient with her rough edges. And she's learned to be vulnerable to him. All in all, I'd say they're doing well together."

Neala kept quiet as they wound along a narrow cliff road, then smiled when they turned a corner and the sea spread out below them.

"I'll never get tired of looking out over the water," Neala said.

"There's the island – only one hundred inhabitants." Seamus pointed over Neala's shoulder to an island shrouded in mist on the horizon.

"And how are we getting there? Do you know a guy?" Neala asked, glancing at Dagda. His lips quirked in a smile but he just shook his head no.

"We'll have a chat with one of the locals; I'm sure we can arrange passage. Also, there's probably a ferry," Dagda said.

Within a few moments, they'd pulled into a small carport and parked their cars, all piling out into the damp mist. Grateful for the sweater coat Dagda had purchased for her, Neala pulled it on and snuggled into its softness. It was almost like being cocooned by the man himself, she thought, but forced her mind away from those thoughts.

He was her protector, not her man. It would serve her

well to remember that they were both loners, and a relationship didn't factor into either of their lifestyles.

"It's going to be another night search," Bianca said, crossing the gravel lot to where Neala stood looking out at the increasingly foggy skyline. Moments before they'd been able to see the outline of the island, but now it was nothing but grey and white swirling mists. Neala didn't trust what they'd find buried in the fog either, which made her anxiety kick up a notch.

"Are you certain we should cross in this? It looks quite dangerous," Neala said, chewing on her bottom lip as she studied the horizon.

"The local lads should know what they are doing. I think we'll be fine," Fiona commented as she joined them. "Though it certainly looks menacing."

"You're coming with?" Neala asked in surprise, glancing at the older woman.

Fiona had pulled a grey wool sweater over her shirt and a tightly-knit wool cap over her head, tufts of white hair poking out from beneath the brim. "Naturally. Anything I can do to be of help. We're all in this together," she said briskly. "And I'm stronger than I look, my dear."

"I'm sorry," Neala said, immediately contrite. "I didn't mean to imply that you weren't. I guess I'm just worried for everyone's safety. This is supposed to be my quest, and here everyone is throwing themselves into danger."

"It may be on you to find your treasure, but it involves all of us. We all love Sasha and if you think we'd not help rescue her, you don't really understand the meaning of family then," Bianca said tersely. Then she slammed her palm into her forehead. "Ugh, open mouth, insert foot. I'm sorry, I'm sorry, I'm sorry. I know you don't really have a family. That was an insensitive thing to say."

"You're right, I don't really understand family. But I do understand loyalty and friendship," Neala said, and reached out to squeeze Bianca's arm. "You're a good friend." She looked up to catch Fiona's warm brown eyes studying her closely. "Yes?"

"I like your spirit," Fiona said, then turned away to meet the men who now strode across the small car lot to meet them. Neala felt oddly warmed by the compliment, though she had no way of knowing who or what this Fiona woman really was. However, there was something about Fiona that made Neala appreciate her approval.

"We've got a fisherman who'll take us over. He's just delivering his catch and heading back home – he lives on the island. He has no problem going out in the fog, says he navigates it like this most days," Declan said, zipping his jacket against the damp.

It didn't take long for the fisherman to deliver his catch and soon he was back at his boat, grateful for the unexpected extra income for being a water taxi service. A jovial fellow named Michael, he entertained them with local tales in his thick Gaelic accent as he helped everyone onto his rickety boat and settled everyone the best he could. Squeezed among some lobster pots and a crate of what smelled like seaweed, Neala peered up at him.

"You're certain you'll be fine with crossing in this fog, then?" Neala asked.

Michael beamed down at her. "Aye lass, 'tis nothing I haven't done a million times before. Could do it with me eyes closed," he laughed, "but I won't, I promise ye that."

With that he untied the boat and motored slowly out onto the water, periodically hitting a cowbell that dangled next to the wheel.

"Why the cowbell?" Neala wondered out loud.

"We're all but flying blind here. He'll be using sound and coordinates to navigate now," Dagda said, then held a finger to his lips to indicate she should be silent. In truth, she hadn't noticed that the chattering fisherman had gone dead silent as soon as they'd begun the ride, but now she realized he hadn't spoken for several minutes.

And so they rode in silence, but for the low rhythmic clang of the bell and the water slapping the hull of the boat. Neala felt anxiety creep its way up her spine until she huddled herself into her sweater and looked down at her feet. Just days ago her biggest worry had been whether she could afford to open a second bakery, and here she was huddled on a smelly boat, quite possibly being shuttled to her death.

Glancing up, she caught Dagda staring at her steadily, the mist shrouding him slightly, making him seem almost an ethereal warrior. His gaze held hers, and he smiled – just a hint, but enough to reassure her. It was as though he could sense her anxiety and was sending her good vibes to calm her down. It worked, for she was able to breathe a little easier, and for some reason, having him near made her feel more reassured about whatever awaited them on this foggy, all but uninhabited island.

"Shore's ahead; grab the pole," Michael called, startling Neala from the stillness around her. She watched as Declan held a pole in front of him while Michael and whomever was on shore did a series of clangs back and forth on their bells. Then a hand reached through the mist and grabbed the pole, tugging the boat to a dock. It amazed her, the unique way these people had figured out how to live, Neala thought. But wasn't that the lesson of ingenuity? People don't always know how to solve a problem until it presents itself to them.

Which should be a lesson for her about anxiety, Neala thought. She'd always figured out how to solve any problem that came her way – and why was this venture any different? Granted, it was deadly and there was magick and all sorts of things she probably didn't even know about, but when it came down to it – she had a team of people to help and she had a can-do attitude.

Historically, that had been a winning combination for her. She could only hope that history would repeat itself.

CHAPTER 23

They proceeded single file into the fog, declining Michael's offer of a place to stay. He'd been smart enough – or paid handsomely enough – to not ask any questions, Neala noticed, and he quickly hurried away after offering explicit instructions on which paths to take around the island.

They trudged along, the going slow, their headlamps barely making a dent in the fog. Neala wondered what they were looking for or how they would even know where Sasha was being held. How were they to find this woman when they could barely see a meter in front of their faces? She wished the wind would pick up and blow this fog away.

Neala stopped so suddenly in her tracks that Dagda ran into her, his arm coming around her waist to stop her from toppling over at his feet. For a second, her body molded to his, and a delicious shiver zinged through her before she stepped forward and cleared her throat.

"Um, so this wind thing that I can do? Call down the

wind?" Neala began, and Fiona murmured something inde-
cipherable from behind her. "Can I do that now? Like at
any time? Can I clear the fog, or am I only able to call it
down during battle or in times of extreme duress?"

"Give it a whirl, darling, and see," Dagda said and the
others encouraged her to do so as well.

"But how? What do I do?"

"Close your eyes," Fiona's voice reached her through
the fog and Neala did as instructed. "Now, feel deep within
you. Search for your power. You'll feel it like a warm ball
of light in your core – or perhaps a humming ball of music.
We all feel it a little differently. Once you find it, you'll
know."

Neala kept her eyes closed and went deep within,
feeling safe in doing so with Dagda hovering at her back.
She let her mind go loose and took a few deep breaths until
she centered on a sparkly ball of energy that lit her core.

"It's glittery," Neala gasped.

"Of course it is," Dagda drawled, and Neala almost
lost the ball of light because she wanted to laugh.

"Now visualize using that light, that power, to push the
fog away so that we may see clearly on our journey,"
Fiona continued. "Or because it's glitter, perhaps you can
visualize sprinkling it on the fog like rain and making it
disperse. It's your own personal choice. Just do what feels
right and see what happens."

Fiona's tone was confident and encouraging. Neala
could see her being a good teacher, as she empowered
people without intimidating them.

Neala closed her eyes again and then envisioned her
glittery ball as a big powdered-sugar shaker. She shook the

glitter out onto the fog, forcing it gently from the island in her mind. When she heard Bianca gasp, she opened her eyes to see silvery specks falling from the sky in a blast of wind, which completely dissipated the fog that clung to the hills around them.

"It's like being in a snow globe," Bianca whispered, wiping glitter from her face. The men didn't seem as amused, especially when Neala craned her neck to look at Dagda.

His beard, once brown, was all sparkly silver, and Neala slapped a hand over her mouth to control her laugh. It didn't matter – between his dangerous look, the glitter beard, and Bianca's chuckling behind her, Neala snorted and threw her head back and roared in laughter.

"Perhaps a different vision next time?" Dagda asked, shaking his beard and ridding himself of most of the glitter.

"I think it's charming," Neala said, reaching up to brush a piece from his cheek, but pulling her hand back before she touched his skin. The moment held a beat too long before she turned away and mentally kicked herself for forgetting what she had lectured herself on earlier today. They were both loners. No family, no attachments, forging their own paths. And that's what she needed to stay focused on.

Perhaps her attraction to him was because she'd given up dating almost a year ago to focus on growing her business – which meant it had been just as long since she'd enjoyed any companionship or intimacy in her life. Women had needs, just as men did, Neala reminded herself. And her needs had been largely unmet for quite a while. Reassuring herself that this was obviously the reason for her tug of attraction toward Dagda, she continued down the path they were hiking, delighted to be able to see ahead of them now.

The sun was just setting on the horizon, sending a warm glow across a rolling green hill and the craggy cliffs that jutted out into the ocean. Lights twinkled from a few houses scattered in the cliffs on one side of the island, but the rest of the island was largely barren, aside from what looked to be some stones or ruins tucked among the cliffs at the high point of the island. Which would make sense, Neala thought. If she were to build a fortress, it would be in that spot.

"There," Declan pointed, and turned to Neala. "You agree?"

"Aye, I agree."

"It's an hour's walk at least. Do we have any food?" Bianca moaned. "Our breakfast got interrupted."

"I've got sandwiches in the pack. Why don't we take a short break, fuel up, and begin the climb?" Fiona said, and paused to put her hand on Declan's shoulder, "We'll do you no good if we are fatigued and running on zero energy. Nor will you. Don't be foolish."

"Fine," Declan bit out. They all found shelter behind a tall group of rocks, and Declan helped hand out sandwiches to the group.

"Neala, walk with me a bit," Fiona instructed, and Dagda rose as well. "Not you, Dag. Just Neala."

"I must protect her," Dagda protested.

"I've magick as well, you know. We won't be far. I need to speak with her privately," Fiona said. She stared him down until he nodded a brisk assent, though he clearly wasn't happy about it.

They walked ahead in silence for a moment until Fiona finally turned and smiled at Neala.

"I knew your mother."

CHAPTER 24

Time seemed to stand still for a moment as Neala felt the air whoosh out of her and a weird tingling begin at the base of her neck. Was she going to faint? O'Riordans didn't faint; they were made of stronger stock than that, she reminded herself. She'd just called down the wind and made freaking glitter fall from the sky. Learning about a mother she'd never known and had long since buried in her mind was not something that should shake her so.

Neala shrugged a shoulder, pretending nonchalance as she turned to stare out at the horizon, where the last light of the day was being claimed by night.

"She didn't abandon you, you know," Fiona continued, turning to walk shoulder to shoulder with Neala, giving her time to absorb the information. "None of the Seekers were abandoned by their mothers."

"None of the Seekers have mothers?" Neala asked, intrigued by the concept.

"They have families who took them in and cared for

and loved them, but no, not their actual mothers. You see, you're magick," Fiona said, turning to Neala with a brilliant smile lighting her face.

Neala could see where once she must have been very beautiful – and, interestingly enough, the years didn't detract from her beauty. Instead, when she smiled, they only enhanced it.

"I'm magick?" Neala said, doubt ringing in her voice.

Fiona laughed, delighted with her. "You just called down the wind, my dear. What did you think that was?"

"I don't know. Maybe something just given to me by the fae for this quest?"

"You are part fae, and part goddess as well," Fiona said.

Neala drew up short, turning to look at the older woman. "I'm part goddess?"

"Of course. Your mother is a goddess. That makes you a demi-goddess."

"I… I have no idea what to say right now."

"Your mother was the goddess of home and family – her power was in nurturing others," Fiona said.

"And isn't that ironic?" Neala asked, feeling the old bitterness swell at the way her father had treated her.

"Aye, I understand from what Bianca said in the car that you have no family to speak of. Your father has passed on?"

"From drink. And bitterness, I suppose," Neala said, shrugging a shoulder once again.

"You're angry. I can feel it," Fiona said, pressing a fist to her chest. "With both of them."

"I guess I am. I'm angry at my mother for abandoning

me and I'm angry at my father for never accepting me for who I was. He constantly tried to force me into being what he wanted me to be," Neala said. She realized it felt good to talk about it. She so rarely examined those feelings she had tucked deep inside of her.

"Your father did the best he could with his limited world view. The drink clouded his vision. We all have our own battles to fight and our own lessons to learn. It is part of our journey and path in this realm. He struggled deeply. Perhaps, with time, you'll be able to step back and view him with empathy instead of anger," Fiona said, her tone gentle.

"I'm not sure I know how to do that," Neala whispered, feeling a sheen of tears prick into her eyes. "I just wanted him to love me, but as me – a woman of her own opinions, beliefs, and dreams. Which doesn't make me a bad person."

"No, it doesn't. But to some, especially those who only know one way or thought process – it can be threatening. It's not easy to change your beliefs. It's even harder if you're escaping into a bottle daily. At the end of it, he led a lonely and sad existence that he created for himself, and his soul will have to learn its lessons in another realm now."

"Can you tell me more about my mother?" Neala asked, and followed Fiona when she indicated two large boulders they could perch on. They settled themselves with their backs to the rock wall behind them, sheltered on all sides so that they had a cozy, private nook in which to talk of magickal relations.

"Ahhh, she was a goddess of nurturing. Her powers lay

in giving, making people feel comfortable, caring for others, empathy, and the like. She spent her days helping people learn to care for others, teaching forgiveness and empathy, and nurturing the world."

"She's gone then, from the way you speak about her in the past tense," Neala said, surprised to find she could still feel sadness over a loss she had accepted long ago.

"Of course she's not dead – she's just moved up the ranks in the spirit world. She's completed her duties here and moved on to where she is needed next, is all."

"Oh. I suppose I don't really know much about all that," Neala said, leaning against the rocky wall and closing her eyes for a moment, trying to work through the tangle of emotions that hung heavy in her gut.

"I find it interesting that you opened a bakery. You're nurturing others, you know," Fiona said.

Neala opened her eyes to look at her. "How? I bake scones and serve coffee."

"You make people feel good. You put love into your work and your food, they are happy when they leave your shop, and you've created an environment of home and family. I'd say that's nurturing."

"I suppose. I have always wanted to create a spot just for me – my own little safe haven," Neala admitted, "that nobody can touch or change but me."

"And you could have done that with a house or an office, yet you chose a business that brings joy and happiness to others. Something to think about," Fiona commented.

"If I'm part goddess – what does that mean? Do I have duties to fulfill?"

"You're already doing so. You were born and put here with this path predestined. It's on you as to whether you pick up the sword and fight, though." Fiona crossed her arms over her chest and studied Neala.

"I've accepted the challenge, haven't I? I'm here." Neala feared her tone sounded a bit petulant.

"Aye, you have. But I think you already know what you need to do for the next step, yet you're deflecting me at every turn," Fiona said, not backing down.

Neala's shoulders slumped. "Sometimes I think it's easier to hold onto the anger. I'm comfortable with it. It gives me power in the situation."

"That's the tricky thing about anger. You think it is you holding the power when you're angry with someone, but it is really them holding all the power. The only power you can claim comes with forgiveness. If it is control you crave, it will come through letting go."

"How does letting go give me control? I control my story and my emotions around it right now. Letting go of that means... I don't know." Neala flapped her hands helplessly in her lap. "It means I have to write a new story. Reframe it. I'm comfortable with my story. Or I was until a few days ago. Now I don't know who or what I am anymore."

"You're still you. But the only thing consistent in life is change. Your old story, the anger you've held onto for years – it doesn't play well in this story. In fact, it works against you. Sasha had to learn the same."

"What do I do? Will you help me?" Neala whispered, turning beseeching eyes on Fiona. "I don't want to let anyone down."

"You won't let anyone down, so long as you stay open and try your hardest," Fiona said.

"Head up, heart open," Neala murmured.

"What's that?"

"Dagda told me that, before we rescued Clare."

"He's a smart man. And a handsome one at that," Fiona commented. "You could do worse."

"I... he's not for me. It's not like that. We're both loners and I don't see a relationship fitting into our lifestyles. He likes the open road and I have a business to run. It would never work," Neala said.

"Love always finds a compromise," Fiona commented, and Neala scoffed.

"I was just thinking of bedding the man. Not love," she huffed.

"Aye, that looks like it would be great fun too," Fiona commented, and despite everything they had just talked about, Neala found herself able to laugh until tears pricked her eyes.

"I like you, Fiona."

"I like you as well, Neala. You've got spirit and a good heart. For that, I'll give you a gift for your journey," Fiona said. "Give me your hands. Both of them."

Neala turned and clasped Fiona's hands in hers. The hands, though their skin was wrinkled and papery, were firm and warm beneath Neala's palms.

"Close your eyes and focus on that ball of resentment in your gut. Lead me to it. Open your heart and let me heal you," Fiona ordered.

Neala closed her eyes, focusing on her gut, where

resentment and anger over past hurts twisted and seethed like a ball of angry snakes.

"Do you forgive, Neala? Can you look at others with empathy and understanding – and send them love and light – even if they have wounded you?"

Neala took her time before answering, testing the emotion of forgiveness, working on building a new story in her mind – and when she said the words, she meant them.

"Aye, I forgive."

With those words the snakes of resentment seemed to shatter in her core, pulling forth from her and splintering like shards of glass into the night sky. Neala's eyes flew open in astonishment; she'd never seen or felt anything like this in her life.

"What was that?" Neala gasped.

"Just a touch of healing and magick, my dear," Fiona chuckled, patting her arm. "How do you feel?"

Neala took a deep cleansing breath and searched her heart, her mind, and her soul.

"You know what, Fiona? I feel pretty damn good. This forgiveness thing might be just fine after all."

"If only more people felt that way," Fiona said and stood, stretching her arms above her head before holding out a hand to Neala. "Come, your man grows restless. We've tarried too long, and Declan is also champing at the bit to get to Sasha. But we needed to accomplish this before we could rescue her. I wasn't sure if you were ready for it."

"He's not 'my man.' I wish you'd stop saying that,"

Neala said, not ready to talk about the forgiveness thing again. It was still just a wee bit tender in her heart.

"And I wish you'd keep your head up and heart open as your man instructed. I wonder if he was telling himself to do the same as well," Fiona commented.

Great. Now she'd be looking at Dagda and wondering.

CHAPTER 25

"What was the magick you used?" Dagda demanded the instant they were back in speaking range.

Neala cocked an eyebrow at him, refusing to be intimidated by his attitude. "It was Fiona's. And it's personal," she said, brushing past him to where Bianca offered her a canteen of water.

"Personal? There is no personal. We're all in this together now," Dagda said, stomping after her.

"Well, I say it's personal." Neala held her ground, rolling her eyes at a grinning Bianca as she took a swig of water from the canteen.

"Let her be, Dagda. If it was Fiona's magick, I trust it," Declan sighed, raking his hand through his hair, and all but growling out the words as he paced.

Dagda looked like he was going to argue, but then thought better of it and instead bent to pack the satchel and swing it over his shoulder before striding off down the path leading to the ruins.

"What's his deal? He's certainly having a wee snit now, isn't he?" Neala wondered out loud, staring after where the giant man trounced down the hill.

"He's worried about you," Bianca said, patting her shoulder. "The magick looked pretty intense from here, and it was hard to tell at first who it had come from. Dagda was halfway up the hill, sword in hand, when he realized it was Fiona's magick. Methinks he likes you…" Bianca sang out the last few words, like a schoolgirl singing a song about two people kissing in a tree.

"He's worried the goddess will kick his arse if he fails," Neala amended as they fell in line behind the others and continued their hike up the hill into darkness.

"I don't think so. He's got all eyes on you," Bianca commented, cheerful despite the damp night and potential for danger on the horizon.

"Listen, I get it. All the other Seekers and protectors ended up together. It would tie this little quest up in a nice, neat package of romance, wouldn't it?" Neala said over her shoulder to Bianca. "But I'm telling you, our lifestyles are not compatible. Dag's a wanderer. He likes the open road, doesn't like being tied down, and he certainly doesn't want to be in a relationship."

"And you think that can't change? That men can't eventually decide they want something different when they meet the right woman? From what I've seen, men will go to the ends of the earth to make love work," Bianca said.

"I don't think that will be the case here," Neala laughed. "You're talking like this is some great love story instead of me, a small-town bakery owner, having met a man – a fae, at that – just days ago. Love doesn't happen like that. It takes time, and grows, and you go on first dates and learn what your favorite music is or what your likes and dislikes are. I think you're a romantic, Bianca, and I admire that. But I'm a realist, and I can tell you that this is not love you're speaking of."

"You think love follows a formula?" Bianca asked.

"Well, maybe not a formula, but there is no love at first sight or anything. It's fun for the movies, but not in real life." Neala shrugged.

"Have you ever been in love before?" Bianca asked, continuing her line of questioning as they arrived at the crest of the hill.

"No, I can't say I have," Neala admitted, and the thought made her feel just a little bit sad, and kind of like a loser for never having been in love. "Never quite found a man that was worthy of that, I suppose."

"Or perhaps you've been following the wrong formula," Bianca sing-songed.

Neala wrinkled her nose in disgust. "I can push you down this hill, you know," she commented.

Bianca smiled. "Try it. I'm little, but I'm fierce."

"I'd be tempted, but I've seen you fight. You are fierce," Neala muttered, just a little annoyed by the topic of conversation, but also enjoying Bianca.

"If you ladies are going to wrestle, might I suggest bikinis and a mud pit? I'd pay to watch that," Seamus said over his shoulder, and they laughed at him.

"In your dreams, buddy," Bianca called back.

"Silence," Dagda ordered from the front of the line, putting the kibosh on their fun.

Neala rolled her eyes again, but followed his order as

they approached the half ruins of the old castle. It looked as if it had once been a small stronghold, with a run-down tower in one corner and a few rooms of various sizes with missing parts of their walls. Only one part of the fortress remained intact – and judging from where their lights shone on the walls, there was no way in or out.

"I don't like this," Dagda declared, bringing the group together in a tight circle. "It feels like a trap."

"Everything is a trap and nobody plays fair in war," Declan said, his eyes scanning the building. "But I can feel her inside this fortress. We just have to find a way without the walls coming down on her."

"Divide and conquer," Fiona suggested.

"I don't know if I like that either," Dagda said.

Neala realized his voice sounded odd, like it was getting further and further away. She'd stepped a few feet away from the group to shine her light around the corner of the fortress, looking for another way into the ruin. The light had fallen upon a small door in the side that they must have missed.

She turned to point it out to the group, and was surprised to see how far she had ventured from them.

"That's odd," Neala said, and raised her voice to shout to the group. "Hey, everyone, there's a door right here."

They all turned in shock, and Neala squealed as she was sucked into the hallway of the fortress, the door disappearing. She now stared at a rough stone wall just inches from her face. Whirling, her light shone down an empty stone hallway, with no way in and no way out. All she could do was walk forward.

Cursing herself for her stupidity, Neala reached for the only weapons she had – the Stone of Truth and her dagger.

She was on her own now.

CHAPTER 26

*D*agda's heart skipped a beat as Neala was sucked into the fortress, the wisp of Domnua magick still curling in the air after the wall slammed shut behind her. Time seemed to stop as he roared her name, to no response from within.

"I knew it," Dagda shouted, racing to pound on the wall Neala had disappeared into. "I knew this was a trap."

"We'll get them both out," Declan said, right at his side and banging against the stone wall just as hard.

"Easy for you to say. This isn't on your head," Dagda grunted, testing the wall for any weakness, running his hands over the stones and looking for cracks.

"It's on all of us. And I'll remind you that it isn't just your woman in there; mine is as well. So stop your bitching and let's figure out how to save them," Declan said.

Dagda whirled on him, so furious with himself that he needed an outlet for his rage. "Bitching? I don't bitch.

Back off or I'll make you back off," he seethed, catching Declan by the throat and pushing him against the wall.

The first blow from Declan bounced easily off his chest, but the second – a direct hit to his gut – had him wincing a bit.

Raising his arm to hit back, Dagda winced as he was cuffed on the back of his head.

"Knock it off, boys. Immediately. We've trouble on our hands," Fiona ordered.

Dagda rubbed his head and turned to see Fiona wielding her walking stick like a club. "Stubborn old woman," he muttered.

"Testosterone driven imbecile," Fiona shot right back, and Dagda shrugged. She wasn't entirely wrong. "Either you can kill each other or the Domnua can. But I think they'd delight in you doing the job for them, seeing as they're just sitting there watching ye all turn on each other."

"Where?" Dagda growled, and turned to see an army of Domnua, standing in stillness on the crest of the hill behind them, with Bianca and Seamus between them, swords raised.

"Shite," Declan cursed.

"Shite, indeed," Fiona said, "Time to work some magick, boys."

"What about Neala?" Dagda said, helpless not to look over his shoulder at the wall behind him.

"She's on her own for now. You can't fight all her battles for her. Sometimes protecting someone also means letting them go out on their own. Can't coddle too much," Fiona admonished.

"I do not coddle," Dagda said, fed up with the lot of them, ready to murder all the Domnua, tear down the fortress wall, and sneak Neala away to safety.

"She's on her own. I've given her all the tools I can. Now, help me with some magick – I need fae input for this," Fiona said. She began to rattle off some magick, centuries old, that Dagda had learned around the fire in his youth. He chimed in, and Declan did the same, and then they began to send their magick forth, praying it was enough to take down the Domnua army currently staring them down.

Or, if they couldn't take them down, at least hold them off until Neala conquered whatever faced her deep inside the walls of the fortress behind him.

CHAPTER 27

eala crept forward slowly, the dagger in one hand, the stone in the other. Grateful for the headlamp and the light it provided while leaving her hands free, she wondered whether she should call out for Sasha or not. Deciding against drawing any more attention to herself than necessary – though certainly the bad guys knew exactly where she was, since they'd drawn her into their trap – she moved along, her steps quiet on the damp stone.

When her father stepped in front of her, Neala gasped.

He looked much the same as he had in the years leading up to his death – dark hair gone to grey, wrinkled brow, and a bulbous nose, ruddy from too much drink. His eyes narrowed as he looked her from head to toe, then spat on the ground in front of her.

Neala squirmed, trying so hard to hold onto the gift of lightness and freedom that Fiona had bestowed upon her. But it was virtually impossible to look upon her father and not feel the old resentments surface.

"Look at you running around with a dagger in your hand. That's a man's weapon. You never did know your place anyhow." Her father glared at her.

"My place is exactly where I want it to be," Neala said, raising her chin and the dagger. She knew this had to be a trick of the Domnua, but everything about it felt as real as if she had just seen him yesterday.

"You always did have a mouth on you, speaking too much nonsense. How women should be able to run their own businesses and get birth control if they wanted. What kind of good woman speaks like that? You should have taken care of our home, then found yourself a man and taken care of him and his home, and kept your opinions to yourself."

"'Should' is such a shite word, isn't it?" Neala asked lightly, inching a little closer to her father. "There are a lot of things people *should* do that they never seem to follow through with. For example, you should have been a better father to me."

"You had food to eat, didn't ye?" her father protested.

"Aye, which I went and got with money from me after-school job. Food I cooked and prepared for you. Which you barely ate since your nose was so deep in a pint," Neala retorted, glancing behind him to see if she could get around him, but his broad shoulders took up most of the hallway.

"At least it taught you how to cook. You wouldn't be owning a bakery anyway if you were shite at cooking. You should be thanking me."

"There's that should word again," Neala said and

stepped forward, more boldly this time and then paused as a thought occurred to her.

"You'll not be passing me," Her father loomed closer and held his ground, his eyes angry in his face.

"You're right, Da" Neala said, eyes on her father's face. "Thank you for teaching me to be a self-reliant and strong woman who, despite everything, can cook, run a business, and maintain healthy relationships with friends. I forgive you for not being what I needed you to be. Because I found myself on my own."

With that, Neala held up the stone, and it began to pulse gently in her hand. Her father's image wavered a bit, growing almost watery around the edges, and his face contorted in rage.

"You'll never amount to anything! You'll see! You should have done as I said." His shouts grew softer as she held the stone up, ignoring him, and looked at it.

"Domnua, show thyself," Neala ordered, and the image of her father faded away to show a smiling silver fae dancing in glee in front of her. "Just as I thought."

The smile died on his face as she threw a knife at him, impaling him directly through the heart, and he dissolved quickly into a silvery puddle on the floor. Bending over the puddle, Neala grimaced as she gingerly pulled her knife out and wiped it clean on her jeans. Not something she'd particularly enjoyed, but she wasn't stupid – she'd seen how ruthless the Domnua could be.

"Well, that was certainly interesting. I suppose that was the forgiveness lesson Fiona was trying to teach me. Not a fun one, that's the truth of it then," Neala said under her breath. She pocketed the stone and continued carefully down the hallway, dagger ready and waiting for what surely would be another trap.

It didn't take long, but this time she wasn't sure what vignette she was stepping into.

Neala hung back, watching as a couple approached her, a man and a woman, both in flowing purple robes and carrying the telltale tinge of purple that marked them as Danula. Relieved that she finally had assistance, she smiled at the couple.

"I'm glad to be seeing you then, as I'm in a fierce pickle," Neala said, smiling gratefully at the man and woman.

"We're certainly not glad to be seeing trash like you," the woman snipped, and Neala backpedaled, holding the dagger higher in front of her.

"Really, I can't understand why Dagda must trifle with these humans. They are so low-class," the man said, shaking his head at the woman beside him.

So these were Dagda's parents, Neala realized, and examined them more closely. From what she understood they were still living, so she'd need to tread carefully here in case these were, in fact, his real parents and not just some Domnua-fueled apparition. Reaching one hand in her pocket, she palmed the stone.

"Apparently he must think we're fun," Neala quipped.

The couple shuddered in disgust. "He'll dilute our bloodline with the likes of you," the woman sniffed.

"Because being half-goddess is so bad?" Neala asked, raising an eyebrow as she studied the couple. She could see where Dagda got his striking looks. Both of his parents were tall, his dad was similar in size to Dagda, and he had his mother's striking eye color.

"That hardly matters. You've been tainted with human blood. I honestly can't imagine what Danu was thinking giving the role of Seeker to humans. She might as well be condemning the world to destruction for all their ineptitude," Dagda's father complained.

Neala wanted to bury her face in her hands. No wonder Dagda had taken off and roamed the world. With parents who were so closed-minded and judgmental, it must have been virtually impossible for him to have any real intellectual growth. She admired him even more now for having forged his own path and made himself his own man.

"Oh, I'm not sure about that. We humans tend to have a surprisingly resilient spirit. You'll be seeing us celebrating when this is all over," Neala said cheerfully, and held up the stone. "But I'll be forgiving you ahead of time, just in case this is part of my lesson too."

"Forgiving us? We've done nothing wrong," Dagda's mother held a hand to her robe, offended at the thought that a human could imply they were wrong about something.

"I'll be forgiving you anyway, as that's the kind thing to do when small-minded people sprinkle their limited, rigid opinions everywhere. Let's chalk it up to lack of education and world experience. I wish you the best of luck, though. Perhaps we'll have a glass of wine when I see you next," Neala said.

She looked at the stone, now glowing in her hand. Dagda's parents were fixated on it, their gazes growing hungry with lust, and the purple tinge slipped a bit to show the silver beneath. "For now though, I'll be saying my goodbyes."

In two quick motions, Neala pivoted forward and dealt quickly with the Domnua masquerading as Dagda's parents. Two more silvery puddles slid to the floor, and once again Neala cleaned the dagger on her pants. She grimaced at the thought of the bloodshed, but it didn't seem real to her. Bright silver blood just didn't make her think of death in the same way human blood did. It was as if she were in a dream or playing a video game.

Edging forward, she turned a corner – and screeched, ducking an instant before a sword swooped overhead.

"Holy shite, I'm sorry. I thought you were a Domnua."

"You must be Sasha." Neala glanced up, panting, from her crouch on the floor.

"Aye, I am. And I'm more than pleased to be making your acquaintance."

CHAPTER 28

*S*asha looked like a warrior; Neala could see why Bianca had found her to be a bit troublesome at first. Dressed in black pants and a fitted black tank, with black hair that fell straight down her back and eyes that lit up her face.

"Seeker?" Sasha asked, still brandishing the sword.

"Aye," Neala said, showing her the stone.

Sasha nodded, bringing the sword down to rest at her side. "I'll be apologizing for that then. It was hard to know who was around the corner when the door in the wall appeared."

"I can understand that. I've just had a few weird run-ins of my own," Neala said. "I'm Neala, by the way, and I'm guessing you are Sasha."

"Aye, that's me. Run-ins? Any more to worry about?" Sasha asked, peering over Neala's shoulder, ever the warrior on alert.

"Not that I saw, but I can't promise anything. I

honestly have no idea how I got in here, or where we are inside the fortress," Neala admitted.

"You know more than I do. I was dropped into the middle of this room by a supremely angry goddess. At least you know where we are. Speaking of – where are we? Have you heard from Declan? Is he safe?"

"Aye, he came to find us with Fiona. We're on Cape Clear Island, in a ruin of an old fortress," Neala said. "And Declan is sick with worry over you."

"Ahhh, Declan." Sasha rubbed her hand over her heart. "He's a good man."

"He seems to be. A handsome one too."

"Doesn't hurt either." Sasha shot Neala a quick smile, then scooted forward to peer down the dark hallway. "My vote is we keep moving. You first, as you've got the light, and I'll bring up the rear."

"What if something comes up behind you?" Neala asked.

"Don't worry about me, I'll handle it," Sasha said with absolute confidence.

Neala believed her. Sasha carried herself with a 'don't mess with me' attitude that Neala found particularly appealing. If she had to go back down a dark hallway potentially full of murdering fae, she could have worse at her back.

"How did you get in here anyway?" Sasha asked as Neala began to walk down the hallway, proceeding cautiously with dagger in hand again.

"One moment we were all outside; the next I saw a door. I had barely started to approach it before I was just sucked inside. I don't even know how it happened," Neala admitted. "I fear I'm not the best Seeker for the job."

"You're exactly the right Seeker for the job. Each one of us was picked for the goddess's own reasons. You wouldn't be here if you didn't have what it takes, so enough with the pity party," Sasha said.

Neala surprised herself by laughing. "Thanks, I needed that. Considering I just killed several Domnua on the way in and unlocked whatever portal it was to get you out, I should be patting myself on the back instead of talking down to myself," she said as they reached a turn in the corridor and cautiously peered around it.

"That's the way of it. Show no mercy. They'll take you down in a second. Nasty buggers," Sasha said.

"That helps. I keep thinking they are people, but maybe I need to look at them like cockroaches."

"I view them as cyborgs. No conscience, just blindly following their master. It's not like they're going back to family and friends at home. They are from the under-world," Sasha said.

"That's even better. Okay, I can do this." Neala blew out a breath.

"Good, because you're about to have to do it several more times," Sasha said as they pulled up short at a group of Domnua who hovered in a room. On a fierce bellow, Sasha dove into the fray, mowing down Domnua with the sword, while Neala did what damage she could with her little dagger. It was over moments after it had started, with Neala and Sasha breathing heavily in the middle of the room.

"That's going to get old real quick," Neala commented, trying to slow her racing heart.

"It does. But not much longer and we'll be past all this," Sasha said, then tilted her head. "Shh... listen."

They both heard Bianca's shout at the same time and ran in unison toward the end of the room, where a window now stood in the wall. Down below, they could just barely make out the scene of a battle, illuminated only by the moon and the headlamps their friends still wore.

"Once more into the breach," Sasha commented and swung one leg over the window, dropping lightly to the ground a floor below. Neala didn't land as gracefully, but rolled and caught herself in time to fend off another Domnua.

"Aye, I'm sick of this already," she muttered.

CHAPTER 29

"Nice to see you, ladies," Bianca called when the last Domnua had been felled. Sasha was saved from answering, as she was already in a heated liplock with Declan, who was refusing to put her down.

"Sorry for the detour," Neala said, trying to catch her breath. The battle had been a fierce one and the first in which she'd fully participated or managed repeated hand-to-hand combat. It was not something she wished to repeat anytime soon. She jumped when Dagda landed in front of her in his haste to get to her.

Dagda said nothing. Instead he ran his hands over her, touching all her curves until she batted his hands away. "Stop it."

"You're safe," Dagda said, ignoring her and testing her limbs, lifting an arm, looking for wounds.

"I'm safe," Neala hissed, trying to step back from his hands. Unfortunately, his touch was having anything but the effect she wanted, and what with the way Declan and Sasha were carrying on, and the lingering adrenaline of the battle, her thoughts were cruising toward a decidedly more sexy direction.

"I shouldn't have let you out of my sight," Dagda said, still searching her body with his gaze, seeming terrified that she was hurt.

"You didn't. I was right there with you. One instant I was and the next I stepped away and was sucked into some sort of magick. It's not your fault," Neala said, surprised to see the anguish on Dagda's face. "I swear to you, I'm fine." She reached up to put her hand to his cheek.

He allowed her to touch him for but a moment before pulling back. "It's my job to protect you. I failed," he said, his face still mutinous.

"You didn't fail. I had to accomplish my steps of the journey inside, on my own. I think that's part of what this is – the quest, you know? I have to do some tasks on my own. And you did exactly what you were supposed to do, which is fend off the army outside as well as protect everyone else. Weren't you the one reminding me that we're all in this together?" Neala asked, crossing her arms over her chest and staring the big oaf down until he shrugged.

"It's different for me," Dagda said.

"It's not, but I'll not be arguing that. I suggest we get off this island and to a safer spot. We can argue all you want then," Neala said, feeling a wave of exhaustion set in. With only a few hours of sleep and several battles in a matter of days, she was ready to drop.

Seeming to read her, Dagda scooped her into his arms and began to stride across the hill, his long legs eating up the distance while everyone followed in line behind him.

"This is highly unnecessary," Neala pointed out, looking up at his mutinous face.

"You're dead on your feet."

"Don't you think you should be carrying Fiona instead? She's much older than me," Neala commented, trying to crane her neck to see behind him.

"She's a tough old bird. She's fine."

"Dagda!" Neala all but shouted and he stopped, looking down at her. The moment stretched between them and Neala felt her stomach quicken as she looked into his handsome face. "Put me down. Please," she said gently, feeling a little out of breath.

Dagda put her on the ground as delicately as if she was a baby bunny, and Neala smiled her thanks at him. Turning, she waited for Fiona and the others to catch up.

"Sorry about that. He was worried because I'm exhausted," Neala said quickly, hoping to move past the knowing looks on Fiona's and Bianca's faces.

"I've got just the place for us to rest this evening," Fiona said, winking at Neala.

"I… I don't think we can join you, though not for lack of wanting to," Sasha said, her pretty face in distress. "But I've been told I'm not allowed on the next leg of the quest."

"You're not," Fiona agreed.

"But… will they really know? Who is deciding this? I see no reason I can't help along the way," Sasha protested, the sword hanging comfortably at her side.

"Clare couldn't come along either," Bianca said, patting Sasha's shoulder in sympathy. "I know how hard it is for you not to jump in on the battle."

"It's not fair," Sasha complained and Declan wrapped an arm around her, pulling her back against his body. They fit together nicely, Neala decided, seeing them like this. She could all but see their bond just by the way they held each other. He whispered something in Sasha's ear that made the look on her face change from one of petulance to instant desire, so hot and fast that Neala felt the punch of it.

"You need to let others fight their battles too. Lessons to be learned and all that," Fiona pointed out.

"Speaking of which – what happened in there?" Bianca asked, rubbing her arms to keep warm against the damp.

"I'll tell you later," Neala demurred, not wanting to get into it or bring up Dagda's parents while they were all standing out in the cold.

"I'm holding you to that."

"In the meantime, I guess I have to give this beauty up once again," Sasha sighed, and held the sword out to Neala, who just gaped at her in surprise.

"I can't take that."

"You have to take it. It's part of the rules. I also have this for you." Sasha handed over another velvet bag and Neala took it, tucking it in her pocket without looking at it, but still refusing the sword.

"I can't take this. I'll kill someone," Neala said shaking her head.

"That's the point," Sasha said, rolling her eyes.

"Most likely myself," Neala argued until Dagda reached over, grabbed the sword, and tucked it under his arm.

"It comes with us. Now move. Michael should be

waiting with the boat if he didn't just take our money and run."

With that, they filed silently to the water, a trail of headlamps in the dark hills, the quiet surrounding them filled with a foreboding promise of danger.

CHAPTER 30

"*I* don't understand. Who is making all these rules? Why can't Sasha come with us? Did you see how she moved with that sword? I'll never be able to use it like she did," Neala asked, unbraiding her hair in the front seat of the car and running her hands through the tangled tresses. Behind her, Fiona, Seamus, and Bianca were tucked into the back seat of the Land Rover while Dagda drove. He'd been silent since their encounter, and Neala hadn't been interested in pushing him into a conversation until his mood had passed. He stared steadfastly at the road in front of them, ignoring the chatter as his eyes constantly scanned for danger.

They'd said reluctant goodbyes to Sasha and Declan, whom Michael had gladly taken into town and secured a car so the couple could head home to Dublin. It was Michael's big night as a tour guide; Neala imagined the man had to be happy for the unexpected windfall of cash. Fishing could be a tough and unsteady industry.

"It's the old way of things," Fiona said. "Curses made centuries ago have rules that must be followed. Magick binds these rules. Applying new magicks on top of old magicks makes it even more complicated. Basically, we need to follow orders. Sure, we could play fast and loose with them – but when the clock counts down and all the treasures are found, or not found, who is to say what will happen? And if it's because we didn't stay within the boundaries of the curse, I'm not looking to be the one to explain that to the goddess."

"It seems silly is all. You'd think we'd want every man – or woman – on deck, so to speak," Neala grumbled.

"I couldn't agree more. But because the fae are who they are, things are always trickier. Nothing is as it seems."

"Is that true?" Neala asked Dagda, who ignored her, but Seamus piped up from the backseat to speak on behalf of his brethren.

"Aye, 'tis true. We fae do love a riddle just as much as we love games and magicks. Combine all three and we'll often have ourselves quite a majestic puzzle to be solving. It brings us great joy, and we also like outsmarting others. In this case, we'd like to outsmart and overpower the Domnua; it's just that this time we are playing for much more than a simple prize or some coin – it's for our world."

"Someone gambled too high of a prize," Neala commented.

"Maybe, but we don't know what other game would have been set in motion if it hadn't been this one," Seamus said, at ease with the trickiness of his people.

"Either way, it's the hand we've been dealt. However,

I'd say we're doing pretty damn well," Bianca said. "And I, for one, look forward to kicking more Domnua arse and saving our world from darkness and gloom."

"That's the spirit, my dear," Fiona said, and directed Dagda to go left at a fork in the road.

"Where are we going?" Neala asked. She'd been so caught up in the goodbyes and Dagda hurrying them along that she'd forgotten Fiona had a place for them to rest for the night.

"Why, my favorite place in the world – a little town called Grace's Cove."

"Yay!" Bianca clapped her hands and leaned forward to touch Neala's arm. "You'll love Grace's Cove. It's this colorful little village tucked at the base of the hill on the water. Wait until we go to Cait's pub – she's a real corker."

"We aren't going to the pub. We're on a quest. There is no time for drinking and letting our guard down," Dagda grumbled.

"I beg to differ," Bianca said, challenging Dagda in a manner that surprised Neala.

"It doesn't matter to me what you want," Dagda said. "My task is to protect Neala and ensure the treasures are found. Period."

"Aye, but we must still rest and we must still eat, and above all – we must live. For if we die on the morrow, well, tonight I want to have a good craic with people I love, surrounded by happy music and a carefully built pint. That, my friend, is certainly worth fighting for."

"She has the right of it, Dagda. None of us are machines and we must conserve our energy. We haven't even met up with Lochlain yet – who's to say when he will join us? For now, we can't make any moves until we have his side of the story and his assistance. Tonight, we'll rest," Fiona scolded.

Neala watched as Dagda hunched his shoulders in annoyance like a small child being reprimanded by his mother.

"Fine," Dagda said, his voice terse.

Neala barely concealed her grin. She could use a pint, some food, and a good rest before she faced whatever came their way tomorrow.

"We'll be there soon enough; Cape Clear isn't all that far. The southernmost points and westernmost points of Ireland aren't too much of a distance from each other. Cait's holding the kitchen open for us, as it usually closes by ten. We'll have food, a pint, and some comfortable beds for the evening," Fiona said, looking down at the phone in her hand.

"Fiona, are you texting?" Bianca asked.

"Aye, I am. I don't particularly like it, but I was taught how to put some magick on it to keep us from being tracked by the Domnua," Fiona said.

"I think they'll track us anyway at this point," Seamus said.

"I've just never seen you text. I didn't think you did that," Bianca said.

Fiona laughed. "I email as well. I was considering opening a Facebook account too," she joked.

Bianca gasped. "It would be my honor to be your first Facebook friend," she said.

"We'll see. You aren't the first to ask, you know,"

Fiona sniffed, and the entire car laughed; even Dagda quirked a small smile.

That was what they were fighting for, Neala thought, that sense of normalcy and fun in the mundane day-to-day that often gets taken for granted.

Because in the blink of an eye, it can all change.

CHAPTER 31

*I*t was too dark to really see the village when they arrived in Grace's Cove, but the twinkling of lights from the buildings lining the streets that wound into the hills looked charming and inviting against the dark night. Fiona directed Dagda to drive along the seafront and up a narrow street. It twisted and curved toward the center of town, where a pub was tucked among several shopfronts.

A sign reading "Gallagher's Pub" hung above the door and light shone from glass-paned windows with cheerful flower boxes below them. A smattering of laughter could be heard from inside, along with the sounds of a fiddler warming up.

"It sounds like a session's on," Bianca said, all but bouncing in her seat.

"Aye, it does at that," Fiona agreed, and directed Dagda to a parking spot around the corner. "Cait will have beds for everyone in the apartments she keeps for vacation rentals, and in low season for people who need to sleep off too much drink."

"Perfect. I would enjoy a full belly and some wind-down time," Neala admitted. She stepped gingerly from the car and stretched, her muscles sore from battle. It wasn't that she wasn't fit – she was used to being on her feet all day – but hand-to-hand combat had certainly tested her muscles in ways she wasn't used to.

"Wind-down time is a perfect time for Domnua to attack," Dagda pointed out, his eyes still scanning the darkness as he stood behind her. He'd kept himself inches from Neala since the battle, and having him so close was unnerving to her. For many reasons.

"Don't you ever take it easy?" Neala said, turning to look up at him.

"Aye, I do. In the bedroom. I like to take it nice and easy there. Slow and relaxed, enjoying every moment," Dagda said, his grin lazy and his eyes hooded as he looked down at her. If he was trying to make her nervous, he was a doing a good job of it.

Gulping down a response, Neala hurried around the corner and to the front of the pub where the others waited, but not before she heard his low chuckle following her. Damn the man, she thought. Every time she'd convinced herself to not be attracted to him, he said or did something that had her thoughts skewing the other direction. And she really wished everyone would stop making comments about Seekers and protectors ending up together. It would be much easier if they could just work their way through this quest, save the world and all that, without romance complicating things.

And wasn't that all romance did, anyway? Complicate life? It was why Neala had given up on dating and focused on growing her business and on pouring energy into her friendships. Those parts of her life were logical; the amount of effort she put into them yielded equal benefits if not more, and there was no muss or fuss. Life was easy that way, and she didn't have to deal with sleepless nights mooning over some man and wondering when he would next call.

A pint-sized woman stood in the door to the pub, a broad smile on her pretty face.

"It's about time. I was going to come after the lot of you meself if you didn't kick some Domnua arse. I've kept a stew on and a few mince meat pies warming. I figured you'd be famished."

"Cait, you're an angel sent to us from heaven and that's the truth of it," Seamus said, beaming at Cait before smacking a kiss on her cheek.

"He's the right of it on that. I'd marry you myself if you weren't taken," Bianca agreed, hugging Cait before disappearing into the pub. Neala waited while Fiona gave Cait an extra-long squeeze and then turned to make the introductions.

"Cait, this is Neala. She owns a smashing bakery in Kilkenny, and she's the Seeker who will hopefully end this silly curse so life can go back to normal. Also, she's part-goddess. Try not to peek into her brain too much. She may level you," Fiona said easily, and breezed past Cait into the pub.

"Try not to peek into my brain too much?" Neala asked, tilting her head at Cait in question. She gasped when she felt an odd brush of power against her mind, like the fluttering of butterfly wings, before it pulled back. "You can read minds? Did you just read my mind?"

"Just dipped in lightly to make sure you are what I think you are. I'll not do it again unless you ask. You've my promise on that," Cait said, making no apologies for her intrusion into Neala's thoughts.

"That's rude," Neala huffed.

"Perhaps, but I protect what's mine. I've got a baby, my family, and all my friends inside this pub. Everyone who walks in the door gets a once-over. Safety first, trust second."

Neala considered her words and wondered if she would use such a power to scan the brains of people who walked into her bakery. Deciding it would be difficult not to use all the tools afforded to you, especially in times like this, Neala accepted Cait's explanation.

"I suppose that's fair. I'd probably be doing the same in my bakery."

"See? I knew I'd like you. And this hulking man behind you? I'm assuming he's your protector?" Cait grinned at Dagda, who loomed in the shadows behind Neala.

"Cait, this is Dagda," Neala said, turning to introduce them.

"Thanks for the hospitality," Dagda said, shaking her hand and then returning to his watch, his eyes constantly scanning the streets.

"Man of many words?" Cait asked.

"Tons. Like 'stop talking. Don't move. Stay close,'" Neala grumbled.

Cait threw back her head and laughed. "Someday the men will fully understand our power. Come, come, let's break bread and make merry and all that. There will be time for battles in the morning," she said, ushering them into her pub and throwing the lock on the door behind them.

Cheers bounced off the walls when she stepped in, and Neala jumped, surprised that the group of people she found there seemed to be shouting for her.

"It's a welcome party. And a good luck party. And basically just a good cheer, good health, kick some Domnua arse party," Cait said, scanning the grinning faces of the dozen or so people huddled around a cake in the pub. "All the women here have a touch of magick in one way or another so you're free to be discussing anything ye'd like about power, fae, and magickal quests. It's nothing new to this lot. Especially this one." Cait pointed down at a baby who toddled over, eyes dancing with delight in a chubby face. "Baby Grace here is nothing but magick and full-on trouble. I feel for Keelin when this one becomes a teenager, I really do."

Baby Grace demonstrated her attitude by lifting a pint glass from the table and making to throw it on the ground. Neala gasped and immediately moved to stop her, but her eyes widened when the glass hovered in mid-air, to the delight of a clapping Grace.

"Is the baby making the glass hover?" Neala whispered.

"Or Morgan. She likes to pull some telekinesis tricks as well." Cait pointed to a young girl, stunning in her beauty, who snuggled into the crook of an arm of a smiling young man – a handsome one at that – watching Grace and the glass.

"Um, should I grab the glass? Will it be okay?" Neala asked, unsure how to proceed.

"It'll be fine. If not, it's not the first glass to be breaking in this pub." Cait shrugged and then pointed to the rest of the group.

"I'm going to get food. Patrick, you're with me to help serve this crew. They're hungry. Morgan, pull the pints," Cait ordered in a no-nonsense tone. The young man wrapped around Morgan disentangled himself so he could follow Cait into the kitchen, while Morgan ducked under a pass-through to the long wood bar that dominated one end of the pub.

"Hi, I'm Keelin." A pretty strawberry blonde woman, with whiskey brown eyes much like Fiona's, expertly scooped Grace into her arms and caught the floating pint glass at the same time. "This firecracker is mine and I'm Fiona's granddaughter," she said with a smile.

"Oh, nice to meet you," Neala said.

"Let me introduce you to the crew. We're all here to help, though Fiona has instructed us that we aren't allowed to really help. No joining you on the quest or any of the like, no matter how much we argued with her. Which is why we decided to throw you a mini-party instead. It's the best we can do on short notice, but at the very least it'll send you off with some love and a warm belly."

"That's incredibly kind of you," Neala said, smiling at baby Grace, who twinkled back at her from Keelin's arms.

"It's what we do. Not everyone knows about or believes in magick, so it's best to support others who have it. We all need family sometimes." Keelin led her to where another beautiful woman – Neala briefly wondered if all the women of Grace's Cove were knockouts – sat next to a buttoned-up man wearing glasses and an easy smile. Neala wouldn't initially have paired them together, for the woman seemed to have a bohemian artsy vibe. She wore a flowing sweater woven in brilliant reds and deep purples, and turquoise earrings that dangled past her shoulders, while the man looked like he'd just come from a day of work in an office building. But by the way they leaned into each other as he whispered in her ear, it was clear they were a couple as well.

"Aislinn, Baird, this is Neala. She's the Seeker on this quest. I'm told she owns a bakery in Kilkenny that is the best around."

"I don't know about that, but I certainly put my heart and soul into what I create," Neala said, offering her hand and a smile.

"Ahhh, an artist of another medium. I can certainly appreciate that," Aislinn said, smiling up at her with stormy eyes. "I'm an artist myself, though I certainly wouldn't catalog my work as the best around."

"You've had quite the success, my love. I wouldn't downplay your work," Baird said, pressing a kiss to Aislinn's cheek.

"She did, at that. She's had several shows up in Dublin now, to smashing reviews. Next she's been invited to show in London. Can you believe that? I mean, I certainly can. Her paintings are stunning. But still, we're all just so proud of her," Keelin crowed.

Neala wondered what their powers were. If one could

read minds and one could lift objects without touching them, what could these two do? Would it be rude to ask?

"Pints are up," Morgan called, and she slid foaming glasses of Guinness across the bar just as Patrick and Cait swung through the kitchen doors with food-laden trays. "As is dinner."

"Let our guests eat. There will be time for talk in a bit. Can't you see they're exhausted? They need food and a drink to replenish themselves. Sit, sit," Cait said, bringing the trays to where they'd pushed several smaller tables together to make one long one. In but a few moments, they were all settled with steaming bowls of chunky Irish stew, warm mince pies, and mashed potatoes in front of them. With a perfectly poured pint, surrounded by the cozy glow of the lamps tucked into corners around the pub, Neala was about as content as she could possibly get.

The only thing missing was a man to cuddle next to her and whisper jokes in her ear, Neala realized. The entire table was paired off but for her, Fiona, and Dagda. She wondered if Fiona had lost a love in her life.

Deciding to keep her questions to herself for the moment, Neala tucked into the stew and let the conversation flow around her.

Content with life – just for the moment – she enjoyed quaint food made with love.

CHAPTER 32

"Fiona, where's John?" Keelin asked as they finished up dinner, having talked of this and that through the meal. Neala learned a lot about the town – everything from the fishing charters that Flynn ran, down to Baird's psychiatry business. They were a tight-knit group and a happy one, and their words ran over each other's, interrupting each other or finishing each other's sentences. It was clear they were family – whether by blood or not didn't matter – and they took great joy in spending time together.

"He's at home with Ronan. I can never leave that dog for too long, you know," Fiona said with a smile.

"Most spoiled dog ever," Keelin commented, but with a smile.

Dinner had been delicious and Neala had groaned when they'd brought out a cake decorated with the words 'Kick some Domnua arse!' across it, which made everyone laugh and cheer. Even though she was full, Neala had to sample a piece.

"I know it's not the likes of your baking, but I do what I can," Patrick said, and Neala tilted her head at him in surprise.

"You baked this?"

"Aye, I did. I like to dabble in the kitchen." Patrick's cheeks flushed.

"He does more than just dabble. He's an excellent chef," Morgan said, clearly proud of her man.

"This cake is delicious. It's sweet but not overly so, and the balance of moisture is just right. I think you've got a winner here," Neala said, scooping up another bite.

"See? I told you it was good," Morgan elbowed Patrick and he flushed again.

"Can I ask a question?" Neala asked, pushing the plate back and scanning the faces around the table. "I certainly hope this isn't rude, but I was told you are all magick or powerful in some way. How did you all get together? Or are you all family? Is everyone in this town magick? I have so many questions," she confessed.

"So did I, when I came here," Bianca said. "This has turned out to be one of my most favorite places in all of Ireland. I was dying to ask so many questions and interview every last one of them. Instead I got dragged into battle." She sighed and crossed her arms over her chest.

"Those are stories for another time," Fiona said from the head of the table, her tone brisk. "And the night grows long. I invite you to come back and stay when this is all over. You're welcome here, and to our stories. But for tonight," Fiona said, looking at a candle flame that flickered in front of the window, "they are close and watching. Let's have ourselves a party."

Dagda had stood at her words, crossing to stand in front of the door.

"They'll attack? Now?" Neala stood as well.

"No. But they wait. And as I always say – if they're going to watch, let's give them something to talk about," Fiona said and clapped her hands. "Shane, with the fiddle please."

Neala's heart thundered in her chest, on alert again for an attack, and in awe of Fiona's attitude. She knew the bad guys were out there and she wanted to make music.

"One more round of pints for the lot of you," Cait ordered, "but no more. Relaxed is good – dulled senses are not."

Morgan jumped to clear glasses while Shane, whom Neala had learned belonged with Cait, eased a fiddle onto his shoulder and began tapping his foot.

"Shouldn't we do something?" Neala whispered to Bianca.

"Oh, you're right. Let's help clear the table," Bianca said, jumping up to begin stacking dishes.

"I meant about the Domnua," Neala protested.

"Domnua aren't our problem until they make themselves our problem. For now, we dance."

Neala scanned the room. Flynn, Keelin's sexy dark-haired husband, dandled baby Grace on his knee, looking completely at ease. Seamus traded jokes with Patrick, while Aislinn and Fiona discussed something about herb growing. Not a one of them looked tense except for her. Turning, she looked at Dagda.

"Do you want us to leave?" Neala asked him. He leaned nonchalantly against the door, his arms folded over his burly chest, seeming for all the world a man at ease in a pub. Neala had quickly learned that his 'at ease' pose was all a ruse, and she wanted to be told straight.

"Here's as safe as any. Relax. I've got you," Dagda said, nodding to where another Guinness had been placed in front of her. Neala flashed back to earlier this week, when she'd downed a pint in one gulp at the pub. It seemed positively ages away from where she was now – or even *who* she was now. She wondered if she'd ever go back to being the same carefree woman who downed pints at the pub on a challenge. Part of her wanted that – to go back to before, where she could live a simple and settled life running her business and meeting friends at the pub. No muss or fuss, but an easy, happy existence that she'd worked hard to build for herself.

Her eyes strayed to the group laughing around the table – Keelin sighing and pulling a floating dinner roll from the air in front of a squealing baby Grace – and she realized that no, she didn't want it to go back to the way it was. Instead, a part of her desperately ached for this type of camaraderie – the type of family that she saw in the connections between the women and men around the table. Even though they were wildly different, and she was certain each had their own magick, they were all accepted and loved in a manner that withheld judgment, and offered only welcome. She wanted this in her life, Neala realized with a fierceness that almost hurt her soul, and she didn't want to do it alone. Glancing over to Dagda, she wondered what he thought of all this, and if it called to him – or if he itched to leave it all and be back on the open road, with no expectations and no responsibilities hanging over his brawny shoulders.

Life was certainly easier that way.

At the first piping strains of the fiddle, the group began to clap and an old familiar tune wafted across the table. Morgan, in a surprisingly beautiful voice, picked up the words immediately, the rest following her.

Her eyes they shone like diamonds,
You'd think she was the queen of the land,
And her hair hung over her shoulders,
Tied up with a black velvet band.

Baby Grace slid from her mom's lap and toddled across the room, her little bum bouncing in time to the music, until she stood in front of Dagda, her arms raised. Neala caught her breath, wondering what the bear of a man would do with this little firecracker of a baby.

Dagda scowled down at Grace, his arms crossed over his chest, and shook his head once.

No.

Baby Grace didn't like the word no, it seemed. She glowered up at him, stubbornly stomping a foot and raising her arms once again. Her pigtails vibrated as she seemed to have a conversation with Dagda, which looked much like scolding, though Neala couldn't hear anything over the song.

Dagda shook his head no once more, and this time baby Grace's lower lip poked out in a pout, and her eyes went big with tears.

Neala wasn't sure if she'd yet seen a look of panic on Dagda's face like the one now as tears began to drip down Grace's face. She'd seen him kill Domnua with less

concern than he now exhibited at the tiny storm threatening to burst at his feet. Quickly, he scooped her up and
bounced her on his hip, doing his best to distract her from
what had looked like the beginning of a full-on tantrum.

"Sucker. She pulls this on all the men," Keelin whispered in Neala's ear.

Neala choked on a laugh, but couldn't seem to tear her
eyes away from the burly warrior holding a teacup of a
baby, doing his best to keep her from crying.

If she hadn't been lost before, Neala was dangerously
close to it now. There was something so sweet about a
strong man holding a baby, doing his best to soothe, that
made her want to snuggle up next to him. Maybe having
Dagda as a protector wasn't such a bad thing. Or perhaps
this was a lesson in teaching her that she could have a man
in her life who complemented her needs and lifted her up –
without trying to take away from who or what she was.
Judging by the men who delighted in their wives and girl-
friends here in this pub, maybe it was possible to find the
perfect partner. Neala's heart began to open to the possibility of more – of love – as she opened her mouth and
sang.

And when Dagda began to sing – in a surprisingly
strong tenor – with baby Grace clapping in delight in his
arms, Neala's heart cracked wide open, filling with a
warmth she didn't fully understand.

Heart open, Neala reminded herself. Head up – but
heart open.

Words of the wise.

CHAPTER 33

*D*agda was finally relieved of a babbling baby Grace – or ticking time bomb, as he thought of her – by a smiling Keelin. Shane played on, moving easily into another favorite, "Fields of Athenry," and Dagda saw Seamus and Flynn head for the back door. Seamus gave him a wave so, once more checking the door was locked behind him, Dagda followed the two men to a small enclosed courtyard out back.

"Smoke break," Flynn said, handing Dagda a cigar. The men sat companionably in silence, Dagda on top of the picnic table so that his view through the back window was unfettered. Should any Domnua break through the front, he'd be there to help in under a second. Relaxing slightly for the first time that day, Dagda tasted the sweetness of the cigar and held it up in his hand.

"Thanks," he said to Flynn.

"No problem. You looked like you needed it after Gracie. She's hell on men."

"You've got a handful there, that's the truth of it,"

Dagda said, charmed despite himself. "She's got a way about her, though. You just can't say no."

"Nope, you really can't. Disciplining her is virtually impossible. She just laughs at you and goes on doing what she wants anyway. But surprisingly, I've found she's not stupid. She wants what she wants, but she never puts us or herself into harm's way. So I've learned to ease up a bit. Keelin's still hovering."

"Women tend to do that," Seamus said.

"Aye, they do at that. Though Bianca seems like she's pretty solid," Flynn commented.

"She's the light of my day, she is. But I've mooned after her for years. Nearly made a damn fool of myself more than once and missed out on dating her several times over. When I finally saw my chance, I wasn't going to miss it. I'm just lucky she felt the same way," Seamus said, at ease with his love for Bianca.

"I feel the same with Keelin. I didn't want to fall for her. I wasn't ready for love. But here I am."

Dagda shook his head. Were the men about to break out their pajamas and have a pillow party and talk about their feelings?

"Neala's a beauty," Flynn said, a smile on his face.

"Aye, she is," Dagda agreed.

"Is she yours?"

"Mine? No, she's mine to protect. But only as demanded by the goddess," Dagda said stiffly, refusing to examine anything that came remotely close to having feelings for her.

"So you're security then, nothing more?" Flynn asked, stretching long legs out in front of him.

"That's the way of it," Dagda said, steadfastly ignoring the underlying question, his eyes trained on the image inside.

Baird, the head doctor, had leaned in to have a chat with Neala, and she threw her head back and laughed. Her face danced, coming alive so that it was as bright as the sun, her hair bouncing in red rivulets over her shoulders. It surprised him just how badly he wanted to be the one who made her laugh in that manner. She was a beauty just going about her business, but when Neala dropped her guard and laughed from the soul, she was breathtaking.

"See how he looks at her?" Seamus said to Flynn.

"The man's a goner and he doesn't even know it," Flynn replied.

"Stubborn though," Seamus said, tapping his cigar on the ash tray.

"Stubborn is for fools. I say make a move. Nobody knows what is destined in our path," Flynn said.

"Do you think he'll realize that?" Seamus asked.

"And admit he loves her?" Flynn studied Dagda. "Doubtful."

Dagda jerked his head, coming back to the conversation, realizing that the men had been talking all along and that he'd been caught, staring like a lovesick fool at Neala through the window. Turning, he saw both Flynn and Seamus beaming at him.

"Shut it," Dagda growled.

"Not gonna happen, my friend," Seamus said, laughing as Dagda glowered at him.

"It's clear you love the lass," Flynn said, gesturing

with his cigar through the window. "Why don't you make your move?"

"I don't... that's ridiculous. I just... she's a pretty woman. That's all," Dagda spat, furious with the lot of them.

"Pretty amazing, too. She's handled all this exceptionally well for being tossed into mid-battle with a bunch of magickal beings that she didn't even know existed last week," Seamus said around the cigar sticking out of his mouth.

"That's a handy quality in a woman," Flynn agreed. "Adaptable and flexible, but has a backbone. All good things."

"That's doesn't mean I love her," Dagda said, shaking his head at them. "I can't love her."

"Why not?" Flynn asked.

"I barely know her. Well, she barely knows me. I know her, but in a weird from-afar way, since I've had to watch her for a while. She doesn't know me. Or understand me. It wouldn't work, is all. It's best not to make things messy," Dagda said, exasperated with the conversation.

"Are you worried she won't love you back?" Flynn asked, his eyes narrowed in consideration.

"That's it. I'm done with this conversation. Cacklin' out here like a bunch of hens. I thought we'd be having a smoke and a men's talk. I'm going back to the women. At least they seem to have some sense," Dagda declared. He stormed inside, leaving the grinning men in the courtyard behind him.

"I'd say our work is done here," Flynn said, raising his pint glass to Seamus.

"Couldn't have done it better if we'd planned it out. The man's family has all but disowned him, from what I understand. I can see where it would make him a wee bit nervous to be taking a chance on love," Seamus said, swigging a refreshing sip of his Guinness.

"He'll get over it," Flynn said, pointing at Neala through the window. "Even if he doesn't want to love her – he'll have to."

CHAPTER 34

*O*nce again, they were paired in the same room and Neala could practically hear the matchmakers singing their way to their apartments, hoping something would transpire between the two of them. Despite her misgivings, Neala hummed as she readied herself for sleep, pulling down the comforter on one of the two double beds in the small apartment tucked in a building behind Gallagher's Pub. Dagda studiously ignored her as he paged through a book, stretched out on his own bed.

They'd ended the night not too long ago, as it was way past baby Grace's bedtime – not that she allowed anyone to put her to bed when she didn't want to sleep, Neala was told. It seemed to Neala that Grace was a miniature monarch, holding court over the lot of them, and she wondered if it was because of her extensive powers or her extensive charm. Perhaps both. Thinking back on how she'd wrapped Dagda around her little finger, Neala laughed.

"What's so funny?" Dagda said from his bed.

"I was just thinking about how baby Grace had your number. She certainly knows how to get what she wants."

"Little terror," Dagda growled, paging through his notebook.

"She's a doll and you know it," Neala said, delighted with him.

"Trouble," Dagda said.

"Oh, that's the truth of it. They'll have a run for their money with that one." Neala laughed again and then bounced her way into the bathroom. Deciding she had enough time for a quick rinse, she undressed, showering quickly but keeping her hair piled on her head. After a quick swipe with her toothbrush, she pulled her white t-shirt over her head, and put the green silk panties back on. Deciding for a moment whether she needed to fully redress just to cross the room to her bed and then undress again, Neala decided against it. They were both adults on a deadly mission. He'd bought her the damn panties, for crying out loud. It wasn't a big deal. They covered as much as a swimsuit would. With that decision made, she left the bathroom and walked across the room, refusing to spare Dagda a glance as she placed her folded clothes on the chair next to her bed.

"What are you playing at?" Dagda asked.

Neala swung around, surprised to find him standing behind her. She'd not even heard him move from the bed. Her heart quickened its beat in her chest and her eyes trailed up his bare chest to his scowling face.

"I'm sorry? I'm certain I don't know what you're implying," Neala said.

"You come strolling past me half-naked, shaking your bum for me to see. What kind of games are you playing?" Dagda demanded.

"I'm not playing any games. I just didn't see the sense in getting fully dressed just to cross the room and then undress again before going to bed. That's all," Neala said, nervously licking her lips.

His eyes zeroed in on where her tongue had just been and Neala felt heat zip through her. She wondered what would happen if she reached up and stole a kiss from him.

"It's not proper. A less honorable man than I could get the wrong idea," Dagda scowled.

"And what idea would that be?" Neala asked.

"That you... that you want..." Dagda raked his hand through his hair.

"Are you saying that what I'm wearing implies I want sex?" Neala asked, raising her chin in anger at him.

"No. And yes. But no. And, no. Not like that. Just... in this situation. Beds, tension, growing attraction..." Dagda all but stuttered in his frustration and Neala found herself completely charmed, once again, by this man who would do anything to stop a baby girl from crying and would worry about men taking advantage of Neala.

"Are you saying you're attracted to me, Dagda?" Neala asked, tilting her head at him in question, seizing on the last part of what he said.

"What? No, I was not saying that." Dagda broke off from what he was stammering about and glared at her.

"Oh? You don't think I'm pretty?" Neala asked. She reached up to pull the band from her hair so that it tumbled over her shoulder, and stuck her lip out in a pout.

"No, it's certainly not that. Of course you're pretty. Even a blind man could know that," Dagda said, raking a hand through his hair once again. "I just…"

"You just what? You don't want me?" Neala asked the question hovering between them. She wasn't entirely sure why she was poking the bear – she wasn't even sure if she was ready for the response she might get, or whether she could handle it. Perhaps it was the Guinness she'd drunk, enough to make her mellow and not worried about her heart hurting. Or perhaps it was watching the closeness and intimacy of all the couples around her tonight and, just for a moment, craving that with someone too.

"More than you know." Dagda's words, said on a rasp, were followed swiftly by his lips, and Neala gasped as his hands dove into her hair, bringing her chin up so that she met his lips.

It was like being devoured by flames, Neala thought, when sane thought was able to slip through her mind again. The man vibrated with energy, his touch on her skin creating a heat like none she'd ever known, and she moaned into his mouth as he coaxed her lips open to suck gently at her tongue.

At her moan, Dagda pulled back, looking slightly stunned as his eyes met hers.

"I've watched you and ached for you… for ages now. Will you let me touch you? I've burned for this," Dagda said, his hands once more at his side as he stepped back and allowed her to make the choice. Neala noted that he said nothing about loving her, but then why the hell should he? She'd certainly had sex with men she'd spent less time with, and been less attracted to, than this man. It would be weird to be throwing the big L-word around after knowing someone a matter of days.

Saying nothing, Neala reached out and took his hands – surprised at how they all but swallowed hers – and brought them to her waist beneath the t-shirt. Stretching up on her tiptoes, she brushed her lips over his, leaning into the kiss. It was all the assent Dagda needed. He growled into her mouth as he ran his hands up her curves, cupping her breasts lightly before walking her backwards to the bed. In one move he lifted her as if she weighed nothing – a feat no man had managed before – and laid her gently on the bed.

Propping herself on her elbows, Neala smiled at Dagda, suddenly feeling a little shy as he stood over her, studying her.

"I think you're the most beautiful woman I've ever seen. I imagine it's how the stars feel when the moon rises. For even though they see thousands of other lights twinkling brightly away in the sky, when the moon rises, the other stars just fade into the background," Dagda said, his voice husky as he straddled her on the bed, his arms coming up on either side of her head.

His words took her breath away and she reached up to run a hand over his cheek. He turned his face to press a kiss to her palm, sending a tingle through her. It was probably one of the sweetest things anyone had ever said to her.

"Dagda… you're…" Neala began, but Dagda cut her words off with his lips, refusing to let her speak – or perhaps unwilling to hear what she had to say. He kissed her until all thought left her brain, until all she could do was surrender to the moment, feel his energy surround her and fill her with heat like no other.

Neala gasped for air as he broke the kiss. He pulled her shirt over her head, but left it so that it wrapped around her wrists, effectively entwining her arms over her head. A moan escaped her as he kissed his way down her neck, his beard scraping her sensitive skin as he first found the soft underside of her breast. As he licked his way around the curve, she arched her back, desperate for him to find where she wanted his mouth. When his hot tongue laved gently at her nipple, Neala moaned, wriggling as heat shot straight through her and to her core.

At her moan, Dagda's head shot up, his eyes burning into hers, a man lost in his desires. In that moment, Neala knew she'd surrender all to him if he let her – even her heart.

Like a man possessed, Dagda kissed his way down her body, his tongue effortlessly finding her most secret of spots, already slick for him, aching for his touch. Delighted with her, he smiled wolfishly up from where his head was tucked between her thighs. As Neala gasped in surprise, and then almost shouted, he bent himself to the task at hand as if he had all the time in the world. Ruthlessly, Dagda brought her to the peak over and over until she lay sweating in the sheets, a quivery mess of nerve endings, her body all but liquefied pleasure.

She thought Dagda would finally claim her then, filling her where she so ached for him. But he picked her up from the bed and carried her to his, tucking her beneath the sheets and pulling her into the crook of his arm, and all she could do was wonder – before sheer bliss combined with complete exhaustion claimed her – why hadn't he taken his pleasure?

Would he not let her love him?

CHAPTER 35

*D*agda stared up at the ceiling waiting for Neala's breathing to change. It didn't take long for her to slip into the dead sleep of someone supremely exhausted. He wanted to kick himself for keeping her awake even longer than he should have, for she needed her rest.

When she'd come out of the bathroom in her white t-shirt, with nothing under it but the green silk he'd purchased for her covering her deliciously round bottom, his entire body had seemed to spring to alert. It was like every nerve ending he had caught on fire at once, and he'd been helpless to not follow her across the room.

And what a fool he'd made of himself, stuttering and stammering like some schoolboy, Dagda thought, not like the man he was – a tough and worldly man who handled whatever came his way. Dagda could have smacked himself, but his arms were wound around the enticing curves that made up the package Neala came in. And what a package it was, he thought, his body still burning with the need for release.

He knew she had expected more – had even been offering more – but he'd only wanted to give to her. To show her that she deserved pleasure, deserved to be worshiped. His needs could wait, Dagda had decided.

Liar, liar, a voice in his mind chided him.

But if he listened to that voice he'd have to crack open a tightly locked box holding all his vulnerabilities from his childhood days – most notably the memory of not being accepted by his family. Which would mean he'd have to admit that he was more vulnerable than he realized and that he was actually scared of loving someone – because what if they didn't love him back?

No, that was something he wasn't willing to examine too closely. He'd lived his life by the "love 'em and leave 'em" rule, and it had worked out well for him thus far. Dagda had always treated women with respect and he'd never led them on. Anyone who'd ever gotten involved with him had known straight up that he kept moving and wasn't one to put down roots. The few who had tried to get him to settle had learned quickly that he wasn't open to that type of relationship.

Which was what scared him so much about this one – the one currently cuddling deeper into his arms, making contented little mewling sounds as she did. For the first time, he could see a future with someone. It had all fallen into place – and it wasn't that he could see exactly what that future held. For him it didn't matter whether they stayed at the bakery or roamed the world.

The future was just Neala.

Which terrified him beyond belief. If he gave her all of himself, would she reject him like the others in his life? Instead, he'd done the only other thing he could, which was to give her immeasurable pleasure and then cocoon her in his arms as she slept.

It was all he could give.

CHAPTER 36

eala blinked awake, going suddenly from a dream that was decidedly naughty to staring at the dark wooden beams of a ceiling that wasn't hers. It took a moment for the last few days to come crashing over her, and to remember the bear of a man who slumbered next to her.

In the night they'd moved apart, sleeping comfortably next to each other, and Neala studied Dagda for a moment. In sleep he seemed vulnerable, and she wondered again why he hadn't allowed her to pleasure him the night before. Wishing she felt comfortable enough with herself to cuddle into him and touch him, she slipped quietly from the bed instead, and crossed to where her satchel sat next to her bed. Something had been bothering her, even last night, and now she realized what she'd forgotten.

Pulling out the grey velvet bag Sasha had handed her, Neala gingerly untied the ribbon that knotted the bag closed. Easing onto her bed in a cross-legged position, she took a deep breath before pulling out a new stone and a scroll of paper. A pink stone, shot through with glimmers of black and silver and cut in the same pattern as the last stone, it looked as though it was the next piece in the set for her pendant. Retrieving the necklace from her bag, Neala carefully fit the stone into the southern point of the quaternary knot, admiring how it looked next to the other stone. She wondered what would happen when she had all four – if something magickal would appear. Fiona would probably know, or at the very least be able to tell her what the stone was.

The slip of paper was a little more concerning.

To love or not to love
To live or not to live
Fire consumeth all
Shame goeth before the fall

"You look beautiful." Dagda's husky voice snapped her gaze up from the clue in her hand to where he lay propped up on one elbow, watching her. Belatedly Neala realized she was naked, and only her long hair covered her.

"Oh, um, good morning." Neala tried to act like she always lounged around naked with men in the bed next to her.

"Did you sleep well?" Dagda asked.

"I did, thank you. I'm sorry, I was out like a light after…" Neala trailed off. She flushed at the thought of his mouth on her, hot in the night, and felt her insides go liquid at the thought of the orgasms he'd given her.

"After I pleasured you? After you came so many times you forgot your own name? After you told me I was the best you'd ever had?" Dagda said, and Neala would have snarled at him if she hadn't seen the teasing light in his eyes.

"Erm, yes, after that," she said, averting her eyes for a moment. She desperately wanted to ask him why he hadn't tried for more, but just then there was an urgent knocking at the door.

"Meet in the pub. We've got company – and he's madder than a wet cat in a bag," Bianca shouted through the door.

"Coming," Neala called.

"Like you did repeatedly last night," Dagda said, still teasing. Deciding to give him a taste of his own medicine, Neala stood and stretched fully, tossing her curls over her shoulder and sauntering into the bathroom. She shut the door on a laugh, hearing his groan of pain.

That'd teach him, she thought. Maybe next time he'd let her participate more.

Feeling decidedly cheerful, Neala got ready to face whatever nonsense was about to greet her down in the pub.

CHAPTER 37

"Well, you certainly look… rested," Bianca observed when Neala and Dagda entered the pub, their satchels slung over their shoulders, their hair still wet from the shower. A comb would have been nice, Neala thought, but she had left her hair to curl wildly around her shoulders as it dried.

"I am, thanks. Dropped like a stone when I saw my bed last night," she said, and bit back a laugh at the disappointed look that crossed Bianca's face. Clearly she'd been hoping for something more, but last night had been too intimate for Neala to share. Plus, she wanted to take some time to figure out just what made Dagda tick, and if she could see herself wanting to spend more time with him.

A man paced the room, startlingly handsome and disastrously angry. He looked like the superhero in a comic book series, all regal good looks, vibrating with rage and a magick he didn't even try to conceal. Whips of power vibrated up his arms like little lightning bolts as he strode the floor and cursed long and loud for all to hear.

"It's glad I am our little ones aren't with us this morning then," Cait said, admonishing the man for his language. "And you'll just be calming right down before I throw you on your arse on the street."

Neala raised an eyebrow as the diminutive Cait went head to head with the enraged man, and Neala could see why she made a good pub owner. It was obvious she'd had to hold her own against many a belligerent customer.

"Try me," the man threatened.

"Don't think I won't," Cait shot right back.

The man stared her down, then finally pinched the bridge of his nose and sighed.

"Listen, I know you're worried about her. But you can't be coming in here throwing lightning bolts of magick around and breaking up my pub because you're scared for her. It does nothing but make me mad and trust me, that's not what you want to be dealing with, on top of everything else on your plate."

"I'm sorry. You're right," the man sighed.

"Lochlain," Bianca said, drawing the man's attention to her.

He strode across the room, fury still snapping around him, and Cait sighed. "I'm putting a full Irish on. Sit. Then you can be on your way."

Soon they were all seated while a sullen Lochlain sat on a bar stool, staring them all down as they shoveled food in their mouths. It was just the four of them this morning; Cait told them that Fiona had gone to her house late last night and would meet with them on their way west. The rest of the Grace's Cove family had said their goodbyes last night, with promises of another big party upon their return, and well wishes and abundant blessings for their journey.

"Sure, sure. Have a lazy breakfast while my Gwen is tortured," Lochlain complained, and Bianca turned to him as she slathered butter on warm cinnamon scone.

"Lose the attitude, buddy," Bianca scolded. "We've just gone through several battles and we're on to your woman next. But if you think we can fight with the courage and heart that's required of us without a few hours' rest and some food, you're wrong. Either we give Gwen our best, or fail her by bringing our worst."

Loch's shoulders slumped and he got up to pace, raking a hand through his hair.

"Can you tell us what happened?" Dagda asked.

Neala nodded. Smart move; keep the man talking.

"It's beyond infuriating, because, as you know, I'm a high sorcerer of my people," Lochlain said.

"What people? I don't know," Neala interjected and then looked down at her tea when he glared at her.

"I'm fae. Danula. And our people live in a village not known to man. I have created a home for Gwen outside the village, so we can have some privacy but she can also enjoy the magick and fun of what the fae world offers, as well as visit the sirens."

"I forgot! There's sirens?" Neala squeaked in delight, and Bianca nodded enthusiastically from across the table, her mouth full of scone.

"I meant to tell you more. We haven't gotten there yet. It's so cool," Bianca mumbled, ducking her head at Lochlain's glare. Swallowing, she mouthed, "So cool!"

"Yes, the love of my life is half-siren. And her family

is made up of mermaids and sirens. I decided we should live by the water so they could visit. Apparently, my wards weren't strong enough to protect her," Lochlain said, furious in his failure.

"Nobody's were. It was the Goddess Domnu who took the women. It doesn't matter what level your magick is. She even stole the treasures back from Danu herself. It wasn't your lack of expertise; it's just that their magick was stronger than yours," Seamus explained, and scooped up some more eggs.

"It doesn't matter. My job is to protect my woman and I failed," Lochlain said, his face set in hard lines.

"What is with these stubborn men?" Neala wondered.

"Irish," Bianca shrugged.

"She'd gone down to the beach to visit with Amynta, her mother. Now that they've found their way back to each other, they try to visit when they can. Gwen is fascinated by the mermaids' story as well as their island home, so she could listen for hours to Amynta's tales."

"So could I," Bianca agreed. "It's beyond what I can even imagine for a fairytale – and that's me saying it, being in a relationship with a fae."

"Oh, I'm dying to know more. You'll tell me everything," Neala demanded.

"Of course. First of all, did you know that the women run the society? And that there are mermen and that the sirens don't actually kill the men after they mate? Such a falsehood. I think it was just wayward sailors they killed after mating. Probably to keep them from discovering the Isle of Destiny, which – oh my goddess – is amazing. There are like five different seasons and night and day going on, all at the same time. I could have spent years exploring," Bianca gushed.

Neala was enthralled. She opened her mouth to speak, but shut it when Loch slammed his fist on the bar.

"Enough! We must go at once."

"But where are we going? Do we have a clue? Do you know where she is?" Seamus asked, calmly continuing to eat his breakfast.

"Aye, I was able to cast a spell so as to track her. But I can't get to her. Apparently I need you." Lochlain's eyes narrowed as he studied Neala.

"That seems to be the theme of things, yes," Neala said.

"Then let's move. Time is wasting," Lochlain ordered.

"Loch, we talked about this," Bianca sighed, pushing her chair back from the table. "I know you're used to ordering people around, but you need us and you can't issue commands like we're your subjects or something. Ask nicely."

Lochlain's expression grew more mutinous, if that was even possible, then he sighed.

"Would you please speed up your breakfast so we can get on the road and save the love of my life, who might very well be hurt and in pain right now?"

"Gwen's pretty spunky," Bianca said. "I suspect she's just fine. But I'm ready to go. Everyone else?"

The table nodded in agreement.

"Let's roll."

CHAPTER 38

*G*wen paced the small room into which she'd been so unceremoniously dropped without a word or any explanation of why she was there. She'd caught a quick glimpse of a goddess who she thought resembled Danu, but that was it. Aside from the Spear of Lugh glowing in the middle of the room, there'd been no clues or any sort of communication.

She'd immediately picked up the spear, delighted to have it in her hands again, and had passed the time practicing defensive moves with it. Her bracelets, still forged to her wrists, worked when she focused on her magick. However, it seemed her magick was useless here, for no matter how often she tried to use it on any of the stone walls that ensconced her, it was diffused somehow. Gwen ran her hand over the stone, feeling the pulse of magick within, and wondered what kind of force field surrounded her. Would Loch even be able to find her? There was no way to send him a message.

It had all happened so fast – she'd really had no

recourse or way of letting him know she'd been taken. She only hoped that he still carried the bond a protector had with his Seeker, where he could sense when she was in danger. Even her mother had been unable to help, only watching helplessly from the water as Gwen had been stolen into another realm. There'd been no warning, no sense of impending danger; just a flash of magick and darkness, and Gwen had been ripped from the beach where she had been happily chatting with her mother, sharing for the first time news she'd been excited to speak of.

Not that she'd had to tell her mother, as mermaids had extra-special senses; Amynta had known even before Gwen had said anything, but had been smart enough to let her daughter speak of it in her own time.

Gwen rubbed her palm across her belly, not yet showing the baby that grew within, and made a promise to her child.

"I don't know for sure what's happening right now. If you feel my fear, please know it is only temporary. We've got a lot of people who love us and will fight for us. This is just a moment in time. Soon we'll be back in the arms of those we love, and you'll feel nothing but joy and song coming your way from me. This I promise you, my little one – we'll be safe soon enough."

She'd only just discovered she was pregnant a few weeks before, and had shyly told Loch the news one night when he'd taken her for a surprise picnic under the stars. The elation on his face had erased any worries she'd had about telling him. They hadn't even married yet or spoken of whether they wanted children, so the pregnancy had brought a slew of nerves with it for Gwen. When Loch had kissed her tenderly beneath the stars and laid his hand upon her belly, promising to love and protect them both for all time, her fears had been replaced with nothing but love and excitement.

But for now she paced, spear in hand, and waited. She wasn't sure how long she'd been in this room, but she knew she was desperately hungry. She would only be able to go so long without water or food before she'd weaken, and her babe needed sustenance.

"We're fierce, little one. This is but a test of our strength. Remember, we come from magick. We'll be able to weather life's challenges in ways others can't." Gwen had been chattering endlessly to her baby, constantly soothing the small soul in her womb while also calming her own nerves. When she had someone else to protect, it took the focus off herself and her own danger.

One instant she was alone in the room, and the next a woman stood before her, seething with rage. Gwen automatically lifted the spear, blocking her body with it.

This was Danu's sister, Domnu, Gwen thought, immediately seeing the resemblance. But where Danu was light and grace, Domnu was darkness and evil. No less beautiful, Gwen observed, but beautiful in the way of a glacier. Lovely to look at, impossibly cold, and quite lethal to try and live with. Her dark hair writhed around her head in frazzled whips of anger and her eyes snapped in a face chiseled from hard edges. Oh, yes, she was beautiful – but in the most intensely dangerous way Gwen had ever seen.

"Those idiots are winning," Domnu seethed, all but pulling out her hair as she stomped a foot on the floor.

"Um, what idiots?" Gwen asked, cautiously deciding to keep her talking.

"Your silly Seeker friends. They must be stopped. They're finding my hiding places too easily," Domnu said, biting the words out as she began to pace the small room.

"Gee, I'm really sorry to hear that," Gwen said, her voice dripping in sweetness.

Domnu shot her a glare. "I'd kill you for that, but I've got bigger things on my mind," she said.

"I don't think you can kill me," Gwen said and then almost slapped a hand over her mouth. What the hell was she thinking, needling the Goddess of Darkness like that? Of course she could kill Gwen. She could wipe out worlds if she wanted. Sometimes there were things that were better left unsaid, and Gwen didn't usually realize that until she'd already said them. This was one of those times.

"I can do anything that I want," Domnu hissed, standing but inches from Gwen now, her eyes glowing with madness that Gwen had missed from across the room. Scary evil goddess was one thing, Gwen thought, going on high alert, but madness was an entirely different game. Proceed with caution, she chided herself mentally.

"I'm certain you can. I'm not sure why I said that," Gwen said honestly. "Sometimes I say things I shouldn't."

"You'll get yourself and your baby killed that way, you know," Domnu said, so casually that it made Gwen's heart skip a beat as Domnu turned away and paced the room once more, muttering to herself.

"I'll work on it," Gwen said.

Domnu shot her a look of disgust. "Work on what?"

"On being better about filtering what I say," Gwen

said, gently this time, as the goddess appeared to be becoming increasingly agitated and erratic, mumbling to herself and tugging at her writhing hair.

"It won't matter much. You're not long for this world," Domnu shrugged, as though killing Gwen was as casual as swatting an annoying mosquito.

"I sincerely hope that isn't the case," Gwen said.

"I'm moving you," Domnu said, having come to some sort of decision in her head.

"What? Where?"

"They are finding the treasures too easily. I'm moving you elsewhere. Frankly, I'd kill you if it wasn't forbidden in the curse. Too easy, I suppose, for us gods to just take you out. The fae do love their little rules. I need to make this more difficult until the time runs out on the curse. We've only a few more days and the curse will have run its course, the treasures won't be found, and the world will be mine once again," Domnu said, her face lighting up with maniacal delight.

"Where are you taking me?" Gwen asked, hoping for any information. She didn't know what she'd be able to communicate via magick or telepathy, but damn it, she'd try.

"I think we need to make things a little more tricky," Domnu said and tapped her finger, studying Gwen.

It happened like before, when she'd been on the beach speaking with Amynta. One instant she was there, and the next her world had completely changed. It was like flicking a switch and turning the lights out in one room, and flicking them on to find herself in another room.

This time Gwen stood alone in what appeared to be a

damp cave, as water rushed in and brushed her feet. Stepping back, she moved into a far corner until her back lodged against a wall and she could tuck herself into a small crevice so that she was protected on all sides. Drawing her knees up, she let her eyes adjust to the darkness. The only light came from a few cracks in a small tunnel, the same one the water was coming through. She watched the water lapping onto the pebbles below. It only took a few moments for fear to fill her heart.

The tide was rising.

CHAPTER 39

The town was as charming as Bianca had described it, and Neala itched to get out of the car and wander the streets to poke her head into various shops or pick up a few items at the market. It was the kind of place you could have a lovely wander in or hole up at the local coffee shop with a book on a misty afternoon.

She'd been relegated to the back seat by an agitated Loch, and frankly, she didn't mind it back here. Neala could secretly watch Dagda while peppering Bianca with questions about the town, though what she really wanted to ask about was the mermaids. Seeing as how they were Lochlain's extended family now, Neala had decided against delving too much deeper, and Bianca had promised a night in the pub to tell her about all the amazing things she'd seen on the Isle of Destiny.

"We'll have to try Flynn's restaurant one night. It takes ages to get a table there, but the seafood is to die for," Bianca said, pointing out a cheerful blue building by the water with fishing nets and pots of flowers decorating the entryway.

"I'd like to come back here. I feel like this village has good energy. I can see why people are drawn to it," Neala said.

"You could open a bakery here," Bianca offered.

"I'd prefer to open one closer to my current shop. Much easier to manage that way," Neala smiled at Bianca.

"I don't know how you don't eat everything in sight," Bianca said. "I can't imagine being around cookies and cakes all day. I'd be ten times rounder than I am now."

"And still just as beautiful," Seamus said, dropping a kiss onto Bianca's cheek.

"Listen to this one. The gift of the blarney he has, that's the way of it," Bianca said, but she flushed with pleasure at his compliment.

"I don't let myself eat anything until I'm done with the baking for the day – then I get one item of choice. It's a rule I had to put in place or I'd be much fatter than I am now," Neala admitted.

"You're not fat, just curvy," Bianca protested.

"I'm definitely not a slender woman," Neala pointed out.

"You've got everything in all the right places," Dagda said from behind the wheel, his eyes on the curvy road ahead, and the car went silent until Bianca let out a little hum.

"Tell me more, Dagda. We'd love to know about her curves. And everything you know about them," Bianca said, a cheeky grin on her face.

Neala smacked her knee. "Would you stop it?" she

hissed, heat rising to her face as she thought about where Dagda's mouth had been the night before. His hands had most decidedly been all over every inch of her body, so he was well-versed on just what her curves held.

At Loch's hiss of disgust, they all shut up, and Neala let her head rest against the window, watching the water spread out before her as they curved their way along a cliffside road. Behind them the hills clambered up and fell away into rolling slopes of green, while below the seagulls swooped near where water broke on the rocks of the shore. Sometimes she forgot the beauty that Ireland could offer, stuck as she was in her day-to-day routine of running her business. She should take a few weekends off and visit places like this. It would be calming for her soul.

"Turn here," Bianca piped up, pointing to where a long stone wall led to a dirt lane that turned off of the main road.

"I don't understand why we're even stopping to see this woman. I understand she's a great healer, but that's of little use to me at the moment. I need to get to Gwen. Immediately," Lochlain said, his fingers drumming a staccato rhythm on the dashboard.

"Because she told us to stop on the way out, so my assumption is that she is giving us something for the journey," Bianca said, glaring at Loch.

"I have everything I need," Loch said, holding up his two hands.

"You might. But our Seeker may not. The more you push against this, the slower things will go. Just hush up and let us get through this so we can get back on the road," Bianca said.

Neala was amazed at how casually she put Lochlain in his place. The man was certainly intimidating, and not someone Neala would want to test her luck with.

"Fine, but let's make this quick or I swear to the goddess I will lay a curse upon this land and all the people within," Loch threatened.

"Yeah, yeah, we'll make it quick," Seamus said, shaking his head at Loch.

The SUV bumped down the lane and turned a corner. Neala immediately smiled at the cottage that sat there, tucked away on the hill, the world at its feet. It was quintessential Ireland, and charming as could be. It made her long to knead bread by the window over-looking the water, a fire in the stove behind her, while her man told her stories as she baked. Neala found herself eyeing Dagda again, wondering if he ever wanted something like that. As much as she prized her independence, it would be nice to share a bottle of wine and talk with someone over dinner. Though she was content with her life, Neala wasn't immune to loneliness.

Fiona came out of the cottage, followed by an older man who must be her love, John. He wrapped an arm around her shoulders, pulling her into him, and Neala smiled.

"Aren't they cute?" Bianca sighed.

"That'll be us someday, love," Seamus said, patting her leg.

"Don't I know it," Bianca said.

Dagda stopped the car and they all piled out. Neala did her best to move quickly, for she knew that Lochlain was about to murder them all if they didn't get on the way to saving Gwen.

"Good morning. You all look well-rested," Fiona said, smiling and introducing John to everyone.

"We need to get on the road," Lochlain said.

Fiona studied him, clearly unintimidated by his blustering. "You must be Lochlain. I understand you're scared for your woman. I have something for you to give her," she said, and held out a small pouch.

Lochlain reluctantly took it, tucking it in his pocket without looking at it. "Thank you," he said, his tone terse.

"Give it to her when you find her. She'll need it," Fiona said, and Lochlain's face went pale.

"Is she hurt? Is she sick? How do you know?" he demanded.

Fiona held up her hands. "I just know what came to me in my dream. She's safe, but time is of the essence. And I know she'll be needing the remedy I've given you. For the babe," Fiona said.

Bianca gasped, clapping her hands together. "Is Gwen pregnant? You didn't say anything." She swatted Lochlain's arm. "Congratulations!"

"Aye, well, I imagine she wanted to tell people herself. And now you can understand why I'm mad with wanting to find them," Lochlain said, his face showing desperation for the first time since Neala had seen him.

"You go over to Flynn's now. I've arranged for him to take you over to the island on one of his boats. It's the fastest way to get there," Fiona said, pointing them over the hill. They all hugged her quickly and said their good-byes before piling back into the SUV.

"I didn't even think about a boat," Lochlain admitted as Dagda floored the SUV, tearing them across the hills over toward Flynn's stables and house, which stood on the opposite end of the cliff.

"Told you Fiona wanted us to come for a reason." Bianca couldn't help herself, but then she reached out and squeezed Loch's shoulder. "Don't worry, Loch. We'll get her. She'll be okay. If Fiona says it's so, it is so. Just bring whatever's in that pouch with you."

Loch patted his pocket and nodded.

"The westernmost point is An Fear Marbh, or the dead man, due to the fact that the island looks like a dead man lying down. It is uninhabited and prime for an attack from the Domnua," Dagda said as he pulled the car to a stop in front of a pretty farm house. "We'll want to be on the alert at all times. No needless conversation, no joking, no distractions. We're nearing the end of this quest and the Domnua are going to be desperate."

He was right, Neala realized, as they got out of the car and grabbed their packs. She tucked the sword by her side. They'd had some downtime, but hopefully it wasn't all for naught. The Domnua could have been ravaging the world while they were drinking and dancing.

Dagda strode across the yard, shaking hands with Flynn, and they had a brief conversation while Flynn pointed out a path which Neala assumed led down to the docks. The door banged and baby Grace tottered out, with a smiling Keelin on her heels.

Neala caught the anguished look that fell over Lochlain's face when he saw the baby, and her heart twisted in her chest for him. She wanted to tell him everything would be all right, but since much of that was riding on her, she didn't feel comfortable doing so.

Why did so much come down to whether Neala found a stupid treasure or not? These were people's lives – their families – and the world at stake. And it all came down to her? What was the point of it all? She was just a simple baker from Kilkenny. Not some demi-goddess or whatever they wanted her to believe. They were wrong to put their faith in her, and it pained Neala to think that she would likely fail these good people.

"Up," baby Grace said at her feet, tapping her palms on Neala's knees.

"I can't, Gracie, I've got to go," Neala said, patting the girl on the head and moving to step around her.

"UP!" Grace shouted, a command, and Neala was shocked to realize she couldn't take a step forward. She was quite literally frozen in place by a steely-eyed angel baby.

"Yes, ma'am," Neala muttered. She bent to pick up Grace, who immediately crowed in delight and released whatever spell she'd held Neala under so that Neala could walk over to join the group.

"Believe. Love. Believe." Grace said before Neala could reach the others.

Neala paused, looking down at the chubby-faced terror in her arms. "Did you say believe in love?" Neala asked, tilting her head in question.

Grace nodded solemnly, reaching up to pat Neala's cheeks with both hands.

"I mean, I do. I know love exists," Neala protested.

Grace patted Neala's chest, where her heart was.

"Love. Believe. Him." Grace turned, pointing to Dagda, and Neala shook her head at the baby.

"I don't love him, Grace. He's a very nice man, but it's not love."

"He loves. He needs," Grace said.

"Needs what?" Neala wondered and then shook her head. She certainly wasn't about to get into a philosophical discussion with a toddler about her needs and love.

"Needs to believe," Grace insisted, holding her eyes steady on Neala's until Neala nodded.

"Okay. I'm not sure entirely how I can help with that, but I'll let him know," Neala said, not sure if that was what the toddler wanted. When Grace beamed and moved to slide down from her arms, Neala assumed she had interpreted it correctly.

The group had started down the path, led by Flynn, while Keelin stayed at the house with Grace in her arms, waving their goodbyes. Dagda hung back until Neala caught up, so that the two of them walked alone for a moment.

"Baby Grace told me that you need to believe in love," Neala said, breaking the silence as they approached the cliff's edge.

"I do believe in love. Just not for me."

CHAPTER 40

*N*eala whirled on him before they reached the group, her hands on her hips.

"How can you say that after what we shared last night?" Neala demanded. She'd been itching for some sort of acknowledgement that things had shifted between them, but ever since they'd left the room this morning, Dagda had treated her like just another one of their group.

"I hate to break it to you, darling, but that wasn't love. That was two people blowing off steam after a particularly tough day," Dagda said, his eyes skirting past hers to the people waiting for them by the cliff's edge. He went to move around her but Neala stopped him.

"No, I don't think it was," Neala argued.

"You can think what you want, but that doesn't change the truth of it." Dagda shrugged.

"You're saying you aren't attracted to me at all?" Neala asked, tilting her head so that she looked up at him, hurt radiating through her.

"Of course I'm attracted to you. I'm a red-blooded

male, aren't I? You're a beautiful woman. I'd be mad not to be attracted to you," Dagda replied.

"But what you said… about the moon…" Neala said.

Dagda looked away. "Just some fancy words. A bit I picked up in a book ages ago. It makes women feel good," he said, and Neala felt the pain slice through her, low and deep.

"I'm nothing more than a conquest, then, am I?"

"Ah, Neala, you weren't a conquest. You were just there. We're two healthy adults with an attraction. There's no need to be reading more into it. Let alone speaking of love," Dagda said, and Neala saw something shift in his eyes.

"That's it, isn't it?" Neala whispered, beyond furious with him. Stepping forward until she was but inches from him, she challenged him. "That's why you wouldn't let me give you pleasure back, isn't it?"

"What is? What's wrong with giving pleasure? I didn't see you complaining," Dagda said, his expression furious now, the shutters drawn on his deeper emotions.

"Because if you give, then nobody can touch you. Nobody can get to the real you. Nobody can hurt you. And most notably, nobody can say they don't love you. You fool," Neala seethed, "you're scared to death of loving someone, aren't you?"

"See, this is why I don't get involved with women," Dagda said. "They always get notions in their heads of something more. You can never just share your bed with a woman and have an easy goodbye. They always want more, more, more. It's why I never stay the night, you know. Because of this." Dagda swept out his hand in anger.

"This? Expectations of speaking honestly of feelings? Like that's such a horrible thing?" Neala asked.

"It is. There's no need to bring feelings into this. We had some fun, now we continue on our way. Stress relief, nothing more," Dagda said, obstinate as the bull that wandered the pasture next to where they stood.

"Sure, Dagda. I get it," Neala said, using every ounce of power she had to not let the tears that threatened seep into her eyes. "You're a coward, is what I understand. Keep it light, keep it easy. That way nobody can hurt you – nobody can reject you again. Like your family did. Well, I have news for you, buddy: I met your parents and I have to say you're letting some pretty awful people control a lot of your potential happiness. But, as you said, you're an adult. I'm sure you already know all that. I'll just move on with the mission and promise not to be getting any ideas in my head."

Neala whirled to stalk toward the group, who were watching them argue with avid interest, and gasped when Dagda grabbed her arm. The sword banged against her side as he whipped her around and forced her to stare up at his enraged face.

"You met my parents? When? You didn't think this was something you should share with me?" Dagda hissed. They stood there, two confused and enraged lovers, the mist falling gently around them as the waves crashed far below.

"It didn't come up," Neala said primly, knowing she was being a bit petty. But damn it, he'd hurt her feelings.

"Tell me everything, immediately," Dagda said, looming over her in his rage.

"Oh, stop with the tough guy act," Neala sighed and rubbed her fingers over her forehead, where a dull pain had begun to throb. "It was when I was searching for Sasha. The Domnua pulled some sly magick – first making an apparition of my father appear. I needed to forgive him to be able to move forward. Next up in their bag of party tricks were your parents. Delightful people, really. I'm glad we aren't destined to be a couple because Christmas dinner with them would be hell, let me tell you."

"What did they say?" Dagda demanded, and for a second, Neala caught that shift in his eyes – a little boy pretending nonchalance – before it was quickly shuttered once more.

"They just wanted to let me know how unsuitable they thought I was as a partner for their little boy," she said. "And that I would be diluting their bloodline if you had children with me."

"Of course. It's always about the perfect bloodline with them," Dagda hissed.

"I told them I forgave them for being small-minded and then went on my way."

Dagda's mouth dropped open. "You said that?"

"Aye," Neala said, watching him carefully.

"To their faces?"

"Yes. I told you that, didn't I?" Neala said.

"I bet they didn't like that," Dagda said, shifting from foot to foot.

"No, they didn't. But I didn't stay to chat, as the Domnua masquerading as them popped forth and I had to fight. Dag, they're awful people. You can't let them decide whether you're worthy of love or not. You can spend your whole life wandering. But don't you want something more? A partner – someone who will stick by you no matter what, someone who can become your own family?" Neala asked, her heart swelling as she realized just how much she'd come to care for this man.

Dagda paused for a moment, looking out over the horizon before once more looking down at Neala.

"It's not worth getting hurt for. I won't let someone have that power over me again," he said, his tone brusque. "I shouldn't have touched you. I'm sorry if I misled you in any way. But there is nothing between us other than what the goddess has entrusted me with – protecting your safety. I apologize for crossing a line that I shouldn't have. It won't happen again."

"But…" Neala said, but Dagda shook his head.

"We've tarried too long. I've said my apologies. We must go."

And that was the end of that, Neala realized, as Dagda stomped across the field to where the group waited, an impatient Loch looking for all the world like he would burst into flames if they didn't get moving.

"What happened to head up, heart open?" Neala called after him, her words carrying on the wind.

Dagda turned.

"That's meant for you. Not me."

"Coward," Neala called, but Dagda just shook his head and kept moving, the walls around his heart locked closed.

CHAPTER 41

*N*eala followed Bianca silently down the steps that led down the side of a cliff to where several boats were docked far below. Bianca had looked over her shoulder a few times, a question in her eyes, but Neala had just shook her head and kept her stony silence.

Perhaps Dagda was right. She'd been foolish to start thinking there was more between them because they'd shared one night together. And it wasn't even like they'd had sex. She'd let him pleasure her and that was that. No big deal. No muss, no fuss. Neala had known from the outset that Dagda was a man made for the open road, not for settling down. She'd been telling herself that repeatedly for a few days now. The fact that they'd shared a moment certainly did not mean there was anything more to it than that – a moment. It must be all this talk of pairing up and the tension they were under with this quest, Neala decided as they reached the dock. The adrenaline alone could get to anybody's head.

Having had the walk down to work through it in her

head and cool off a bit, Neala finally came to the conclusion that she'd been a bit silly. There'd been no reason to push the man about love just because a toddler with magickal abilities had some sort of secret message about it. For all she knew, the message could be for Dagda and someone else in his life. Neala barely knew the man.

What she did know was that relationships led to complications she wasn't willing to deal with when she had an ever-expanding business to run. Circling right back to what she'd been telling herself for a while now, Neala decided she would take the "stress relief," as Dagda had referred to it, as a fun diversion and ascribe nothing more to it.

"Hey," she said to Dagda as they walked out onto the dock. Turning, he studied her silently. "Sorry about all that. You're right. It was just a fun release of tension. You certainly weren't my first, and won't be my last. No worries on all of it, then, okay? Friends?" Neala held out her hand.

Dagda glared down at it, his expression even more furious. "Friends?" he said.

"Yes? Can't we be friends?" Neala wondered where she'd stepped wrong now.

"So you've been with a lot of men? I'm just another one on your path?" Dagda said, his tone low but dangerous.

"I... what? I'm telling you I'm sorry for reading into anything and I think we can be friends. Isn't that what you wanted?" Neala demanded, exasperated with this puzzle of a man.

"Fine," Dagda gritted out, barely shaking her hand

before he stomped to the end of the dock to help load the boat.

Neala blew out a breath and rolled the tension from her shoulders. She honestly thought she'd been giving him what he had asked for, and now he was mad at her once more.

"I need details – and, like, immediately," Bianca demanded, grabbing her arm and pulling her close.

"Not much to say," Neala said, still watching Dagda as he angrily checked out the supplies on the boat.

"That's a load of shite," Bianca commented.

"We had a bit of a moment last night. I thought there could be something more. He doesn't feel that way. I decided I agree with him and that we can be friends, and now he doesn't seem to be happy with that either," Neala summed up as quickly as she could. She rocked lightly on the balls of her feet as she considered the back and forth of what had just happened.

"Och, sounds like the man is scared."

"I don't have time or interest for scared boys in my life. If he decides to man up, I'll consider it. For now, he's just a friend," Neala said, her tone sharp enough that even Bianca stopped talking for a moment, just raising both hands in acquiescence.

"Fair enough, girl. I'm here for whatever you decide or need."

"Thanks, Bianca. You're good for me," Neala said, shooting the blonde a smile before moving to board the boat. "Let's go get Gwen."

"Finally," Loch said.

CHAPTER 42

The ride out to Dead Man's Island was silent, aside from the slap of the waves on the bow and the occasional cry of a gull swooping lazily above them. Neala couldn't help but think how the island really was shaped like a dead man lying in his coffin, with his arms crossed peacefully on his chest. She sincerely hoped it wasn't an omen about what they would find when they searched for Gwen.

She studied the island as the boat drew near, but didn't see any sort of ruins or structures that could easily be hiding Gwen. It was likely that this Seeker was going to be much trickier to find, Neala thought.

"What did the clue say again?" Bianca asked from across the boat.

Neala dug it from her pocket, reciting the lines carefully:

To love or not to love
To live or not to live
Fire consumeth all

Shame goeth before the fall.

"Great, that's just what I want to hear," Bianca said. "Fire? What? She's going to light the island on fire?"

"Maybe it's because of Gwen's cuffs? She can shoot fire?" Seamus asked, giving Neala another thing that she wanted to ask Bianca about. She felt as though she needed at least a week of stories to catch up on all the miraculous things these women could do. And to think, weeks ago she had barely believed in fairies –now there was magick and mermaids and calling down the wind… it was mind-blowing. What a world of possibilities they lived in, Neala mused, leaning against the railing and looking out at the island that now loomed ahead of them. With those possibilities could come so many things. At any turn she could meet a new love or decide to relocate and open a new business elsewhere. Life was about chance, but also about choice, Neala thought, her eyes straying to Dagda and then away. She'd been right when she'd said earlier that there would be another man after him. Perhaps never like him – oh no, she doubted she would ever meet someone like him again. But could she move forward and find someone in the future?

Absolutely.

"There's a small dock ahead," Flynn called from where he was driving the boat. They'd tried to make him stay back at the house, promising they'd pay for any damage to the boat, but he'd refused. Flynn knew these waters like the back of his hand and he felt personally responsible for delivering them safely to the island.

It wasn't long before the boat was tied to the dock and

they all piled off, packs on their backs, Neala with her sword at her side. Turning, she met Flynn's eyes.

"Thanks for the ride. Are you sure you want to wait?"

"I'll be here. If things get dicey, I'll pull away from the dock and come back. I've added some flares to all of your packs. Send them up if you need extra help and I'll call in the crew. We're here for you in any way we can be."

Such simple words, but they meant a lot, Neala thought as they fell into line once more and walked from the dock. They didn't even know the man, nor his family, but the Grace's Cove family had accepted them instantly into the brood as though they were one and the same.

Neala wondered if Dagda thought there was anything to what baby Grace had said about believing in love, which also seemed to coincide with the clue. She wondered just what form this line of questioning would take on their journey on An Fear Marbh.

"Neala, let's go," Bianca called.

She jumped, realizing that the crew had already forged up the hill, Lochlain leading them like a man possessed. "Coming," Neala said, waving her thanks to Flynn and chugging up the path behind Bianca and Seamus, with Dagda bringing up the rear behind her. They climbed in silence for a while, unsure of where they were going, but staying quiet so as to listen for anything or anyone calling out or approaching them.

"It's so quiet," Bianca whispered.

"I know. It's like it really is a dead island," Neala whispered back. It was true, too, as there was no herd of sheep dotting the hills, nor anything else making noise. Just silence, the wind sweeping across the cliffs, and occasionally the falling of a rock onto the shore below them.

Lochlain had stopped at the crest of a hill. More hills dropped behind him to the left, and a second path wound down a cliff's edge to the right. They stood, clustered in a small group, and looked out at the massive island surrounding them. "I think we should spread out a bit," he said.

"No," Dagda ordered.

"He may be right, though," Bianca protested. "Look at the size of this island. If we don't have much time for Gwen, we need to cover as much ground as possible."

"And if you get jumped by the Domnua? What then?" Dagda argued back.

Neala stepped back, cocking her ear as she thought she heard something. Was that someone singing? It was intoxicating, pulling her in, the warm voice and notes of the song seeming to envelop her entire being, warming her to the core. Helplessly, she followed the song, running to the cliff's edge, and with zero hesitation, Neala dove headfirst into the cold water, the song pulling her deep into the sea.

CHAPTER 43

*E*ven the shock of the cold water couldn't shake her from the reverie she drifted in, so entranced by the song was Neala. It was like it called to every aching part of her soul – the shadowy bits that ached for love and acceptance – and promised that if she just opened up and gave love a chance she could be whole. Neala closed her eyes and let herself sink, not caring about anything anymore, so long as she could listen to this song.

When hands grabbed her, she jerked her eyes open, surprised to see what looked to be an arm and fins dragging her from the water, moving so fast that there was no doubt this creature wasn't human.

Neala sputtered at the surface, shocked by what had just happened. She heaved for breath, her entire body shaking in shock.

A woman, stunningly beautiful in a regal, otherworldly way, floated before her in a tunnel that had just enough light for Neala to make out the woman's features.

"That was foolish," the woman said.

"I... I didn't know what I was doing. I felt intoxicated by the song," Neala admitted, finally realizing the depth of what she'd done.

"A siren's song is virtually impossible to ignore. Gwen's is particularly powerful. She was calling to you, and you answered – but at a risk to your own safety. I'm only glad I was here to save you. We must go under, once more, and I'll pull you with me. Can you hold your breath again?" the woman asked, her tone serious.

Neala could only nod, still trying to wrap her mind around the fact that by all appearances it seemed as though she was having an actual conversation with a real-life mermaid.

"Now," the woman – er, mermaid – ordered, and all Neala could do was gulp air before, once more, she was submerged in the salty cold water, being dragged through darkness, until, just as her lungs were beginning to burn with the need for air, she was dragged to the surface.

"Mother!"

"Gwen, you're safe," the mermaid said, swimming to the shore where Gwen crouched and hugged her. Neala stumbled up the rocks, desperate to get out of the water. She stood panting in the pale light of the cave, and looked at the curvy woman crouching by the water.

"You must be Gwen," Neala said.

"Aye, I am. And you're the Seeker?"

"I'm Neala. Was that you singing then?"

"You heard me!"

"Aye, that's a hell of a voice you've got there. I don't suggest you be using that unfiltered anywhere or you'll have thousands of men at your feet," Neala grumbled, pulling off her now-sodden sweater and wringing it out. The cold began to set in and she shivered.

"You're freezing," Gwen said, coming over to examine Neala.

"Water's a bit chilly for my liking," Neala admitted.

Saying nothing, Gwen closed her eyes and turned, bringing the intricately carved bracelets on her wrists together. A flash made Neala throw her hands up, and to her astonishment, a cheerful fire began to burn in the corner of the cave.

"I'm not sure why I didn't think of that earlier," Gwen admitted.

"I'm not sure I've ever seen something so amazing," Neala admitted, moving to sit near the warmth of the fire to stop her teeth from chattering. "Though the mermaid is right up there."

"I am Amynta," the mermaid said, "mother to Gwen."

"Pleased to meet you, Amynta. Might I just say that I think you're one of the most magnificent creatures I've ever seen in my life?" Neala said.

Amynta beamed at her. "That's kind of you."

"It's the truth," Neala said, then looked at Gwen. "I hear congratulations are in order."

"Och! Did that man tell everyone? I swear I'll throttle him when I get out of here." Gwen crossed her arms and fumed.

"I think it just kind of came out. But I've never seen a man as desperate to find his woman as that one. You've got one very scared and very lovesick man on your hands," Neala said.

"I'm worried for him. He can be a bit impulsive, and

will drive himself to the point of injury to get what he wants," Gwen said, biting her lip and bringing her hand to her belly.

"Is the babe well?" Amynta asked, concern wreathing her pretty features.

"Yes, she's a strong one." Gwen dimpled at Amynta's smile. "And yes, I feel she is a girl."

"Aww, congratulations," Neala said. "That's fantastic news. We'll have to throw a baby shower when we get out. I make the best cakes for those types of parties."

"Yes, let's. Perfect – something to think about as we wait. Mother, is there no way for us to leave? Can you not take us out the way you came in?" Gwen asked, her eyes going to where the water line edged closer to their feet.

"Alas, I cannot," Amynta said, sadness crossing her pretty features. "There is strong magick that even I cannot break through. I could bring her in, but I can't take you out."

"Can you go back out? Warn the others?" Neala asked.

"I shall try. Please do your best to stay back from the water line and keep warm. I don't want you to be ill," Amynta admonished Gwen, who nodded. With a flip of Amynta's magnificent tail, she was gone.

"That's seriously amazing," Neala said, shaking her head at where the mermaid had just been.

"Don't I just know it? I about lost it when I found out that I was descended from sirens," Gwen gushed, moving closer to the fire. "I mean, I love comic books, and to find out that basically I had some of the powers that a comic book character does? It was so cool. Now I get to live in this world of magick and fae and mermaids… it's beyond."

"I can imagine. I'm still kind of coming to terms with all this," Neala admitted.

"Tell me what's happened," Gwen insisted.

Neala filled her in as quickly as possible, trying very much to ignore the rising sea levels in their cavern. Leaving nothing out, she brought Gwen up to the point at which she'd dove into the water.

"Do you love Dagda?" Gwen asked.

"I... I don't know if I can answer that yet," Neala admitted, turning to face the fire, trying to warm her front side now.

"That's fair. How about this... do you think you could love him?" Gwen changed the question slightly.

"I think that, given some time and the chance, yes, I could," Neala admitted. "I think he's incredibly attractive, he can be funny when he wants, and he has a deeply developed sense of honor. I also admire his willingness to go out on his own and create the life he wants to live, instead of following his family's expectations of him."

"Do you think he loves you?" Gwen asked, holding her hands closer to the fire.

"No, he's made that abundantly clear. I'll admit there was a part of me that was hoping he would just give it a chance, to see... but, ah well." Neala shrugged.

"If you've had to overcome two other lessons, what makes you think this isn't the third lesson? Like baby Grace said – maybe you need to believe that you're worthy of love. It's something I had to work on," Gwen said, meeting Neala's eyes. "I never thought I was all that pretty. I was always in the friend zone. When I met Lochlain, wow, did I think he was so handsome. Like a superhero."

"He does look like a brooding superhero," Neala admitted and Gwen laughed, her face lighting with love as she spoke of Loch.

"But I was convinced no girl like myself would ever be of interest to a man like Loch. I wasn't some lusty sophisticated woman, you know? I'm kind of a geek and wear baggy t-shirts and spill things on myself."

Neala laughed. "I can see what you mean. I'm like that as well."

"But then I met my mother and learned what I was, and I had to claim my own power. Really claim it – and believe that I was this badass siren of a woman. Maybe you need to do that, too, in order to unlock this portion of the spell," Gwen said. "It would make sense if it was in my comic books."

"But I kind of tried that already," Neala protested. "I was willing to give it a shot with Dagda – even admitting how much I'd already grown to care for him. I do think I'm worthy of love, and I've already told myself that if not with Dagda – well, then, perhaps with someone else. But I'm not scared of it. It's more about my willingness to let it interrupt or complicate the life I've built for myself."

"Deep down, you truly believe that you are worthy of love? And that you are this beautiful, amazing, strong woman who has created an awesome life for herself?" Gwen asked, peering at Neala with a wisdom in her eyes that spoke of centuries of knowledge.

Neala paused and searched herself, testing how the words felt, before she answered.

"You know what? I really do. I'm proud of myself for

what I've created and I think I have a lot to offer a partner. I'm definitely worthy of love," Neala decided.

Gwen turned and looked toward where the water continued to rise.

"Nothing's changed. I don't think that's going to be the key to solving this part of the curse," Gwen said, nibbling her lip in concern as she eyed the water.

Dagda. Believe. Love.

Neala smacked herself in the head with her palm.

"It's not me who needs to believe," Neala said, replaying baby Grace's words. "It's Dagda. We're doomed unless he figures this out."

"Shite," Gwen said, fear creeping across her face for the first time. "Bianca is out there, though. I believe in Bianca, and I believe in Loch. Together they'll figure out a way. We just have to hope it's in time, before this water rises too far."

"Um, and before the Domnua get us. Because if my eyes aren't deceiving me, I think I just saw a flash of silver," Neala said, grasping Gwen's arm and pulling her behind her body, conscious of the baby she carried. Gwen peeked over Neala's shoulder.

"Damn it," Gwen complained. She stepped forward, the spear raised, as Domnua began to pour from the water, an unending gush of evil.

Neala stepped forward, sword raised.

"Let's show these bad boys what we're made of," Gwen said, smiling sweetly at one that ventured forth.

In seconds, battle cries filled the room and Neala knew nothing else but pivot, kick, and thrust with the sword. Over and over they came, filling the room endlessly while she and Gwen battled, never faltering, taking each fresh wave of Domnua with grit and determination.

Neala wasn't sure when she'd ever been more proud of herself or anyone else. In the face of the rising water – now at their knees – and an uncertain future, they fought on, refusing to surrender. Instead, they tackled every Domnua attack as if they'd been born for this battle. And perhaps they had been.

When Gwen slipped, Neala gasped, crying out as a Domnua kicked her full in the stomach. Gwen doubled over in pain. Screaming in rage, Neala raised her sword and finished the room off, Domnua falling left and right, dissolving in silvery puddles that the water quickly absorbed. When she was finished, Neala crouched around a huddled Gwen and pulled her as far from the water as she could go, cuddling the sobbing Gwen to her chest.

"I've got you. Just hang on a little longer. Loch will be here. I know he will." Neala looked over Gwen's shoulder, her gaze steely as she watched for more Domnua in the water and prayed that Dagda would come to his senses.

Every second counted.

CHAPTER 44

*D*agda ran the shoreline, looking for any glimpse of Neala he could catch. Panic raced through him, but for once in his life he didn't know what to do. He'd not seen where she'd gone in, and it would be a death wish for him to dive in the water knowing full well this could be a trap set by the Domnua.

"Does anyone see anything? Hear anything?" Dagda raged, adrenaline coursing through him as he continued to run, slipping on the damp rocks, his eyes scanning for anything that would indicate where Neala had disappeared.

"Nothing," Bianca shouted and the others echoed the same. They'd all split up along the beach and the cliff line, looking for any sign of Neala.

Dagda's heart thundered in his chest, and his mind refused to believe that she was gone. There was no way they'd take her from him – not now, not when he'd finally had a taste of her. From the moment they'd kissed, she'd burned her way into his bloodstream, into his mind, and into his heart. He didn't know if he'd ever be capable of giving her what she deserved in a partner or what she wanted in life. But last night he'd been given just a moment in time, and he'd done everything in his power to make her feel as loved and as safe as he could. It was all he could do, Dagda thought, all he was really capable of giving to her. He'd wanted her to feel cherished, as she deserved to be.

His anger ratcheted up as he scanned the empty waters. She'd said today that they could be friends and she'd move on to the next man. Which was exactly what he'd wanted, and why he'd pulled back from her this morning. Dagda had tried his best to keep it casual, and there she'd been throwing the word 'love' around.

Love, Dagda scoffed; like he could really offer that. He didn't know how to love someone, at least not in the way Neala deserved. As his parents delighted in reminding him, he wasn't good enough. How would he be good enough for a woman as amazing as Neala? If he gave her his love, she'd end up moving on – like everyone in his life did eventually. The risk was just too great.

No, it was best to set her free and give her a chance at life and love in a way that she deserved.

When Loch shouted from above, Dagda's heart jumped in his throat.

"Amynta!" Loch yelled, racing down the cliffside, all but tumbling his way to the shore where a woman – and if Dagda's eyes weren't deceiving him, a mermaid at that – now swam.

"Amynta! Do you have Neala?" Bianca shouted and Dagda raced to where she crouched at the shoreline, waving Amynta closer to them. They huddled as a group at the beach, waiting for Amynta to approach.

"Neala and Gwen are safe," Amynta said without preamble and Dagda felt the air rush out of him in relief. "But they are in trouble. Time is of the essence."

"Where are they? What can we do?" Loch demanded.

"They are in an underwater cavern. Only accessible from the far side of this sheer cliff. The tide is rising and the Domnua are near," Amynta said, flipping her tail in agitation as she swam rapidly back and forth in front of them. Dagda couldn't be entirely sure, but it felt like she was shooting mean looks at him.

"How can we reach them?" Loch asked.

"Can you get to them?" Bianca asked.

"Can you bring us to them?" Dagda asked.

"I can get inside, but I cannot bring them out. The magick is too strong, stronger than I am capable of breaking," Amynta said, staring pointedly at Dagda again.

"The clue!" Bianca exclaimed. "We need to solve the clue."

"Doesn't Neala need to do that?" Dagda argued, suddenly nervous as he recalled the contents of the clue. "Isn't that the Seeker's job?"

"Domnu may have switched things up this time," Bianca argued. "I bet she's angry that we are kicking butt."

"But…" Dagda paused and looked at Amynta again. "Why do you keep shooting me nasty looks?"

"I believe you're the one who can break the magick that prevents me from bringing my daughter to safety. Perhaps if you'd stop arguing your fate and start opening your heart, we could move forward," Amynta said, her words like knives to his gut.

"I'm not sure what you mean," Dagda said, but then recalled Neala, fiercely standing her ground and imploring him to listen to what baby Grace had said. Believe in love.

Thinking back over the clue, he turned and cursed, long and low, and strode a few feet away down the beach as realization ripped a hole in his gut. The clue was for him. One of the biggest hang-ups he had in this life was the shame of being disowned by his parents. It made him feel unworthy of love – of giving or receiving it.

But that wasn't true, Dagda sucked in a breath as he looked out at where the water met the horizon. He had nothing to be ashamed of. He'd been a good son, and he was a strong and honorable man. Even respected enough to be picked to be a protector by the goddess Danu herself. He was worthy of – and even capable of – giving love. If he could believe it.

Baby Grace had been right.

Dagda jumped as Loch clasped a hand on his shoulder.

"Listen, mate, I know grappling with your emotions is a tough thing to do – especially at a high adrenaline point like this. I had to do the same with Gwen. But I promise you, it's not so scary on the other side. Once I believed in Gwen, and that I could have a life filled with love and laughter with her, my life really began. It was like I'd been living in black and white before she'd arrived and she brought color and light into my life. Give it a chance."

With those words, Loch stepped back and gave Dagda a moment to collect himself.

Dagda thought about a life with Neala, one filled with

her laughter, her curling into his arms to sleep each night, having a glass of wine while they made dinner together. He could help her with her bakery, or steal her away, if they found a store manager, and show her some of the world she wanted to explore. And she could show him what it meant to have a home, a real home, and family. Together they'd be their own little unit of light and love. Aye, he could see it.

If she'd have him. And after the way he'd acted this morning, she had every right to never give him a chance again. Dagda swore. But wasn't that what love was? Understanding when someone was scared, forgiving when they screwed up?

"I believe," Dagda whispered. "I believe I can love you in ways you've never been loved before, and that I can make a family with you. I believe we can give this a go – us two outsiders – we can build our own home together. I believe in us. I know we can give love a chance."

At his words, a shimmer seemed to flutter across the water.

Amynta cheered, barely pausing before she dove under the water, her tail disappearing.

"I hope that was enough, mate," Loch said, his face drawn in concern as they all waited in silence by the shoreline. Even Dagda hoped it was enough, for there was nothing else he could say or do. He didn't even know if he fully loved Neala, but he knew he would give it his all.

When Amynta surfaced, what felt like eons later, shouting, Dagda's heart shot into his throat. Neala swam next to her, pulling herself powerfully toward shore and he dragged her from the water. But it wasn't Neala that Amynta had been shouting for.

Gwen was cradled in her arms, her face slack, her skin white against the blue of the water.

"The Domnua came," Neala sobbed. "They kicked her in the stomach."

"The pouch Fiona gave you!" Bianca screamed at Loch who had momentarily frozen in shock. Coming to, he reached into his pocket and pulled out the pouch, dropping a vial of liquid into his hand. Wading into the water, he took Gwen from Amynta's arms and ripped the stopper from the vial with his teeth. Letting Gwen's head hang back over his arm, he poured the contents of the vial into her mouth and then brought his head down to her chest and prayed.

They waited, silence stretching out, until Dagda wanted to scream.

When Gwen coughed, wriggling in Loch's arms, they all cheered. Bianca began to cry, and so did Neala.

Dagda wrapped his arms around Neala, bringing her close so he could wipe her tears.

"I'm sorry," Dagda said, pressing his forehead to hers. "I'm sorry I'm stubborn, and difficult, and often closed off. I'll do my best not to be in the future. I want to try for this, I really do. I will give you my all."

"That's all any of us can do," Neala said.

CHAPTER 45

*J*t didn't take them long to hustle back to the boat, Lochlain carrying Gwen the entire way despite her protests. There was no need to linger on Dead Man's Island, especially when Neala reported that the Domnua were close and described the attack they had weathered in the cave. Amynta followed by water, and Neala couldn't help but delight in the way she zipped along the surface of the water, her magnificent tail sparkling like jewels in the sunlight that filtered through the clouds. It felt like a dream, this moment, and Neala wondered if she was going into a bit of shock from the cold water and the battle, or if her life really was this surreal.

She and Dagda hadn't spoken since he'd first pulled her from the water, but he stayed close, always touching her in one manner or another. Neala found herself feeling a bit shy as she shot him glances. It wasn't that he'd said he loved her, she reminded herself as they scaled the hill and raced down the path that led to the dock where Flynn was moored with the boat. It was that he would give them – as in, them as a couple – a real chance.

Wasn't that all anyone could do, really? Have hope? Give love a chance? It never really started out as love, Neala thought. Instead it was like baking. You had to put the right ingredients in, then give it some time to bake before you were rewarded with a beautiful cake. Love was much the same. It started with ingredients like hope, trust, admiration, and respect. With time, that could grow into something so much more, she mused. "Just need to sprinkle some hope in," she said.

Dagda shot her a confused look that immediately turned to concern. Stopping in his tracks, he lifted Neala into his arms, cuddling her close to his chest as her teeth began to chatter.

"I think she's going hypothermic," Dagda shouted, and Flynn ducked below a hatch, pulling out blankets and an emergency kit, while Bianca began to unlace Neala's sodden shoes. In a matter of moments they had stripped her of her wet clothes and wrapped her in emergency blankets and tons of heavy wool fisherman's blankets. Bianca was opening hand-held warmers and slipping them beneath Neala's blankets as soon as they warmed up. Neala just wanted to close her eyes and sleep, so massive was the wave of exhaustion that threatened to overtake her.

"I need you to stay awake," Bianca said briskly. When Neala ignored her, she smacked her lightly in the face, making Neala's eyes pop open. She glared at Bianca.

"Rude."

"It would be rude of me to let you die, wouldn't it?" Bianca asked, and brought a cup to Neala's lips.

"What is it?" she asked as the boat pulled away from Dead Man's Island and began the trek home.

"Whiskey, naturally," Bianca said. "Down the hatch."

It burned straight to her core, but it was a good whiskey and soon enough began to work its magic, heating her insides as her core temperature began to return to normal. Dagda hovered over her, never leaving her side, while Lochlain cradled Gwen and murmured into her ear.

"Is Gwen well?" Neala whispered to Bianca, too terrified to ask about the baby.

"I think so, but I'm giving them a little space until we know for sure," Bianca whispered back.

Neala leaned back, cuddled into her warm cocoon, and tried to process everything she'd just gone through. From the mermaids to Dagda deciding he wanted to give their relationship a chance – it was a lot to take in. For now, all she cared about was knowing if Gwen's baby was safe.

"Neala," Gwen called, and Neala sat up straighter, peering across the boat to her.

"Are you okay?" Neala asked, her eyes hopeful.

"I am. Whatever Fiona gave Loch was the right thing to take. The baby's safe. She's a tough one," Gwen said.

Loch's face lit with joy. "She?" he asked, nuzzling his face into Gwen's neck.

"Aye, I feel it," Gwen said.

"She will be a warrior queen among her people," Loch declared. They all cheered, delighted that there was some good news coming out of their scare.

"Oh, thank the goddess," Neala said, pressing hands to tearful eyes. It was all a little much to take in, and she knew the journey was not yet over. Her emotions seemed to be running higher than usual.

"You did good in there, whatever you did," Dagda said, patting Neala's shoulder awkwardly. She'd noticed he hadn't much spoken since they'd gotten on the boat, and she wondered if he was feeling as awkward and unsure as she was.

"I fought as hard as I could. When they kicked Gwen in the stomach... well, I kind of lost it. I was so furious that these stupid dark fae were going to take something so joyful from her," Neala said.

"You did amazing," Dagda said, wrapping his arm around Neala and pulling her into the warmth of his body. It felt good to snuggle in like this, comfortable.

And right.

CHAPTER 46

*I*t had actually pained Neala to say goodbye to Fiona, baby Grace, Gwen and the rest of their new friends. Her spirit wasn't broken but her body was tired, and she'd wanted just another night to rest up before they continued on their way. Gwen had been the one who had finally convinced Neala that they must continue on.

"We've only a few days left before the curse is up. You can rest when this is all over. Please, I beg of you on behalf of my daughter and the world she is to live in – please hurry."

You couldn't really argue with that type of plea, Neala thought, leaning against the window as Dagda headed north.

"You've time to rest," Dagda said, looking over at Neala with a new softness to his gaze.

"I will. I just need a moment to go through some stuff in my head," Neala said, then sat up straight as she remembered the pouch Gwen had pressed into her hands when they'd hugged goodbye. "I almost forgot – the pouch!"

The Land Rover now held three of the four great treasures of the Tuatha de Danann and Bianca was beside
herself with delight as she held each one and examined all
the intricacies and beauty each held. It was as if all her
Christmases had come at once. For Bianca – someone who
had studied these myths and given tours around Dublin
speaking on their history – to actually hold and study each
piece of magick was like finding the Holy Grail.

"Nobody will ever believe this," Bianca mused,
holding the Spear of Lugh in her lap and poring over the
carvings on the handle.

"Watch where you point that thing," Seamus grumbled.

"Sorry, my love. This is just beyond, though…"

Neala pulled a stone from the pouch along with
another small scroll of paper. Holding the crystal up, she
let the light shine through, illuminating the deep blue of its
hue. The last gem had been rhodonite. Pulling the necklace
out from where it draped beneath the loose sweater Fiona
had given her, Neala fastened the stone into the Celtic knot
pendant. The range of colors looked pretty together, and
she wondered what the next stone would be.

Look for the light
Find the will to fight
For at the darkest hour
One must understand true power

The poem on this scroll held a different tone than the
last, as though if the goddess knew they'd only have a few
precious moments left before plunging into battle.

"That one doesn't seem to be written by Domnu,"
Bianca commented, leaning over Neala's shoulder to look
at the stone in her necklace. "The others had sort of a sing-

songy schoolgirl feel to them. This clue seems more intense."

"This is also Neala's treasure to find, so perhaps it is back to what the original clues were?" Seamus asked.

Bianca patted him enthusiastically on the knee. "That's my man, using his brain. He's probably right. The other clues were to rescue the seekers that Domnu had kidnapped. But, in all likelihood, she probably doesn't know where this last treasure is. Which means this is a clue from our favorite goddess, Danu."

It seemed like all of Neala's thoughts were cramming together in one giant traffic jam of confusion and contradiction. She needed an hour of downtime to turn it all off and not speak to anyone.

"We're certain of where we go next?" Neala asked, glancing at Dagda.

"Aye, Malin's Head is the northernmost point. I've an idea of where we go from there. Close your eyes. You had a pretty big scare. Rest now," Dagda soothed.

Grateful that he was there, Neala smiled at him once before dropping almost immediately into sleep.

When she dreamed, it wasn't restful.

Her shop, once gilded and beautiful – a warm haven of welcome scents and glorious baked goods – lay burned beneath her feet. A line of hungry people, wearing nothing but rags, clambered outside, sifting through the ashes, looking for anything, even a scrap of food, to eat. Neala stood in the midst of it, turning in all directions, wanting to help.

"You see? You have nothing to give," Domnu said from behind her.

Neala whirled to see Domnu holding the Cauldron of Plenty, the people lining up behind her, crying for food. "The other treasures mean nothing if the world starves. And I will be the one to choose who gets to live, and who will die."

Domnu tossed a look over her shoulder at the people clambering behind her, their ravaged cries of hunger begging her for but the smallest sip from her cauldron.

"Don't you see? All I have to do is feed them and I'll have their allegiance forever. It won't be so difficult to take over the world once the treasures are mine. I'll control everything, and you will all bow to me."

Domnu winked from sight and the people cried out, dropping to their knees in anguish as she left them behind with not a crumb to eat.

Neala sat up on a gasp, blinking rapidly at the glow from the dashboard, trying to place where she was.

"It's okay, you're with us. Just a dream, love," Dagda said, running one hand down her thigh while the other continued to steer.

"I saw Domnu in the dream," Neala said, forcing herself to bring her breath under control. "She's going to use the cauldron to control people's allegiance to her. She's going to starve everyone if she wins this battle."

"She won't win. It's a common tactic the gods and goddesses like to employ," Dagda said, his voice serious as he talked Neala down. "A bit of psychological warfare, if you will. Showing up in a dream can shake someone's confidence quite a bit. Personally, I take it as a good sign."

"How?" Neala said, turning completely to look at him. Bianca and Seamus were curled together in the back seat, taking what rest they could, with only Dagda keeping watch in the early hours of the evening as they drove.

"It means you've shaken her. You've got her running scared. She wasn't thinking we'd get the treasures back, let alone be on our way to collect the fourth. We'll need to be prepared for her to pull out all the stops. And you are going to need to stay as mentally resilient as you can. This isn't a normal fight. They'll use magick to mess with your thoughts."

"How do I do that? How do I know what's a trick and what's not?" Neala asked, tucking one foot under her thigh as she studied him, reaching up to pull her hair down from the rough knot she'd put it into after her swim. Now she began to untangle it over her shoulder, running her hands through the length of it as Dagda spoke.

"Head up, heart open," Dagda said, sliding a glance her way. "I've told you that before."

"It's not always the easiest to do," Neala argued back.

"Sure it is. You've just got to trust what feels right to you – no matter what – and have faith it will all work out. I'd say it's like following your own true north."

"True north," Neala murmured. "My true north."

"Aye, which technically speaking isn't like the North Star or anything. But poetically speaking, I think it means that our soul is our compass. Your north and someone else's north might be wildly different – but neither are wrong. However, in the situation we find ourselves in, it's going to be your true north, your soul that will lead you on the correct path."

"That's a hefty lesson, no? The fate of the world is in your hands so just listen to your soul," Neala scoffed, starting to braid her hair. "Don't you think it would be easy to second-guess yourself?"

"You can second guess yourself until the day you die. Is that the life you want to live? Commit to a direction and move forward with it. I don't see this as being too difficult for you. Look at all you've accomplished on your own thus far, just by following your own path," Dagda said, smiling at her.

"Yeah, but I've made plenty of mistakes along the way too," Neala pointed out.

"And I'm sure you've learned from them. We all make mistakes. It's only a failure if you don't learn something from it," Dagda said.

"I'd really prefer not to be making one of those mistakes when the fate of the world rests on my shoulders," Neala said.

"I'd really prefer we didn't have an army of dark fae tracking us and trying to kill us, but hey, that's the way of it right now. I'd much prefer to be in a cozy pub with a pint while a pretty girl with a beautiful braid entertains me with her stories," Dagda said.

Neala felt herself growing warm inside. "I'd like that too," she said, feeling almost shy again.

"It's a date, then. When this is over, I'll take you to the coziest pub I can find and we can talk for hours about nothing or everything," Dagda promised.

"Greece," Neala blurted out, then pinched herself. A first date should not be a trip to Greece.

"Greece?"

"Aye, I've always wanted to see Greece. I feel like if we save the world, we should get to go see the pretty blue waters of Greece," Neala said, feeling her cheeks flush in the darkness of the car.

"That's fair, pretty lady. When this is over I'll take you to see the pretty blue waters of Greece."

"Awww, that's so sweet," Bianca chimed in, her voice still thick with sleep. "Can we come?"

"No!" Dagda growled.

CHAPTER 47

"*H*ell's Hole?" Neala asked in disbelief, looking back over her shoulder at Bianca.

"That's correct. Hell's Hole in Malin's Head is the northernmost point of Ireland, unless we start going out onto some of the wee rocky islands and such. But knowing the fae, I suspect they'll have picked Hell's Hole because they do have a flair for the dramatic," Bianca said, looking pointedly at Seamus.

"What? I'm pretty even-keeled, I'd like to think," Seamus protested.

"You have your moments," Bianca said.

"Not as much as you, my delightful sweet muffin," Seamus said, and Bianca chuckled.

Neala caught Dagda looking at her with a considering eye. "Don't ever call me 'sweet muffin,'" she said, and he laughed – a real laugh, robust and filling the car.

Even Bianca paused for a moment. "Wow, the man actually laughs," she stage-whispered.

"I laugh more often when I'm not on a mission to save

the world, I'll have you know," Dagda said. "However, I feel like it's important for me to take my post seriously."

"I think it's exactly the right time to be laughing," Bianca argued. "What's the point of all this fighting if we don't enjoy life along the way?"

Bianca's words echoed in Neala's head later that night when they pulled into an encampment in the far north of Ireland. Dagda had said he had some friends who would put them up for the rest of the evening, but Neala hadn't expected this. Bianca crowed with delight as the SUV bumped down a dirt road and its headlights shone on several tents with a group of people gathered around a fire. A woman, easily eighty years old if she was a day, stood in the beam of the headlights.

"Clodagh! We stayed with them one night when we were searching for the sword," Bianca said eagerly. "They have the coolest tents."

"Travelers?" Neala asked.

"Got a problem with travelers?" Dagda asked, raising an eyebrow at her.

"Not in the least. I think they'd be the perfect people to show you the back roads of where we're going," Neala answered honestly.

Dagda smiled at her. "Glad you aren't the judgmental type."

Clodagh, the old woman, had welcomed them immediately into the camp, kissing Dagda like he was her long-lost son, and feeding them a hearty stew around the fire. When she passed a jug of whiskey around the fire, Neala paused and looked at Dagda. He stood just outside the circle, on guard as always. But he gave her the nod, and she took a healthy swallow, promising herself that would be it for the evening.

The group was a merry one, with much laughter and even some dancing breaking out around the fire, Bianca and Seamus merrily joining in. Neala considered doing so, for Bianca was right – if we may die on the morrow we should dance tonight – but Clodagh settled on a stump next to Neala.

"You've got yourself a mighty battle ahead of you," Clodagh said without preamble.

"I suspect we do, at that," Neala admitted, meeting the old woman's eyes, which held the wisdom of her years.

"Is he your man?" Clodagh said, nodding her chin at Dagda, who stood just outside the circle.

"I don't quite know how to answer that," Neala said, which was the truth – she didn't. They hadn't laid claim to each other, necessarily. They'd only made a promise to try.

"You don't have to have all the answers to trust it will all work out the way it is meant to," Clodagh said, tapping one foot in time with the drumbeat.

"Easier said than done," Neala said, tugging on her braid as she looked at the fire, worry racing through her.

"Worry is for another day. Now is the time for giving," Clodagh said gently, nudging Neala with her shoulder. "Give your man love."

"I don't know that I love him. Or that he loves me," Neala protested.

"You must give love to get love. Remember that. Now, to bed with everyone. We can dance when the battle is won," Clodagh said, not allowing Neala any further comments. With one clap of her hands the music ended and everyone shuffled off to their various encampments. Clodagh had shown her their tent when they'd first arrived and Neala made her way to it, saying goodnight to a giggling Bianca as Seamus dashed with her to their tent. There was no doubt in her mind how they would be using the time before morning.

Perhaps she should take a cue from Bianca's book. Live in the moment, for tomorrow will bring what it brings. And, as Clodagh had so carefully reminded her, she needed to give love to get love. Remembering how Dagda had been so willing to give of himself the other night, but refusing to take, she decided it was time to turn the tables on him.

An oil lantern burned brightly in the corner, and Neala crossed to it and turned the wick down until only a soft glow lit the tent. She had to hand it to the travelers; though they were in a tent, it was anything but shabby. With a nice floor and a double bed stacked with soft blankets and tons of pillows, it was as cozy as one could ask for.

Glancing at the front flap, she quickly pulled off her clothes and unwound her hair from the braid so that it tumbled over her shoulder. Then she climbed into bed, pulling a sheet over her body. Her pulse picked up a beat as she waited for Dagda to enter the tent, knowing full well that he was still patrolling the outside and checking for any trouble spots in the perimeter. When the tent flap finally pushed open and Dagda ducked inside, Neala felt her whole body flush from wanting him.

He paused, ducking just slightly because of his height, his eyes on hers.

"I can sleep outside," Dagda decided, and made a move to go back out.

Springing up, Neala stomped to him and grabbed his arm, pulling him around so that he looked down at her, a furious woman in all her glory before him.

"You will not be sleeping outside tonight. You will be joining me in this bed," Neala ordered, and began to undress him. At first, he protested, but with each stern look she gave him and each garment she pulled from him, his protests died. By the time she had him standing before her – and a more handsome man in the flesh she'd never seen – they were both breathing harder from excitement.

"Neala, I…" Dagda said, his eyes straying to the front flap again, "I should be outside, watching over you while you sleep."

"No, you shouldn't be," Neala said, raising his hand and pressing a kiss to his palm. She led him to the bed and pushed him gently down until he sat before her while she stood. "I need you right here. With me." Saying no more, she brought his hand to her heart, and pressed her lips to his mouth.

"But… we're in battle," Dagda said, once more trying for honor.

"And battle we shall on the morrow. But tonight… I want to give you my love," Neala said, her breath soft against his lips. "Let me show you."

"No, I should give to you," Dagda said, his hands coming to rest on her hips, his face mulish.

"I'm in charge tonight, Dagda. As my protector, I demand that you listen to my orders," Neala said, her voice stern.

Dagda's mouth dropped open, working for any words, any sense of control he had over the situation. When he realized it was futile, he dropped his face to her chest and hugged her.

"There's my man... my bear," Neala whispered. "Lie back now and let me love you."

CHAPTER 48

Dagda trembled as he stretched out on the bed, his muscles rippling down his body as he reached out his hands for her.

"Nope, I'm in charge. Cross your arms behind your head," Neala ordered, faking a bravado that she didn't necessarily feel. This man was far more experienced than she, and his lazy sensuality was both a turn-on and an intimidation for her. When he reached up and crossed his arms behind his head, following her orders, Neala felt her mouth go dry at the sheer masculine strength displayed before her.

Give love, Neala reminded herself. Show him.

Crouching on the bed next to him, she bent her head and let her hair trail over his chest, touching her lips lightly to the muscles found there. Slowly, she teased a row of kisses up his chest, letting her breasts swing lightly across him, her nipples perking as they brushed his skin. Needing a better position, Neala boldly straddled him.

Dagda moaned just a little, and pulled his hands back from his head.

"Hands up top," Neala ordered, and he groaned, but did as she said. Sitting back a little, she just looked down at the amazing man below her, and reveled in all that was Dagda. For days now she'd been watching him and noting how confident he seemed in every situation, handling things with quiet control or fierce bravery. The only time she'd seen him unnerved was when he'd had to admit to a willingness to be vulnerable.

To her.

And here he was, once again gifting her with his own vulnerability, by letting her take control. She smiled at him, so brilliantly, as light seemed to flood her entire being, and helpless not to, he beamed right back at her.

Bending, Neala slid her hands up his muscular chest and nuzzled into his neck, teasing kisses along the way, reveling in his scent – so musky and manly – and nipping lightly at his ear. When she finally found her way to his mouth, Dagda moaned.

To make a strong man moan – well, that was empowering, and intoxicating, Neala decided as she became entranced with his lips, kissing him until they both panted for breath, the slow slide of tongues a dance of heat and anticipation. Neala writhed against him, already wanting more, her body crying out to let him touch her.

Ignoring what her body wanted, Neala broke away and began to slowly kiss her way down his body.

"Have I told you how handsome I find you?" Neala asked, stopping to pay attention to his nipples, scraping them with her teeth just enough so that he jerked against her mouth.

"You haven't," Dagda said, his breath ragged.

"Ah, I'm sorry for that," Neala said, continuing to lazily explore his chest, her tongue running along all the grooves and ridges, her hands caressing the strong muscles of his arms. "Have I told you how much I love that you take care of me?"

"Ah, you have not," Dagda said, groaning just a little as she reached his abs, her tongue sliding along the eight-pack she found there.

"Have I told you how I think you have a good heart?" Neala asked, pausing to look up at him under heavy lids.

"You have not...Neala, you don't have to say this stuff..." Dagda's words trailed off at her glare.

"Have I told you that I think you're amazing beyond belief and that I've never met anyone like you before?" Neala asked, her eyes still on his.

"No," Dagda said, the word a ragged plea on his lips.

"I suppose I'll have to show you then," Neala said, and kissed her way down to where he wanted her most, sliding him deeply into her mouth so that he gasped in ecstasy. Taking her time, she enjoyed the feel of him, heavy in her hand and mouth, as she licked her way toward completion, growing just as excited as she felt him becoming.

"Hey!" Neala gasped, surprised to find herself lifted from him, his arms most decidedly no longer crossed behind his head. Sitting up on the bed, he pulled her to him so she straddled him, and his eyes met hers dead on.

"I've never wanted someone so much in my life as I do you, Neala. You glow for me – you're my light, my true north, my everything. I've ached to be with you," Dagda said, his stormy eyes holding hers.

"I want to show you my love, Dagda. I feel it. It scares me. It feels too soon or... I don't know, but I won't let fear stop me from knowing what I feel. And I know that I'm falling for you, if not already fallen," Neala said, melting against him as he cradled her in his arms.

"I fell for you the instant I saw you. You've captivated me like no other," Dagda said.

"Be with me, Dagda, make me whole," Neala said, and he filled her in one delicious thrust. She threw her head back, her hair tumbling over her shoulder as she moaned in delight, her muscles clenching around him instantly. Burying his face in her breasts, Dagda paid careful attention to the sensitive peaks, sending her so quickly over the edge that she cried out, pure ecstasy filling her as together they claimed each other as one.

And when it was over, Dagda started all over again, showing her how much he also liked to give, until Neala, spent with love and lust, passed into a dreamless sleep, snuggled on his chest and feeling like she'd finally found home.

CHAPTER 49

"ull moon tonight," Clodagh informed her the next day. It was mid-day already and the travelers were packing up camp, readying themselves for the travel ahead. Both Neala and Dagda had been shocked by how long they'd slept; Dagda had even had a few angry words with Clodagh about it.

"Your man worries," Clodagh said, pointing to where Dagda packed up with a studied precision that belied the anger he was keeping tamped down.

"He wasn't happy that we slept so late. I think he feels he needs to be awake at all times, constantly protecting me," Neala said on a shrug.

"Rest is good for the soul too. As is lovemaking," Clodagh said, her eyes crinkling at the corners. "I see you gave him your love."

"I did," Neala said, flushing a little as she thought of their night together.

"Good. Tell your man not to worry. The battle is for

this evening. We'll all go," Clodagh said, rising and stretching.

"Wait, how do you know it is tonight?" Neala scrambled up, surprised.

"I listen to the wind. As should you, pretty one, since you control it. The curse is over at midnight this eve. You'll not fight this battle alone tonight."

"Wait…" Neala's mouth fell open as complete shock coursed through her. "I thought we had more time. What do you mean it's up tonight? How do you know this?"

"We've had a few missed days over the centuries to account for, my dear. Fae calculations can often be a little off. Trust me when I say… tonight, we fight."

Neala didn't wait to hear any more, and she raced across the camp to where the others stood by the SUV.

"It's tonight. They say the curse is up tonight. At midnight. Big battle tonight," Neala gasped, almost trembling with her worry.

"We just heard," Bianca said, pulling Neala into a hug. "It's going to be fine. The gypsies will come with us. We'll have backup."

"We need more than the travelers! We need an army! We don't know what we're walking into," Neala said, feeling panic bubble up from deep inside, threatening to choke her.

"No, we don't," Dagda said, pulling her to him so that he had his hands on her shoulders, her face tilted up to his.

"We do. It's too much. I can't do this alone," Neala gasped, dangerously close to tears. She'd grown to like all these people she'd met along the way, and the fear of letting them down – of destroying the future for Gwen's daughter – all of it, threatened to overtake her.

"You're not alone. No matter what," Dagda said, brushing his lips gently over hers. "Remember, you gave me your love. And I gave you mine. No matter where you stand, I'm with you."

His words steadied her and Neala nodded, hoping that when the time came she was capable of living up to everyone's belief in her. Because at the moment, she wasn't feeling all that confident that she'd have the right answers, or even be strong enough to withstand the onslaught of dark fae who so desperately wanted to run free in this world.

"We're with you too, Neala," Bianca said from behind her, and Neala turned to send her a watery smile. "I know we may not seem like much, but we've held our own thus far. What's one more battle?"

"I think you guys are magnificent," Neala said.

"You hear that, Bianca? I'm magnificent," Seamus said, elbowing Bianca.

"I think she meant me," Bianca pointed out.

"She said us," Seamus argued, following her around the car as they continued packing up. Just like that they were back to joking and laughing, and the heaviness of what lay ahead was pushed to the back.

Neala held that feeling with her through the afternoon and into dusk as they drew near the infamous Hell's Hole. Why, oh why, did this battle have to occur in a place with such a name? It was as though the Domnua knew it would mess with her head. Psychological warfare, Dagda had reminded her, could be just as powerful as real warfare.

Dagda pulled the SUV to where Clodagh stood, a long walking stick in hand.

"Here's far enough. The rest we'll go on foot."

They'd decided to approach Hell's Hole from a roundabout back way, instead of the direct route. From what Neala gathered, it was a deep crevice cut into the cliffs that looked like a deep watery blue grave. When conditions were right, the waves would slam into the rocky walls, sending towers of water shooting toward the sky, their force sucking down anyone stupid enough to stand nearby. Sounded like the perfect place for a battle, Neala thought – rocky, dangerous, and unpredictable. Great.

They fell into line, picking their way along the rocky terrain, the sun's last rays lighting the way for them. Neala felt keyed up, ready to jump at anything, and she continued to run through everything she'd learned along the way. She felt like she was about to go take the exam of a lifetime and she'd been given the wrong notes to study from.

"Sooooo." Bianca drew the word out, falling back so that she walked in front of Neala. "Give me details."

"On what?" Neala asked, still distracted.

"Duh, on Dagda. It's obvious you two did more than sleep last night. Are you kidding me? I almost jumped Seamus again based on all the sexual energy pouring off the two of you this morning," Bianca fanned her face and, despite everything, Neala found herself smiling.

"It was amazing," Neala admitted.

"I'd say. Just look at the man," Bianca agreed.

"I did. And more," Neala smiled again, remembering his hands all over her body and his promises of love.

"Did the L-word come up?" Bianca asked.

"It did. We're… we feel the same," Neala said and Bianca squealed, turning to grab Neala in a quick hug. The whole line of people turned instantly and Neala held up her hand.

"Sorry, sorry. Everything's fine. Keep moving," Neala said, blushing furiously at the knowing look in Clodagh's eye.

"I'm sorry. I just get so excited. I want everyone to be as happy as Seamus and I are," Bianca said, with such an open and giving spirit it made Neala's heart melt. She had only known this woman less than a week and here she was, crowing in delight over Neala's happiness. It was a gift, and a power, to have such a giving spirit, Neala thought.

"I appreciate that, I really do," Neala said. "Not to change the subject, but can you tell me again how I'm supposed to know how to find this cauldron?" It had been a sticking point with Neala for days now. They were going to go into battle and she was supposed to just… what, scurry around until she found some glowing cauldron somewhere? It didn't make any sense to her.

"The Cauldron of Plenty," Bianca hummed, twirling a finger in the air. "Nobody goes away from it hungry. It can feed nations upon nations, armies upon armies. It was an exceptionally sought after treasure, for even with the best weapons one can wield in battle – like the sword and the spear you now carry – nothing matters if your army or your people starve to death. It serves the most basic, and yet one of the most important, of needs."

It gives, Neala thought. It had been a recurring theme on their journey – giving. Giving of love, generosity of spirit, giving of time, giving of friendship, giving of food –

all of it was about giving. She wondered if that was a key she would need to unlock this riddle. Was it giving the power that the clue spoke of?

There was no more time to think, as a shout went up from the front of the line. They'd drawn to a stop at the rise of the cliffs, the water sweeping out to the left, and a downward slope before them leading to the crevice that Neala knew must be Hell's Hole. But it wasn't the impending doom that she saw there that made her almost weak in the knees – oh no, it wasn't. For as the sun blew its last kiss to day and night claimed them, the sight before Neala was like nothing she could have prepared herself for.

"They're here."

CHAPTER 50

*T*ears pricked Neala's eyes, and Bianca clenched her arm in shock as they took in the army before them, and the leaders who stood in front.

Clare and Blake, Sasha and Declan, Gwen and Lochlain – all stood, arms locked, heads held high, with the goddess Danu in front, her purple glow lighting the field around them. And oh, for acres, it seemed, a faintly glowing army of Danula stood at the ready.

"Look!" Bianca gasped, and pointed to the sea below, where the water teemed with mermaids and mermen. Tridents galore glinted with magick, a veritable water army at the ready.

Neala could only shake her head at the magickal beings, mermaids, fae, fairies flitting by – and was that a leprechaun? Humans, gypsies, and goddesses alike stood at the ready, all to have her back and to help fight for the light in the world as they knew it. For the first time, hope bloomed in Neala's soul and she let go of Bianca's arm, striding forward to meet the goddess Danu.

She looked like her sister, Neala thought, as she came to a stop and bowed her head before the goddess. Fiercely beautiful, but in a warm way. Where Domnu's beauty had been lethal, Danu's seemed to envelop and coax warmth into your soul. She was the bright side of the moon, the rainbow after the rain – and being in her presence made Neala want to weep with joy.

"Goddess," Neala said.

"Seeker, you've done well for yourself. You'll see hardship before the night is over. Trust yourself," the goddess Danu said, then whirled when a cry shrieked across the land. Ice shards of evil rained upon them as the Domnua poured from Hell's Hole, in a tidal wave so great it was blinding.

"Head up, heart open," Dagda said, grabbing her into one soul-searing kiss, then he stood before her, sword at the ready, as the battle descended upon them like a bomb had exploded.

Neala had no frame of reference for this. It was like a cloudburst – no, a hurricane of evil, unleashed with such tremendous force that she couldn't even think. All she could do was react. She decided upon the spear as her weapon, for she'd been told no battle could be won against it, so she let the sword hang at her side and plunged forward, dropping anything that had a hint of silver glow and even so much as looked at her.

Battles may seem glorious in movies, but in reality they were intensely scary and left no time for Neala to catch her breath, let alone look for the cauldron. Try as she might, she couldn't seem to see past the wave of Domnua that fought their way forward. And the screams – oh, the screams of the dying were enough to chill her to the bone and she prayed that none she loved would be hurt this night.

Just as she thought they were gaining some headway and that the army was receding, they dropped from the sky, winged beasts of silvery fury. Neala was plucked from the ground in the claws of a vulture beast, the talons digging so deeply into her sides that blood ran in rivulets. The last thing she saw was a panicked Bianca screaming to the sky, and then Neala was dropped from on high into the teeming pit of Hell's Hole itself.

CHAPTER 51

*T*he silence shocked her the most. Not the pain of the landing on a sharp rocky cliff, nor the magickal wounds at her side that burned as though hot pokers had been stuck into her ribs. Neala struggled to breathe, blinking her eyes against the darkness, confused as to where she'd landed.

"Foolish humans. They always fight like they actually have a chance."

Neala coughed, struggling to her feet, one hand grasping for purchase on the ledge where she stood, the other holding the spear in front of her.

The Goddess Domnu stood in front of her, her head high, her eyes whirling in madness, matching the hair that swung in riots around her head. Neala glanced up to see that she'd been dropped into Hell's Hole, but her landing had been broken by a ledge that stuck from the otherwise sheer rocky cliff. She could just barely hear the cries of the battle above, but she couldn't hear the water below her at all. It was as if she were cocooned inside some magickal bubble.

A snow globe, she thought dumbly, shaking her head. Like she was inside a snow globe of magick, and now she faced down the ice queen herself. Glancing below her, she saw the mermaids trying to break through the magickal force field that Domnu had thrown up, confirming her suspicion that the final battle – the real battle – was going to be just between Neala and the dark goddess herself.

"We make our own chances," Neala parried, vying for time as she tried to catch the breath that had been knocked out of her from the fall.

"Nothing is chance. Don't you understand that it is all preordained? And here I have you, delivered up to me with all the treasures I need. The clock ticks down as we speak," Domnu said, twirling a lock of hair around her finger and laughing when she pulled it away, silver blood dripping from her finger where her own hair had bitten her.

"We've time yet," Neala said, her eyes on the madness of Domnu.

"Time moves faster in magick. What is a minute in your realm is triple that here," Domnu shrugged, unconcerned.

"You still don't have the cauldron. You can't win without it," Neala said, fairly certain she was right, but not entirely sure. Nobody had briefed her on what happened if all four treasures were not found.

"That's why you're here. Don't you see? Once you give me the cauldron, I will have won. The power will be mine. I can feed myself and whomever I choose forever.

There will be no famine if I say so. If I'm displeased, the world will die in hunger. That's the beauty of the power I will now wield. I get the say," Domnu crowed, all but dancing on the ledge in front of Neala.

But that's not power. A thought niggled deep in Neala's brain and she fought through the mind fog to try and reach it.

"I don't have the cauldron. You have no power," Neala said instead, still searching her mind desperately. What had the clue been about again?

"You do too have it! Give it over!" Domnu shrieked, and then Neala could think no more. The goddess whipped magick at her, slicing across her chest and down her legs, wounding her so deeply that blood began to pour from her. Neala gasped as her life's stream began to seep from her body, staining the rocks at her feet. When the goddess raised her arm again, Neala struck out with the spear, slicing the goddess a blow that sent her tumbling, slipping from the ledge and bouncing to the rocks at Neala's feet. A look of shock raced over the goddess's face as she looked up at Neala, her hand coming to her chest where silver blood gushed from the wound.

"You'll never win. Your friends are already dead. Your man? He's gone. I've sent a special army after them. You'll have nothing and die for nothing. The time is up for the curse, just now – I can feel it. I shall rise and the power will be mine – mine and my people's," Domnu gasped, clutching at her chest.

Neala raised the spear for the killing blow, beyond mad with the rage of knowing that all the good people she loved above were to die because of one woman's quest for power. And as she swung, she remembered Dagda's words.

Head up, heart open.

Neala stopped the spear inches from Domnu's throat as the answer poured into her and the final seconds of the curse counted down.

She looked at Domnu and held out her hand.

"You... you fool," Domnu gasped, her face lighting with delight.

"No, I'm not the fool; you are. Power doesn't come from taking from others. True power comes from giving – giving love, giving generosity, and giving chances. You may call us humans stupid for doing so, but I'm claiming my power. The Cauldron of Plenty isn't meant to be used as a tool for power to hurt others. Its only wish is to give. And so, Domnu, I won't fight darkness with darkness. I give to you my light and I will help you stand."

Domnu threw back her head and howled, the bubble of magick shattering around them, the sounds of the battle above and below roaring down into the cavern, the walls shaking with Domnu's rage as the cauldron appeared at Neala's feet and Domnu disappeared from sight, vanquished once more to the dark underworld that would forever be her prison.

Neala dropped to her knees, wrapping her arms around the cauldron, as tears flowed from her much like her blood still did. For though she'd saved the world, she'd failed her friends. With nothing left to live for, she closed her eyes and let the unknown claim her.

CHAPTER 52

"Wake now. Wake, my blessed one," a woman's voice crooned to her.

Neala struggled, not wanting to open her eyes, sadness weighing her down. "I don't want to," she said, turning her head away from where a cool hand pressed to her cheek.

"You must. The tide rises and you're still needed," the voice said again, more firmly this time, and something cool was pressed to her lips. Neala gulped the liquid, which tasted like she supposed starshine might, and felt her insides go liquid with joy at whatever filled her.

Blinking her eyes open, she saw a woman kneeling before her, angelic in her beauty. Neala was still huddled on the ledge in the cavern, the famous treasures at her feet, and the last moments of battle slammed back into her mind.

"My friends…" Neala struggled to sit up, but the woman held her back with just her hand.

"Shh, give the magick a moment to work." The woman

smiled so lovingly at her that Neala looked more closely. She seemed oddly familiar.

"Mother?" Neala squinted, seeing now why the woman seemed so familiar. They shared the same eyes and mouth.

The woman nodded. "Aye, my blessed and beautiful daughter. I'm bursting with joy at the lessons you've learned on this path. Not many could have nurtured someone so dark the way you did."

"I didn't nurture her," Neala protested.

"As the goddess of nurturing and family, I say you did," her mother laughed, a tinkling sound of joy. "You could have given her punishment, but chose to give her love and forgiveness. That's nurturing if I've ever seen it. I'm so proud of you. You've done well this day, and we're forever indebted to you."

"I... well, I just did what I thought was right," Neala protested, embarrassed by the praise, but lapping it up like a kitten being given warm milk for the first time.

"You did. You trusted your heart, your true north, and you saved us."

"Is... what happened above?" Neala's voice cracked. She was so scared to ask about Dagda and her friends.

"Why don't you see for yourself?"

"I can't get out of here on my own." Neala looked up at the sheer cliff walls, and her mother laughed the tinkling laugh once more.

"My gift to you, my daughter: I will bring you up. Come now, put your arms around my neck and I shall carry you once more, as I did when you were but a baby." With that Neala's goddess mother gathered her into her arms, along with all the treasures, and brought her to the cliff's edge, depositing her gently on the rocks, far from the edge of Hell's Hole.

"I'm scared to turn around," Neala whispered.

"Have faith. All will be well." Her mother kissed both her cheeks, and as quickly as she had come, she was gone. If Neala hadn't seen it with her own eyes, she would have thought she'd been hallucinating.

"Neala!"

Neala choked out a cry, bringing both her hands to her face at Dagda's shout, tears pouring from between her hands. All she could do was turn, so scared was she to move or to uncover her face and look at the destruction before her.

"Neala! You're safe. Holy shite, you're safe. I've died a thousand deaths since you went over the edge. You saved us. You saved us all. Butterfly, my beauty, my angel, look at me. Please look at me," Dagda whispered, crooning to her until Neala dropped her hands so she could see his face.

Aye, the man looked like he'd been in battle. As dirty as if he'd ridden a hundred days on a horse through muck and mud, with scrapes and bruises, and a cut lip just beginning to swell – but he was in front of her and he was in one piece.

"You're really here? I'm not dreaming?" Neala whispered, raising one hand to gingerly touch his cheek, wiping a smear of blood she found there.

"I'm really here," Dagda whispered, dropping his forehead to hers, his breath coming out in anxious little puffs. "I thought I would die when I saw you go over the edge."

"You're safe? You're not hurt?"

"Och, what's a few scrapes here and there? But you?" Dagda stepped back and ran his hands over her body, making sure for himself that she was safe. "There's a powerful lot of blood on you, lass. We need to get you to a medic."

"No, I'm safe. My mother... the goddess. Magick. Oh, Dagda," Neala said, tears falling again. Dagda, not caring about his split lip in the slightest, claimed her mouth in a bruising kiss.

"I love you, Neala. My fierce and kind warrior, my heart. I love you for all time," he whispered against her lips.

"And I you, my mighty warrior." Neala smiled at him, but immediately sobered. He was too large for her to see around. "But... what about everyone else? Did they..."

"See for yourself, lass," Dagda said, sweeping Neala into his arms and turning her so she could see.

And there, in the light of the full moon, her friends cheered, the army of Danula echoing them so that the cries of happiness shook the land, and the mermaids danced in the waves that crashed far below.

Forever after, when the full moon rose over Hell's Hole, visitors could hear the cries of joy as light once more drove out darkness, reminding all who heard it that love will always be the answer.

EPILOGUE

"*W*hy are we here again?" Neala complained, annoyed that she couldn't just go sleep for days and days like she wanted to. Though her mother had given her a healing magick, her body still needed more recovery time from what should have been a fatal blow by Domnu.

"Them's the rules, kid," Bianca smiled at her, completely comfortable with following all the silly fae twists and turns that had guided this mission they'd all found themselves drawn into.

They'd hightailed it back to Grace's Cove that same evening, arriving as the sun broke the skyline, heralding a new day of peace. People went about their business, getting the newspaper, opening the tea shop, and sending their children to school, completely unaware that their world would have been forever different had Neala and the other Seekers been unable to break the curse. Neala wondered briefly if not knowing of the evil in the world was a better option than knowing, but decided it wasn't. She supposed she'd rather know what they were up against, and had defeated, than remain blissfully unaware of all the magick that was out there.

And so much magick it was! Neala had a lifetime of learning to catch up on, and Bianca had promised to school her in some of the finer points of fae magick. But for now, they stood on the beach of Grace's Cove, a supposedly mystical beach which Neala had been told was heavily enchanted. She figured it must be, since each of them was required to stop and offer some sort of gift to the cove before they were allowed to set foot upon its shores.

Except for baby Grace.

She'd raced for the water's edge the minute they'd reached the beach, and nobody had tried to stop her. Now, she skipped and danced her way through the edge of the surf, her chubby toddler's legs making her waddle as she went. It seemed that the cove had no issue with Grace.

The lot of them stood on the beach, battle-weary, covered in dirt, scrapes, cuts, and bruises, and waited. Neala was about to open her mouth to ask a question when a soft blue light began to emanate gently from the depths of the cove.

"Whoa," Neala whispered, and Dagda clenched her hand tightly.

"Neala." The goddess Danu stood before her. Neala wasn't sure if her heart would ever get used to people appearing out of thin air, and she puffed out a breath of surprise before bowing her head to the goddess.

"Goddess."

"You've done our people a great service. We are indebted to you. Remember that, should you ever need help, you've only to whisper it on the wind and we will come," Danu said. So saying, she held out her hand and gestured to Neala's pendant, which hung outside her torn shirt. Neala slid it off and handed it over, feeling oddly bereft as she did so.

Danu slid the stone she held in her palm into the last part of the quaternary knot and then held the pendant between her closed palms. A light flashed, and Danu murmured over it before kissing it once and handing it back to Neala. The last stone, which looked to be an emerald, shone brightly in the true north position. The pendant was now closed, the metal soldered around the stones, with no way for them to come loose. Neala smiled, delighted at the piece, and slid it back over her head. It felt different somehow, lighter, and it snuggled warmly at her chest.

"This necklace is to remind you to always look for the light – and that no matter what, family is near. You've only to place your hand upon it to feel the love."

The goddess stepped back and smiled at the group on the beach. Bending, she sheathed the Sword of Light in a special carrier on her hip, and pocketed the Stone of Truth in a pouch at her side. Holding the Spear of Lugh in one hand and the Cauldron of Plenty in the other, she looked ready for any battle – no matter what.

"My Seekers, my protectors, and all the helpers along the way, you are forever favored in the eyes of my people – both the fae and the gods and goddesses alike. To my Seekers" – Danu met their eyes each in turn – "I'm sorry for the scare at the end when I allowed Domnu to capture you once more. There was a caveat to the last treasure. If the Seeker wasn't able to overcome each lesson along the way, then she wasn't deserving of the treasure. There was a level of selflessness that was required that could only be obtained in that manner. I know I frightened you, and for that, I apologize. Please know you're the favored ones now, and your lives will be blessed with the luck of the fae."

Neala opened her mouth to protest or to ask more questions, but as suddenly as she had come, the goddess was now gone.

"I suppose she can't tarry too long with those treasures," Gwen said.

"Still makes me mad that she let you get kidnapped," Loch said, holding Gwen tightly in his arms. "I'll have words with her at some point about this."

"Och, let it be, man. Now is the time for a party!" Gwen said, turning to kiss Loch.

"Yes, I'd like to formally invite you to a private celebration at Cait's pub tonight," Fiona said. "You'll rest for the day and we'll see you this evening for a celebration."

They all waved goodbye to the cove, which for some inexplicable reason still glowed blue, and began the climb back up the cliff wall. Neala kept glancing behind her, watching baby Grace dance in the sand, the ever-watchful Keelin hovering at a distance.

"That Grace is magick, isn't she?" Neala asked. "Like real magick beyond what we know."

"I believe so. It's hard to read her. She's not fae; she's

something else entirely. It'll be fascinating to watch her grow," Dagda said.

"You're going to watch her grow?" Neala asked, raising an eyebrow at him as he lifted her into his arms, seeming to sense her exhaustion.

"What do you say we settle down here? I quite like the vibe, and Flynn's already spoken to me about a job on the boat. Seems to me you were quite charmed with the village. Do you think you could leave your bakery in Kilkenny?"

Neala gaped at him, caught totally off-guard. Pausing, she looked around at where the cliffs kissed the sky and Gracie danced in the magickal water far below.

"Aye, I could leave it. Sierra's been dying to get her hands on running it."

"I say we do it then," Dagda said, sealing his words with a kiss.

NEALA SLEPT LIKE THE DEAD, curled into Dagda's arm, until a banging at the door of the apartment woke her.

"Go away," Dagda murmured, causing Neala to laugh.

"I will not go away, Dagda scarypants. We've got a party to attend and we even get dresses!" Bianca shouted through the door.

Neala sat straight up. "Dresses?"

"Aye, Fiona didn't want us to have nothing to wear. She even sent a surprise. Open!"

Neala stumbled to the door, wrapping a robe that had been left on the bed around her, and opened the door to a beaming Bianca and a man she'd never seen before.

"Oh, honey, you are fabulous," the man said, pursing his lips as he took in the rumpled hair that fell almost to Neala's waist.

"This is Maddox, and he's brought clothes for us. I've kicked Seamus out to the pub. Meet us in my room in ten," Bianca giggled, delighted with a girl's night, if even for an hour, and tugged Maddox to her apartment.

"I've got a girl's thing. Dresses and whatnot," Neala said, eyeing up Dagda, who looked wickedly handsome lying in bed with the sheets twined around him. "But I feel like my energy is back…"

"Don't start something you can't finish. And if I know anything at all, I know that blonde will be back banging on the door in ten minutes if you aren't at her apartment and ready." Dagda smiled, his stormy eyes lighting with love. "But, I promise you, I'll be taking my time with you tonight."

His words sent a shiver through Neala that still warmed her when she thought about it later as they readied to go to the pub. True to his word, Maddox had arrived with dresses galore and had delighted himself in dressing all of them exactly as he wanted, while refusing to listen to any complaints from the ladies. The end result was nothing short of spectacular. Maddox had dressed each of the Seekers in rich jewel tones that complemented their coloring, with a deep emerald green for Neala, her hair hanging loose in ringlets to her waist, and a headband of rose gold woven through her curls.

For Bianca, he'd chosen a gown in the softest blue, almost a white, making her blue eyes pop in her face, and had woven her blonde hair into a braid at the crown, tucking sapphires amongst the braid. She looked like a seductive maiden of yore, and Neala quite fancied it. She wouldn't wear something like this normally, but it seemed fitting, after a magickal fairy quest, to don a beautiful gown and go dance the night away with the ones she loved.

"Come, my beautiful birds. It's time to dance with the fae." Maddox clapped his hands. "You get to meet more of my people. What fun!"

They all followed him down the steps of the apartment and into the pub.

"Are we the first ones here?" Sasha wondered, tugging at the deep red gown that hugged her slim curves like a glove.

"They must be out back," Maddox hummed, and they followed him. Neala knew something was up when he paused and threw the door open dramatically.

Instantly, Bianca began to cry.

The courtyard was lined with hundreds of candles, and magickal fairy lights hung suspended in the air. The tables had been removed and nothing remained but rows of chairs with an aisle leading to an altar. Flowers climbed the birch branches that created an awning sparkling with gold and magick, beneath which Seamus kneeled, a ring box in his hand.

"Ohhhhh," Neala breathed, and Gwen squeezed her arm. Clare wiped tears from her eyes and they all waited on Bianca.

"Bianca," Seamus said and Bianca rushed forward, barreling past the surprised people sitting in the chairs who laughed at her enthusiasm.

"Seamus! You didn't!" Bianca gushed, wiping her tears.

"You're it for me, my love. I've wanted a life with you since the moment I saw you. I've bided my time, but I don't want to wait a moment longer. Will you make me the happiest man of all time and be my wife? Will you light up my life for all eternity?" Seamus asked, still on bended knee.

"Of course I will. I didn't even understand what love was until I met you," Bianca said, and Seamus stood, capturing her lips in a kiss.

"Ahem. I didn't say to kiss the bride yet." Fiona stood there, regal in a deep blue gown with flowers pinned to the bodice.

"We're getting married!" Bianca squealed, turning to wave to the girls. Maddox dutifully handed off bouquets of flowers, and before she knew it, Neala was standing as a bridesmaid at one of the prettiest and most loving weddings she'd ever had the privilege of attending.

And when it was over, they danced into the wee hours of the night, the fae singing a merry tune, the pints flowing. The music carried outside to where Neala had paused to catch her breath and look up into the starry night sky.

"There you are," Dagda said, coming forward, a pack on his back.

"What's the pack for?" Neala said, straightening her shoulders, and preparing herself for a goodbye. She should have known. The man was a wanderer and always would be.

"For us," Dagda said, bending to kiss her lips.

"Us?"

"I promised you a date in Greece, didn't I?" Dagda demanded.

"I... you did at that," Neala said, and found the light inside, brimming over until she laughed in complete joy. "We're going now?"

"That we are. I wouldn't let my woman down."

So saying, he swept her into his arms and Neala gasped as they winked out of sight, Dagda employing the fae magick she'd seen him use once before. Hanging on, she let her head rest on his chest and listened to his heart, knowing that what the goddess had said was right.

Look for the light, for love is always the answer.

DID you fall in love with the Isle of Destiny series? Join my newsletter and you can celebrate Christmas all year round with a trip back to Grace's Cove. As a welcome gift, I will send you a copy of Wild Irish Christmas right to your inbox.

https://offer.triciaomalley.com/4fgv74bn6q

Readers are raving about this feel-good novella where the worlds of Isle of Destiny and the Mystic Cove meet. And don't worry - fan favorites Bianca & Seamus make an appearance!

WILD IRISH CHRISTMAS
Lily finds herself inexplicably drawn to a small village,

and every night has vivid dreams about a handsome Fae prince. These dreams meld into reality when she's suddenly faced with a harrowing rescue of her dream prince in real life. Only she can save him in time, forever sealing their fated bond – but first, she must bring herself to believe in her own fairy tale...

Imogen, Captain of the Irish charter boat Mystic Pirate, has little time for friends and doesn't trust her lovers.

A brand new series from Tricia O'Malley!

Read on for a sneak-peak of chapter 1 from Song of the Fae
Book 1 in the Wildsong Series

CHAPTER 1

The door to Gallagher's Pub slammed open with such force that the musicians tucked in the front booth fell silent and the crowd gaped as a man strode in from the storm that raged outside.

The Prince of Fae had arrived.

Judging from the furious wave of energy that crackled around him, as though he controlled the very storm itself, Prince Callum was ready for battle.

"Oh shite," Bianca breathed from where she sat, tucked in a booth next to her husband Seamus, along with Callum's right-hand man, Nolan. In seconds, Seamus muttered a complicated spell and threw a magickal bubble across the room, concealing Callum from the view of the crowd. For a moment, everyone looked around in confusion, and then a woman jumped up and ran to close the door. From outside the spell, it would look as though the group at the table continued to enjoy an easy-going conversation.

"Just the storm blowing the door open." Cait, owner of

Gallagher's Pub, shot Callum a look from where she manned the bar and the music commenced.

Thunder roared overhead, shaking the windows of the pub, and Cait ducked under the passthrough and went head-to-head with the Prince. Though she wasn't Fae, Cait had a magickal bloodline that fueled her confidence.

"That's enough of that now. You'll be replacing any windows you break." Cait's voice was low. Callum brushed her aside like she was a gnat and Bianca's swift hiss of breath was enough to assure Nolan that very few people were ballsy enough to treat Cait that way. Not to mention the fact that it was rare for Callum to be out-right rude.

Which meant something was very, very wrong.

He'd never seen the Prince like this before. In all the years he had stood by his side, both in battle and in over-seeing the royal court of the Fae, Prince Callum lead with a cool head. Except when it came to his fated mate and one true love...Lily. The hair on the back of Nolan's neck lifted, as though darkness slithered over him, and his eyes held Callum's as the prince skidded to a stop at their table.

"Prince." Seamus bowed his head.

"Lily's missing." Callum's words fell like an icicle shattering to the ground.

Nolan was the first to speak.

"What happened? I can leave immediately. What should we do?"

Cait surprised Nolan by appearing at Callum's side once more, and she did something that no Fae would ever dare to do – she tugged Callum's hand until he was sitting on a chair in front of the table and handed him a whiskey.

"Tell us," Cait insisted.

Bianca's eyes darted to Nolan's, the pretty blonde having picked up on the break in Royal protocol, and he made a mental note that she might be useful for whatever lay before them. Because if something bad *had* happened – here in Grace's Cove and not in the Fae realm – well, they would need help navigating this world. Both Bianca and her husband, Seamus, had successfully supported the Seekers on their quest to save the Four Treasures from the Domnua, the evil fae, over two decades ago. It looked like they were about to be recruited for another quest.

Pulling his eyes back to the Prince, Nolan waited until Callum had swallowed the whiskey and then schooled his breathing. Outside their magickal bubble, the band played on and a few people had pushed chairs aside to throw themselves into a measure of complicated dance steps. Any other night, and Nolan would have joined them. When he was on duty – Nolan allowed nothing to distract him from the job. But, like all Fae, Nolan loved celebrations and where there was music, there'd often be Fae dancing just outside the awareness of humans.

"It's the Water Fae." Once more Callum leveled a fierce look at Nolan, and his insides twisted. The Water Fae were the faction of elemental Fae that Nolan commanded. It was his duty to oversee and manage their concerns and needs – which meant something, likely the Domnua, had forced the Water Fae to act out.

"You're certain?" Nolan asked, his words sharp.

"Aye, sure and I'm certain. Didn't they already try to kill me?"

It had come as a great surprise to everyone in the Fae

realm, particularly those in the Royal court, when the Water Fae had launched a surprise attack on Prince Callum, nearly drowning him on his mission to find his fated mate. Luckily, Callum had survived and had mated with his beautiful Lily, and Nolan had been left to clean up the mess with the Water Fae.

Which, he'd *thought* he'd handled...

"Sir, I met with the leader just this week."

"And what was the resolution of this meeting?"

"I met with the Water Fae on their turf – in their protected cave deep in the sea. I was quite confident that we'd left the meeting with a mutual respect and under-standing. They'd brought up some concerns for me to address, and I've already made good on one of them."

"Which one?" Callum asked, his fingers clenched tightly on the whiskey glass. The rest of the table remained silent, their eyes bouncing between Callum and Nolan like they were watching a tennis match.

"They desired that the path of the human's cargo ships be amended slightly as it crossed too closely to their nurseries in the kelp. I adjusted the currents of the ocean to force the boats to give a wider berth to that particular area." Nolan had been proud of this particular feat, as it had taken careful manage-ment of many natural elements, not to mention adjusting human behavior without them being aware of it. He'd also been pleased to be able to help the Water Fae quickly, so they would understand that he was working on behalf of them as a representative in the higher realms of Fae Court.

"And that's all? Nothing else...untoward happened in this meeting?"

Nolan was shocked by the note of suspicion in Callum's voice. Not only had Nolan proven his allegiance to the prince numerous times over, but they were also friends. The accusing look in his eyes sent a shiver across the back of Nolan's neck. While Callum was known for being fair, he could also be ruthless. If there was any reason for Callum to suspect that Nolan was involved in Lily's disappearance – he'd be dead before the end of the night.

"No, sir. It was one of our better meetings. Frankly, I'm surprised by this. I was quite pleased with the results of our negotiations, and it had sounded like the elders were as well. Please, can you tell me what happened?" Nolan took a careful sip of his whiskey, the liquid burning a hot trail to his stomach.

"I only left her for a moment." Callum's voice was ragged, his eyes haunted. "I'd promised her I was going to try to light a fire like humans do." Callum waved his hand in the air. "You know, with the wood, and the flame, and the tinder…all that nonsense. She wanted to see if I would have the patience to try it without my magick, you see. It was a game, really. We were having fun…laughing. I went outside into the storm to get the firewood from the shed. She'd…she'd been standing in the doorway, just a touch in the rain, laughing out at me because she wanted to watch me do manual labor."

Bianca looked as though she wanted to make a comment about if building a fire was really manual labor but shut her mouth when Seamus touched her arm briefly. The two worked beautifully together, and were so in tune that Nolan was surprised that Seamus had even had to physically correct her.

"When I came back...wood in my arms...she was gone." Callum slammed his fist down on the table and a flash of lightning lit the sky outside the pub. In seconds, thunder followed, shaking the room with its wrath. "The door was wide open. And...just this."

Callum pulled out a piece of parchment paper and put it on the table. Nolan leaned over, not touching it for Fae magick was tricky on an easy day – and read the words.

We trade a love for a love. You've stolen our power. Now we steal your heart.

Below the words was a sketch of a talisman etched with an intricate Celtic knot. It was a drawing of the Water Fae's amulet, which was unimaginably powerful in the wrong hands, and only worn by the leader of the Water Fae. Each faction of the elemental Fae had a ruling talisman such as the amulet, and the leader always had it on hand lest it be stolen and used for wrongdoing. Panic slipped through Nolan as he met Callum's eyes.

"The amulet. It's missing."

"Aye, and they think *we* stole it."

Song of the Fae

AUTHOR'S NOTE

I'm honored that you have taken a chance on my stories –
it means the world to me that you've followed this series
to its conclusion. And, because I love writing about Ireland
so much – I couldn't help but start a spin-off series.

The history behind the beginning of the Mystic Cove
Series:

On a warm, sunny day in September, I hiked up The
Saint's Path located on Mt. Brandon in Dingle, Ireland.
The Stations of the Cross lined the path and led to the
highest point of the peninsula. At the top, the winds were
fierce and the view almost heartbreaking in its staunch
beauty.

Days later, I awoke to the bells of the Christchurch
Cathedral in Dublin, in a lovely hotel room. A dream
tugged at my mind. So powerful, so insistent, that for the
first time in my life, I was compelled to write my dream

down, worried that I would lose the threads of the story that had captivated me in my sleep.

Soon, my dream had expanded from one book into a seven book series.

Sometimes, you just have to follow that moment. That brief hint of inspiration that lights you up inside. That... something... that keeps niggling at your brain. The Mystic Cove books are those stories. The ones that I think about when I'm doing yoga or in the yard playing with my dogs. The ones that make me ache to return to the shores of Dingle and spend many a day soaking up the beauty and charm that the small village has to offer.

Thank you for taking part in my world, I hope that you enjoy it.

Please consider leaving a review online. It helps other readers to take a chance on my stories.

Be sure to check out my website at www. triciaomalley.com. From here you can also sign up to my newsletter for information on new releases, fun giveaways and updates on my Island life!

THE WILDSONG SERIES

ALSO BY TRICIA O'MALLEY

Song of the Fae

Melody of Flame

Chorus of Ashes

"The magic of Fae is so believable. I read these books in one sitting and can't wait for the next one. These are books you will reread many times."

- Amazon Review

Available in audio, e-book & paperback!

Available Now

THE MYSTIC COVE SERIES

Wild Irish Heart

Wild Irish Eyes

Wild Irish Soul

Wild Irish Rebel

Wild Irish Roots: Margaret & Sean

Wild Irish Witch

Wild Irish Grace

Wild Irish Dreamer

Wild Irish Christmas (Novella)

Wild Irish Sage

Wild Irish Renegade

Wild Irish Moon

———————

"I have read thousands of books and a fair percentage have been romances. Until I read Wild Irish Heart, I never had a book actually make me believe in love."- Amazon Review

A completed series.

Available in audio, e-book & paperback!

THE SIREN ISLAND SERIES

ALSO BY TRICIA O'MALLEY

Good Girl

Up to No Good

A Good Chance

Good Moon Rising

Too Good to Be True

A Good Soul

In Good Time

A completed series.

Available in audio, e-book & paperback!

"Love her books and was excited for a totally new and different one! Once again, she did NOT disappoint! Magical in multiple ways and on multiple levels. Her writing style, while similar to that of Nora Roberts, kicks it up a notch!! I want to visit that island, stay in the B&B and meet the gals who run it! The characters are THAT real!!!" - Amazon Review

THE ALTHEA ROSE SERIES

ALSO BY TRICIA O'MALLEY

One Tequila

Tequila for Two

Tequila Will Kill Ya (Novella)

Three Tequilas

Tequila Shots & Valentine Knots (Novella)

Tequila Four

A Fifth of Tequila

A Sixer of Tequila

Seven Deadly Tequilas

Eight Ways to Tequila

Tequila for Christmas (Novella)

"Not my usual genre but couldn't resist the Florida Keys setting. I was hooked from the first page. A fun read with just the right amount of crazy! Will definitely follow this series."- Amazon Review

A completed series.

Available in audio, e-book & paperback!

THE ISLE OF DESTINY SERIES

ALSO BY TRICIA O'MALLEY

Stone Song

Sword Song

Spear Song

Sphere Song

A completed series.

Available in audio, e-book & paperback!

"Love this series. I will read this multiple times. Keeps you on the edge of your seat. It has action, excitement and romance all in one series."

- Amazon Review

ALSO BY TRICIA O'MALLEY

STAND ALONE NOVELS

Ms. Bitch

"Ms. Bitch is sunshine in a book! An uplifting story of fighting your way through heartbreak and making your own version of happily-ever-after."

~Ann Charles, USA Today Bestselling Author

Starting Over Scottish

Grumpy. Meet Sunshine.

She's American. He's Scottish. She's looking for a fresh start. He's returning to rediscover his roots.

One Way Ticket

A funny and captivating beach read where booking a one-way ticket to paradise means starting over, letting go, and taking a chance on love…one more time

10 out of 10 - The BookLife Prize

Pencraft Book of the year 2021

CONTACT ME

I hope my books have added a little magick into your life. If you have a moment to add some to my day, you can help by telling your friends and leaving a review. Word-of-mouth is the most powerful way to share my stories. Thank you.

Love books? What about fun giveaways? Nope? Okay, can I entice you with underwater photos and cute dogs? Let's stay friends, receive my emails and contact me by signing up at my website

www.triciaomalley.com

Or find me on Facebook and Instagram.
@triciaomalleyauthor